D1553373

Please proceed
to the
Nearest Exit

Please proceed
to the
Nearest Exit

JESSICA RAYA

McClelland & Stewart

Library and Archives Canada Cataloguing in Publication

Raya, Jessica, 1971–, author
Please proceed to the nearest exit / Jessica Raya.

ISBN 978-0-7710-7320-5 (bound)

I. Title.

PS8635.A9396P73 2014   C813'.6   C2013-903199-5

Typeset in Minion Pro by M&S, Toronto
Printed and bound in the USA

The lyrics on page 1 are from "We've Only Just Begun," words and music by Roger Nichols and
Paul Williams. Copyright © 1970 IRVING MUSIC, INC. Copyright Renewed. All Rights
Reserved Used by Permission. *Reprinted by Permission of Hal Leonard LLC.*

McClelland & Stewart,
a division of Penguin Random House Canada Limited,
a Penguin Random House Company
www.penguinrandomhouse.ca

1 2 3 4 5   21 20 19 18 17

For Julia

Only fools, liars and charlatans predict earthquakes.

—Charles Richter

1

This will probably come as a surprise to many, but not once in all the time that I knew her did Carol Closter ask me if I believed in God. She simply assumed I did, the way I once assumed that everyone listened to the Carpenters. Which isn't to say that I didn't believe in God, only that I didn't believe in Carol's God. Back then, my God was a sort of Santa Claus, a kindly robed hippie who went around granting good grades and sweet-sixteen convertibles. But, like I said, in the two years that I knew her, Carol Closter never asked and I never offered. If I reached spiritual enlightenment by listening to "We've Only Just Begun" over and over until my mom pleaded with me to please, please, please stop before she threw herself off the roof, well, that was nobody's business but mine. *We've only just begun to live / white lace and promises.* I'm sure the Bible has some catchy lines, but God's no Karen and Richard. My dad's favourite line: *We're all just one bad decision away from disaster.* You won't find it in a Carpenters song. That one was pure Jim Fisher.

"We're all just one bad decision away from disaster." This was the epilogue to every story about another poor sap who'd gotten himself maimed or blinded or worse. Jim Fisher sold insurance, and being a man who didn't know how to talk to children, including his one and only daughter, he spoke to me as he would a client, spouting the facts of life, death, and dismemberment the way other men did baseball scores. Being a girl who didn't know how to talk to men, especially her one and only father, I listened, my tender mind whirring to catalogue these catastrophes under Bad Things That Happen to Other People. I grew up knowing that more toddlers drowned in backyard pools like ours than in the canal that split our town in two. I knew my chances of choking on a hot dog or slipping in the tub. For years, I thought "stop, drop, and roll" was a game all families played. My mom thought this kind of talk would frighten me. I thought his knowledge of the world's secret workings would keep us safe. So I kept my dolls mummified in bubble wrap and cut my hot dogs into bite-sized pieces and waited for my Barbie Dreamhouse life to take shape.

By the time I met Carol Closter I'd stopped worrying about the kinds of things you can insure yourself against. I was fourteen years old at the start of 1971, and as far as I could tell each new day was another chance to completely screw up my life in ways my dad couldn't even imagine. What was a little earthquake or electrocution compared to the daily hazards of high school? Anyway, by then the man was living in a pool house. He was hardly in a position to be offering advice.

I used to blame Neil Armstrong. The night he walked on the moon, my family had camped in front of the television like the rest of the country. It was July 1969, and some of us still believed the stars had all the answers. Mom had bitten her Patti nails and wept quietly. She wasn't one of those mothers who cried all the time. When Nixon was sworn into office, girls at school said their mothers had blubbered like babies. Mine had turned off the TV and gone to bed with a headache. My mom was from Canada and Canadians couldn't vote. If my history textbooks were right, Canadians didn't do much of anything. She probably cried on the night of the moon landing because she realized nobody from her country would ever step foot off this planet. My dad, on the other hand, was one hundred per cent American. He sat quietly gripping the arms of his favourite chair as if he was sitting up there in the Lunar Module between Buzz and Neil. When Old Glory was planted in Swiss cheese, Dad stood and saluted the set. "Well, how about that?" he said. "How about that." Then he picked up a throw pillow and took his own earth-bound steps through the sliding doors. He spent the rest of the night outside on a lounge chair, gazing up at Neil's moon. The next night he was there again, wrapped up in an old sleeping bag. By September, he'd claimed the thin mattress of the pool house cot. One small step for man, one giant leap for Jim Fisher.

In the weeks that followed, under cover of dark, Dad ferried his things quietly across the yard. He took his two favourite books: the latest edition of *Morbidity & Mortality*, which arrived at his office every December wrapped in plastic like someone's warped idea of a Christmas present, and *Natural Disasters for Insurance Sellers*, a depressing door-stopper with the physical charm of a phone book. They were followed by a box of Cuban cigars and the misshapen clay ashtray I'd made in fifth grade. Next went his plaid dressing gown and clock radio. Inch by inch, Dad was planting his own flag. One morning I saw him shaving over the pool, the unreliable reflection his mirror, ropes of white foam falling into the water.

My mom said nothing of Dad's migration. She preferred to express herself through the art of interior decorating. The less time he spent in our house, the less she liked it. Suddenly every chair and sconce offended. The brass chandelier clashed with the tweed sofa, the floral sofa with the plaid stair runner, and so on. *Sprucing*, she called it. "Just sprucing things up!"

The neighbourhood women were in awe. "You could decorate professionally," they told her. "You could be in one of those magazines." But nothing satisfied her for long. Eventually she'd come home with a stack of paint chips. Our house was like Heraclitus's river: you never stepped in the same room twice.

Of the bills, my dad only said, "Well, hell, Americans buy things." This was nowhere more true than in Golden, California, a town built on the optimism of young families who fled the city for three-bedroom, two-car homes promising luxury for him and leisure for her. Dad had ordered our own white rancher over the phone, at a time when buying things you'd never laid eyes on seemed like a swell idea. Now the house was my mom's domain, in body if not in name, and he had the pool house, his own Lunar Module at the back of the yard. When I told my best friend Melanie D'Angelo about it, she said, "I guess your parents are as nuts as mine." What else was there to say? The Fishers were like the D'Angelos were like everyone we knew. Looking too closely at your family was asking a question you didn't really want the answer to.

My parents had met in Santa Barbara, where she was on exchange for a semester and he was selling life insurance door to door. My mom was the first woman in her family to go to college, but she wouldn't be the first to finish. "That's how things were. Half my friends were engaged, or engaged to be

5

engaged, whatever that meant." That was all she ever said about their courtship, not that I wanted to know. Like most parents I knew growing up, mine were not what you'd call happy. They didn't fight like other parents, but probably only because they were rarely in the same room. There were the obligatory functions, dinners with clients, community fundraisers, but even seated side by side under long white tablecloths, my parents maintained their distance. At home, they danced around each other, bodies circling but never meeting, graceful as the sparrows that lived in our lemon trees. If hands accidentally met reaching for the coffee pot, apologies ping-ponged between them—*sorry, sorry*, as if everything was a mistake. It had been like this for as long as I could remember. Dad's move to the pool house simply formalized their arrangement.

A few times a year, when the country club ordered complicated centrepieces and hired a band and life could be viewed through the bubbles in a champagne glass, there would be an extra appointment at the hair salon, a new dress for her, a freshly pressed suit for him. She would tell him he was handsome. He would put his hand around her waist and call her babe. For a few days after, they would be attentive to each other, flirtatious even. But within a week the curtain would be drawn and the delicate ballet would begin again. *Sorry, sorry.* These extravagant evenings were the tenterhooks on which their marriage hung.

That Valentine's Day—V Day, as I've come to think of it—seemed no different from the others. I barely glanced up from the television as my parents said goodbye, drifting out in a haze of cigarette smoke and vodka-loosened smiles. "Don't wait up," Mom giggled. I didn't.

When I woke the next morning and made my way, yawning, to the bathroom, I heard my mom's bedroom door open. Dad crept out, dinner jacket slung over one shoulder, a red rose hanging limply from the lapel. He was carrying his black tasselled loafers like a birthday cake.

"Oh," he said quietly. "Morning, sport."

Around the time he moved into the pool house, Dad had started calling me sport, kiddo, champ. I guess he thought it made us sound like buddies. I thought it sounded like he couldn't remember my name.

"Morning, Cap'n," I said. "Nice shoes."

He cleared his throat but didn't say anything. Jim Fisher was from a generation of American men who didn't say more than was necessary, men who invented Liquid Paper, network television, and the hydrogen bomb. He'd been to Korea, but he never talked about it, which is probably the only thing you can say about something like that. "Your father loves you very much," Mom was always telling me, as if she'd married a deaf-mute. On the rare occasions when he hugged me, he came at

7

me from the side, one-armed and by surprise. It had all the warmth of a noogie. Dad said having to shake hands all day was worse than mining coal—come five o'clock, he didn't have anything left to give. You wouldn't know it by looking at him, at that capable square head on those wide, straight shoulders, the steady brown eyes, the practical sideburns. Jim Fisher looked like he'd been born in a blazer. His salesman smile, when he turned it on, was a hundred watts of California sunshine.

He gave me one of those smiles now. "Okay," he said and hurried away in his socks.

I took my time showering, giving Dad plenty of time to make a run for it. While I got dressed, I heard my mom shuffling down the hall, her groans like little curses. I grabbed my book bag and followed her to the kitchen.

Mom stood at the sink in her slip, waiting for her glass of Alka-Seltzer to stop fizzing. She'd fallen asleep in her makeup. A hair fall clung to the back of her head. If my dad was like the California sun, Elaine Fisher was like the sun-tanning lamp she kept in the garage. Having the misfortune to be born Canadian, she worked harder at being American than any American I knew. She read biographies of dead presidents, straightened up before the cleaning lady came, and could spend more time with a *McCall's* magazine than I ever did with a textbook. But beneath the Miss Clairol blond was just a girl from Alberta who refused to wear girdles and couldn't see the appeal of a gelatine mould. She drove her Buick Electra with her head tucked into her neck, squinting at the road as if unsure where she was and how the heck she'd got there.

"Is that what you're wearing?" she said, finally noticing me.

"Is that what *you're* wearing?" I said.

"Why? Where do I have to be?"

The toaster started smoking. She lifted the lever, pinched two pieces of hot toast between her fingers, and flung them at a plate. "There's something wrong with that thing," she said, as if we didn't eat black toast most mornings. The only person I knew less skilled in a kitchen was me. Dad said we were the only two people on earth who could burn air.

As I scraped and buttered, Mom reached into the drawer where she kept her cigarettes and her calculator. She always had to convert recipes from four servings to three. For years she blamed her cooking on poor math skills. The cigarettes were in a small black enamel box along with her silver lighter. She coaxed a Salem from the pack, lit up, and inhaled extravagantly, as if to say, now *this* is breathing. I bit off a corner of charred bread. Now *this* is eating, I thought.

There was a pile of loose coupons in the open drawer. Mom reached in with her free hand and dug around until she found what she was looking for: the brochure our house had been ordered from. I used to look at that brochure all the time when I was little. Except for the baby brother, that was my family and our house. I don't remember my first home, the Santa Barbara bachelor pad where we lived for a year before those student protesters killed a caretaker and Governor Reagan called in the National Guard. To me, my life began right there on page 12. I liked to imagine myself delivered in a giant box along with the terracotta tiles and self-cleaning oven. Later, I imagined Dad taking one look inside that box and saying, "What? I didn't order this." It's not that I thought my dad didn't love me. I just didn't think it would have occurred to him that he had a choice in the matter.

"Did you see your father this morning?" Mom said, staring down at the brochure. "Did he say anything to you?"

"About what?"

Mom nodded slowly, as if she understood something. If she did, I wished she'd explain it to me.

I chewed the last bit of toast and swallowed. It stuck in my throat halfway down. There was a cup of black coffee on the table. Dad's coffee. I swallowed again, preferring to scrape the toast down dry. Mom got a glass from the cupboard and filled it with milk. I drank it in one go. When I put the empty glass on the table, the cup of coffee was gone.

Mom handed me my bagged lunch. "We ran out of sandwich meat," she said. "I got creative."

"I'll alert the school nurse."

She half smiled, smoke streaming from the corner of her mouth. Then she put the brochure and the enamel box back in the drawer, and shut it a little harder than necessary. I wondered if she thought the same thing I used to—that without that baby brother, we would never be the kind of family you could use to sell things.

By the time I got to school, I'd missed homeroom and, according to Melanie, the most important moment of my entire life. She pulled me into the bathroom. Jamie Finley had asked someone to ask someone what my story was, she said, "*for a friend*." Her eyebrows went up, or what was left of them. She'd started plucking recently.

"I have a story?"

"A friend, Robin. A *friend*?" Melanie rolled her eyes. She did this all the time now that we were mature high school students. "Troy Gainer, Robin. Troy Gainer likes you!"

Troy Gainer was a junior and a jock, one of the guys on the swim team who had Nautilus machines in their garages and all the personality of a dead man's float. Half the girls at Ronald Reagan High School would have thrown themselves on a landmine just to get a ride in his red Mustang. I knew this for a fact. They confessed it in bathrooms and whispered it in the halls. They wrote it in notes passed between desks, their cursive slanting dreamily, their lowercase *i*'s dotted with hearts. *I would die to have him like me. Wouldn't you die?* I'd heard Melanie say it more than once. She thought Troy Gainer was a stone-cold fox. More importantly, he was popular. He was practically a god.

"Why don't you look happy?" she said. "Do you know what this will do for our social life?"

"But Troy Gainer's never even talked to me."

"Of course not. Good-looking boys don't have to make the first move. But remember how he smiled at you in the stairwell that time?"

"That was a month ago, and he was laughing, not smiling. I think I had toilet paper stuck to my shoe."

Melanie gave me a teacher's look, one I was all too familiar with. *You can do better than this*, it said. *You'd better.*

I ratcheted up the corners of my mouth. "Troy Gainer!"

Melanie turned to the mirror and slicked her smile with strawberry lip gloss. "Troy and Robin," she sang, "sitting in a tree."

A half-hour later I sat in social studies, doodling *RF + TG* over and over on a sheet of foolscap, hoping that if I wrote it enough times my hand could convince my brain that it was true. My stomach was getting in the way. We were learning about ancient Asian cultures and our teacher, Miss Blumberg, was wearing a red cheongsam with a chopstick speared through her bun. Much as I tried to concentrate on Troy Gainer and the long and beautiful life we'd have together, I kept thinking about egg rolls.

Two seats over, Joyce Peyton stared at me like she was doing algebra in her head. Since getting her teeth fixed, she'd become what some considered pretty. She was what I considered a jerk. She managed a small cabal of girls that some days included Melanie. Melanie didn't like Joyce any more than I did, but she said it was important to get in with the right crowd. We used to have friends. Now we had *crowds*. The word was enough to make me feel claustrophobic.

My stomach growled. I ignored Joyce and took out my lunch. Rona, as Miss Blumberg insisted on being called, said we were adults and didn't need permission to eat or use the bathroom. Most of the adults in second period chose to sleep. Peeling back the wax paper, I remembered Mom's warning. American cheese and cocktail olives. I lifted the sandwich to my mouth. I'd seen worse.

"Don't eat that."

A small girl stood in the doorway, dressed, it seemed, in someone else's clothes. Even with a bucket hat perched on a nest of strawberry-blond curls, she wasn't five feet tall. The sleeves of her blouse grazed her knuckles. The cuffs of her patchwork jeans had been rolled at least twice. You could've made another outfit with all that extra fabric. What skin you could see was a milky pink not found in Golden, where even the newborns had tans. She walked over to my desk, reached out a freckled hand, and plucked a cigarette butt from underneath my Wonder Bread. "Don't you know that cigarettes are bad for you?" Her laugh was like a bell.

Miss Blumberg bent down to address the child. "Are you lost, dear?"

The girl took in the teacher's getup and held out a green slip of paper. "No," she said. "Are you?"

"Well, class, it seems we have a new student. This is Carol Closter from Montana. Who can tell us the capital of Montana?" Our teacher's hopeful smile met twenty-two blank stares. We'd never seen anything like Carol Closter. She might as well have been from Mars.

"Well, it's nice to meet you, Carol. I'm Miss Blumberg, but you can call me Rona."

"Do I have to?" Carol Closter said, hugging a purple binder to her chest.

"Well, that's fine. That's your prerogative. Does anyone know what 'prerogative' means?" More blank stares. "A right or privilege belonging to an individual or group. Okay, then . . . Carol? Why don't you take a seat." She scanned the cramped classroom. "There, by the window."

"I'm supposed to sit near an exit," Carol Closter said. "I have an abnormally small bladder." She thrust another piece of paper forward. "I have a note."

Mouths fell open, but not the faintest chuckle left our lips. It was like watching someone leap off a bridge.

"Well, I'm not sure what to do here, Carol. Maybe someone wouldn't mind switching?" Miss Blumberg appealed to Joyce, who stuck her tongue against her capped teeth and sucked.

"You can have my seat," I said. Carol Closter beamed at me as if it was the nicest thing anybody had ever done for her. Joyce frowned at me like I was a quadratic equation. I shrugged and gathered my books. Poor math skills were another thing I'd inherited from my mom.

In my new seat I could see all the way from the parking lot to the football field. The late-winter sun glinted off windshields. Lemon trees rustled sweetly in the breeze. Another nice day— yippee. Vice-Principal Galpin was on a ladder, peeling paper hearts from over the school doors. The ones he didn't catch fluttered to the ground like red and pink butterflies. He looked down at those fallen hearts for a long time. Melanie's older sister had told us Mr. Galpin used to be everyone's favourite teacher. She said he'd show up at dances in a tuxedo T-shirt and bow tie and get everyone doing the Chicken. He'd cracked jokes all the time. Then he lost his wife and daughter in a car accident. One day he came to school with only the left side of his face shaved. That was the last day he'd taught anyone anything. Now he went around peeling little pieces of tape off paper hearts so they could be used again next year. He reminded me of my dad, of all the dads, with his dirty-blond hair and beige blazers and the look of someone who's realized life's given him the old bait and switch. Moody Miller, perched up above on the corner of the roof, nodded as if in agreement. That and his hand lifting a joint to his lips were the only moves he made. It was Moody's seat I was in, though I couldn't remember the last time I'd seen him in it. He preferred the school roof to classrooms and the company of Mary Jane to other kids. He could sit up there all day if he wanted to. He often did.

Below Moody, the door to the gym opened and Jamie Finley stepped outside. He put his hands on his hips and scanned the parking lot like he was having a wonderful day. I held up my middle finger and waited for him to turn my way.

I didn't have anything against Jamie Finley personally. I didn't even really know him. We had gone to the same junior high, but we were two years apart, which might as well be twenty at that age. Jamie was on the swim team with Troy

Gainer, but he wasn't like the other jocks, who stalked the halls punching lockers and hooting like apes. I'd never once seen him stuff anyone in a locker, though I'd have bet he'd seen the inside of one himself at some point. He was tall but skinny—ten pounds soaking wet, my dad would've said. When he slung his gym bag over his shoulder, its weight spun him like a top. *Jamie Thinly*, kids called him. Not that I was one to talk. My own arms were violin bows without the elegance. There was no escaping my Johnson dowry. We had the long, tapered fingers of pianists, Mom said. Or serial killers.

As Jamie untangled himself from his gym bag, Mr. Galpin smiled at him. He almost laughed. Jamie Finley should get a medal for that, I thought. He should get his own page in the yearbook. When Jamie smiled, a dimple appeared on his right cheek, as if somebody had poked it with the tip of a protractor. You couldn't see that dimple and not smile yourself, not even if you were hungry and in a lousy mood. Then I remembered that Troy Gainer had a cleft in his chin. It looked like someone had nicked him with an axe. He was probably on the other side of that gym door right then, snapping at people with a wet towel.

I scrutinized my sheet of doodles. Someone had written *JAMIE* in bubble letters on it. I crumpled up the page. My hand was as useless as my brain.

"I heard that. Say it again, freak."

Everyone turned to look at Joyce, who was twisted around in her seat, glaring at the new kid. Carol Closter sat with her head bent over her clasped hands.

"I wasn't talking to you," she said.

Miss Blumberg put her hand on Joyce's shoulder. "Who were you talking to, dear?"

Carol Closter lifted her head slowly. "I was talking to God."

Gasps. Whispers. What was the protocol for prayer? This was worse than the bladder thing.

"She's doing it again," someone said. "She's praying."

Joyce jumped up so fast her chair fell over. "I am not sitting next to some Jesus freak."

"People, please." Miss Blumberg held her hands in the air. Her voice was getting squeaky, the way my mom sounded when one of the country club women popped by and found her in a pair of jeans. "We're all adults here. Let's talk this out." Everyone groaned.

The bell rang. Kids shot out the door, shouting with relief, saved from another Rona Blumberg share circle. Our teacher followed, waddling awkwardly in her cheongsam, just as anxious to get away. When she was gone, Joyce turned sharply in the doorway and pointed her push-up bra at Carol Closter. "Don't ever look at me again. Okay, freak?" She didn't wait for an answer.

Carol Closter folded herself tightly around her purple binder, cotton handkerchief balled in one fist. Her breath was loud and shallow, like she was trying not to cry.

"Don't take it personally," I said. "That's just Joyce."

"It's allergies," she said. "I'm allergic to this town." She blew her nose as if to prove it.

I peered into the hall and saw what I always saw—the field of blond hair, the plains of bronzed skin, the oceans of blue eyes, the mountain range of ski-slope noses. Golden was the only home I'd ever known, but that didn't stop me from feeling as foreign as my mom. I was brunette and bony. I'd never learned to feather my hair. Left to its own devices, my mouth preferred a flat line. In class photos, beside my sunny classmates who beamed at the camera in a flawless row, I stuck out like a rotten tooth. Melanie said I didn't give myself enough credit. "You're not unpopular because you aren't pretty," she'd recently assured me. "You're unpopular because of your personality. But some lemon juice in your hair now and then wouldn't hurt."

This from my best friend since sixth grade. A girl who prayed and carried a handkerchief didn't stand a chance.

Joyce and two other girls leaned against a bank of lockers, sneering at us. When Melanie joined them, they closed ranks around her, whispering loudly.

Carol Closter blew her nose. "I hate it here already."

"It's not so bad," I said.

Behind her, the huddle broke. Joyce and the other two girls slouched against the lockers, their arms crossed as Melanie waved me over frantically. She mouthed Troy's name. When that didn't move me, she held a finger to her throat and sliced.

I turned my back to her. "Maybe just don't . . ."

"Be myself?" Carol Closter smiled with one corner of her mouth, a sly grin reminding me that, small or not, she wasn't actually a little kid.

"Well, anyway," I said. "Turn the other cheek, right?"

"Right. And if that doesn't work, kick them where the sun don't shine."

I smiled now. Maybe she'd be okay after all.

Melanie was suddenly beside me, grabbing my arm. "We're late for gym."

"We already had gym."

She pulled me down the hall anyway.

"You really are hopeless, you know. If it wasn't for me, you'd end up like one of those old ladies who get eaten by their cats. You'd end up like that loser Moody Miller."

I glanced over my shoulder. Carol Closter was still at Miss Blumberg's door. Mr. Galpin was talking to her now, a stack of fallen hearts wedged under an arm. One was taped to the back of his beige blazer. Someone had written on it in felt marker,

If lost please return to Reagan High. When Carol saw me looking, she lifted her handkerchief into the air as if one of us was going off to war. Either that or she was ready to surrender.

"Moody's not a loser," I said. In fact, I was beginning to think Moody Miller might just be the smartest person I knew. "He's a loner."

"What's the difference?" Melanie said.

I didn't know the answer. Losers, loners, Jesus freaks, jocks—in the end most of us would end up members of the Golden Country Club. Some day Troy Gainer would probably sneak out of my recently redecorated bedroom, carrying his shoes.

2

Why the Closters left Big Sky Country for the Golden State was at one time a subject of some national debate. In one supermarket tabloid, a woman from Montana claimed she had spilled coffee on an atlas at Mrs. Closter's house and both women had watched, wide-eyed, as the profile of Jesus Christ took shape over Southern California, with my town smack dab where his eye would go. The article included a grainy photo of a thin woman in a cheap wig holding up what looked like a gas station map. The stain on it did resemble the saviour rather impressively, but also a young Jerry Garcia. I heard it was sold to a collector in New York who was neither religious nor a Grateful Dead fan. An article in *Newsweek* later discredited the woman's story, among others, and set the record straight. But back when I first met Carol Closter, it was still a bona fide mystery, like how they made Spam.

We were not what you would call a God-fearing people. In

a town where just about everything had a store-bought glow, what churches we had were low-lying, bleached, and forgotten six days of the week. My family went to church four times that I can remember, all on Christmas Eve so my mom could hear the children's choir and Dad could shake hands with the minister, who signed the cheques for his staff's life insurance. When Mrs. D'Angelo dragged Melanie to confession, they had to drive an hour to the city, where people knew something about shame.

Founded at the turn of the century by a man with a gold rush fortune and redeveloped fifty years later by men with business degrees, Golden had risen preternaturally from rock and clay. Our kidney-shaped swimming pools, nitrogen-spiked golf courses, and air-conditioned mini-malls were nothing short of a miracle. Every day blue skies, every year a new tax loophole. The Kent State shootings and Manson murders were tragedies watched from the temperate safety of Freoned living rooms, the Vietnam War was "that unfortunate business over there," and the civil rights movement had no effect whatsoever on the healthy supply of immigrant labour. We still had the PTA, the NRA, and thank our lucky stripes for the CIA. So nothing against religion, we just didn't have much need for it. If all else failed, there would always be barbecues and office picnics, cocktail soirees, canapés, and two kinds of fondue. It was Sodom and Gomorrah, only with nicer cars.

How could we explain Carol Closter, who said grace over her tater tots and dropped scripture in class like she was quoting Shakespeare? Every Friday, she invited her classmates to her super-fun Bible study group. "We've got beanbag chairs!" she'd say. It was as if she'd never been around human beings before.

Jesus Freak. Carol Cloister. Sister Carol. In a place like Golden, she was an abomination, as repulsive and fascinating as the fetal pig locked in the biology cupboard. As much as you didn't want to look at the pulpy pink glob, you couldn't help yourself. Wherever Carol went, sniggering trailed her. Banana peels and sandwich crusts collected in front of her locker like tumbleweed. Kids rode her about her hair, her clothes, her hats. Those hats! She wore one everywhere, even inside.

"Do you think she ever takes them off?" Joyce said. "I bet she doesn't. Not even to go to bed."

"She probably sleeps in one," Melanie agreed.

"She probably wears one in the shower," Joyce said, though no one knew for sure since Carol was always the last one to shower after gym class.

"She probably showers with all her clothes on," Melanie said.

"Wouldn't you?" Joyce said.

Carol, walking a few feet ahead, pulled her shoulders back and lifted her hatted head a little higher.

"You guys sure are fascinated by what other girls do in the shower," I said.

They sucked their lips shut and kept them that way.

The truth was, I sort of liked Carol. There was something commendable about her obstinacy, her constancy, her unwavering Carolness. Guys were always knocking those hats off her head and throwing them in the trash or out windows, but the next day she'd show up with another one, like that Dr. Seuss character. Until I met her, I hadn't known it was possible to pity and admire someone at the same time.

When Carol found me in the library the next day, her hat was the same bright yellow as her overalls. She looked like a baby chick bounding toward me. I hid my smile behind my notebook. Maybe I liked Carol, but she didn't have to know that.

"Fancy meeting you here," she said, grinning at me with her hands on her hips. "What are you doing? Do you want to study together?"

"You don't have any books."

She held out her hand and showed me a white book not much bigger than a deck of cards. The pages were gold-edged. A thin red ribbon marked her page. I'd never seen a Bible that small before.

"I get a free block to study scripture," she said.

"Well, I don't. I'm actually pretty busy. I have to hand in this biology report today. So if you don't mind."

I picked up my pen. At the top of the blank page I'd written *Plant reproduction is very important to plants.* I was supposed to write two hundred words and draw the anatomy of a flower with all its parts, but I couldn't bring myself to do it. The dozen red roses Dad had given Mom on Valentine's Day had sat in a vase on the dining room table ever since, their heads drooping so quickly that if you stood there long enough you'd see one nod. But Mom refused to throw them out. Every day she took the bouquet into the kitchen and carefully rearranged it, brittle leaves rustling as she worked. "There now," she'd say, palming the fallen petals. "That's not too bad. I think we can get another day or two."

Then that morning while Mom was busy scraping the toast, Dad had scooped up the vase, opened the cupboard under the kitchen sink, and chucked the whole thing into the garbage. "That smell is enough to put a man off his coffee," he said. When she turned around he was already shin deep in the bin. She'd burst into tears and fled to her bedroom. "Well, it stunk, didn't it?" he'd asked me and I'd had to agree. But I still didn't like the sound of their stems cracking under his shoe like the fine bones of a small animal. Now, thanks to my biology textbook, I knew that roses had ovaries. I didn't even want to know what a pistil was.

"I'm really good at reports," Carol said. "I could help you. It'd be fun."

But I didn't want help with my report. What I wanted was to keep an eye on Joyce, who was talking to Allen Wendell a few tables away. Allen was one of the kids who languished in the portables at the back of the school. Guys like Troy Gainer thought it was hilarious to high-five Allen in the halls, but girls gave him a wide berth. If you laughed at one of his dirty jokes to be nice, you'd never hear the end of them. He knew hundreds. I think he memorized them from books. Joyce was always saying what a pervert he was, so what was she doing sitting next to him, whispering in his ear?

"Earth to Robin! Are you there? Come in, Robin!"

The librarian rang her bell in our direction. Joyce glared our way.

"Jeez, Carol. I'll talk to you later, okay?" I made a big show of flipping through my textbook, hoping she'd get the hint.

"Are you okay, Robin? Are you mad at me or something?" Carol wasn't much for subtlety.

"Since you asked."

When I looked up, Carol was biting her bottom lip, clutching her Bible so tightly she nearly folded it in two. Joyce was gone, and Allen sat alone with a big smile on his face, carving something into the table with a thumbtack.

"No, Carol, nothing's wrong. I just really need to get this done, okay?"

"Sure, Robin. Okay. I'll leave you alone. See ya later, crocodile."

She bounded away as happily as she'd come. Allen Wendell followed her with his eyes. When he saw me watching him, he grinned and grabbed his crotch. I closed my book and gathered my things. I'd had enough biology for one day.

I had planned to tell Melanie about Joyce and Allen as we walked home that day—had been looking forward to it all afternoon, in fact—but Joyce beat me to the punch. She'd told Melanie that she'd seen me talking to Carol Closter. Her pair of twos trumped my ace.

"I told her you're only being nice to Cloister because you feel sorry for her," Melanie assured me. "But you better watch it. People are going to think you're actually friends."

"Maybe we are," I said.

"That's not even funny." Melanie stopped and crossed her arms. "Have you even talked to Troy yet?"

She knew I hadn't. It had been two weeks since Jamie Finley asked what my story was, and Troy hadn't so much as glanced at me in the halls. I was fine with this arrangement, but Melanie, apparently, was not. My apathy was getting in the way of her complete and total happiness, which depended, she explained now, on Jamie Finley falling in love with her.

"You like Jamie?"

"Sure," she said. "Why not? He's a junior and he's on the swim team, and he's sort of cute, don't you think?"

"Why don't you just go out with Troy?" I said.

"Because that's not the way it works. Troy likes you, so I like Jamie. I don't make the rules."

I tried to pay attention while Melanie explained just what those rules were. She had older sisters, so she knew about these things. If we were still in junior high, at least we'd be having this conversation on the swings. Mr. D'Angelo had hung a tire swing in the backyard for Melanie and her sisters, but she preferred the swings at our school, where she didn't have to worry about her mom listening through a window. We used to spend whole afternoons nestled in those snug canvas seats, doing our favourite songs grave injustice and sharing the kinds of things only twelve-year-olds would call secrets. If Melanie had a crush on a boy, which was all the time, she'd plan their wedding, laying out the details for me slowly, as if I were taking notes. Four groomsmen in pale grey tuxes, four bridesmaids in full-length lavender tulle, lavender roses on everyone and everything—you could dye the white ones any colour you wanted, she'd told me, just like carnations.

Mrs. D'Angelo had seen blue roses at a cousin's engagement party once, tinted perfectly to match the bride-to-be's eyes. Melanie would wear white, of course, and her hair up so God would see the delicate gold cross necklace she'd gotten for her first communion. As she descended the church steps as the new Mrs. So-and-So, a hundred white doves would be released while Richard and Karen sang "Close to You." That last one was my idea. I couldn't imagine my own wedding, so I elaborated on hers.

Melanie applied her planning skills now to the Troy Gainer problem. Once again, she had it all figured out. Weekends, the swim team held court at The Place, an abandoned house in an old development slated for demolition where kids went to drink and make out. We would go and act sexy and Troy would finally ask me out and Jamie Finley would ask out Melanie. Then the four of us would fall in love and drive around in Troy's red Mustang, and our lives would be a chewing gum commercial.

"The Place?" I said. "Grade-twelves go there." Stories had circulated of small, dark rooms with mattresses on the floors.

"That's the point," Melanie said. "We're not kids anymore."

Looking at her, I could see she was half-right. Melanie wore matching bras and underwear. I still wore a training bra, though what I was training for wasn't clear. Melanie had started shaving her thighs. I hadn't started shaving anything— I figured I'd have plenty of time to enjoy razor burn. It felt like these changes had happened overnight, while I wasn't looking. Somewhere along the way we'd gotten out of sync. Instead of trying to catch up, I kept digging my feet in. Melanie said high school was our time to spread our wings. But I didn't want to spread my wings for Troy Gainer, or anything else for that matter.

"Are you trying to ruin my life on purpose?" she said. "Maybe I should cut my wrists now and get it over with."

"Pills are a more common choice."

I was only trying to make her laugh, but Melanie didn't think it was funny. We walked the rest of the way in silence. I could hear the swish of her cords.

As we neared our corner, I tried to remember the last time we'd been to the swings. I couldn't remember when it was exactly, only that it was the summer before high school. If I'd known it was the last time, I would have paid more attention. I'd have smelled the metal on my hands as I fell asleep that night. I'd have saved some of the sand from my shoes.

"Hey," I said. "Let's go to the swings."

Melanie scowled at me sideways through a wing of perfectly feathered bangs. "Swings? How old are you? God, Robin, get a clue."

She turned sharply and started down her street. I stood there for longer than I should have watching her walk away, embarrassed by how bad I was at letting go of things, amazed at how easy she made it look.

When I got home, my dad's car was in the driveway. It wasn't even four o'clock. Seeing it there before six was like hearing a phone ring in the middle of the night.

Dad was in his overcoat, banging on Mom's bedroom door. I could hear him from the foyer. "Goddammit, Elaine, you made me come home early. Now you won't talk to me? I've got things to do. What the hell is going on?"

Mom's door opened a few inches. She was still in her house-coat. A single roller clung to the right side of her head.

"What's going on?" he said to her, softening now. Nobody could yell at someone that pathetic.

"I need to talk to you," she said through the crack.

"So talk. By all means. I'm dying to hear what you have to say."

"Did you have a nice day?"

"Did I have a nice day? Is that what I cancelled three appointments for? My day was wonderful and this is the cherry on top. How was your day, dear? Did you talk to the gardener? Did you take in my tasselled shoes to get fixed? Did you even get out of bed? It must be nice to have nothing to do all day. Is it your time of the month or something?"

She started crying.

"It's the roses," I said from the hallway. "You shouldn't have thrown them away."

Dad gave me a look. "Not now, kiddo. Your mother's not feeling well."

"How would you know what I'm feeling?" she said and slammed the door shut. A second later, it opened again. Dad's loafers were hooked by the fingers of one hand. The other held a pair of scissors. She snipped off the tassels and handed him the shoes. When she slammed the door this time, we heard it lock.

"For Christ's sake, Elaine, take a Midol. Take a Valium. Take *something*."

"She just wanted to keep them a bit longer," I tried again. "She put 7-Up in the water every day."

Dad sighed and bent down to pick up his shoes. He took them and a bottle of Scotch out to the pool house. I thought maybe I should tell him that you could buy roses in any colour you liked, in case he wanted to get her new ones. But then I remembered that the red ones were Mom's favourite. Despite all appearances to the contrary, she wasn't a woman who was hard to please.

——

For the next week, Dad ate his meals at the office, showered at the club, and came home late. Mom slept in and went to bed early, with migraines, she said. She must have felt better during the hours I was at school and Dad was at work. Fabric swatches and paint chips accumulated on the dining room table while we were gone. At night, when the sound of Mom's crying came through the wall, I slept with my radio and let David Cassidy wonder into my ear why he was so afraid to love me.

If I wanted to worry about something, I would've started with my own screwed-up life. In the mornings, Melanie wasn't waiting for me at our corner anymore. After school, we didn't walk home together either. In between, I would find her sitting on the back field with Joyce Peyton, picking at their sandwiches and slicking their bare legs with baby oil. Seeing me, they'd clam up and smile like cherubs, shiny knees touching, they sat so close. "We're working on a group project," Melanie said. Beside her, Joyce grinned, smug with secrecy.

I spent more time in the library, where you could nap uninterrupted at one of the carrels that lined the back wall. When Carol found me there this time, my geography paper was pasted to my cheek with drool. We were studying the Ring of Fire, twenty-five thousand miles of oceanic trenches, island arcs, and volcanic mountain ranges that encircle the Pacific basin. It's the secret earth beneath our feet, a land of angry plates and ancient crusts, pushing, stretching, grinding away at our solidity. Periods of calm go on for years, decades, millennia, and then one day, snap—the world splits in two. I didn't know why they bothered teaching this stuff. Every Californian knows about the Ring of Fire, but most still go on with their lives as if the worst thing that can happen today is gridlock on the 101. For the daughter of an insurance salesman, it was just another bedtime story.

"I knew you'd be here." Carol peeled the page from my cheek.

"Who told you that—God?"

Carol flattened her smile. "You shouldn't joke about Him."

I yawned. "What do you want, Carol?"

She looked around, as if someone might be listening, but the library was empty. Only losers went there at lunch. Even Allen Wendell had better things to do.

"God did tell me something," she said. "He told me to tell you not to be sad about those girls. He told me to tell you they aren't really your friends."

"Do I look sad?" I gave her the biggest smile I could manage—forty, maybe forty-five watts. The school nurse had assured me that it was normal to feel bad all the time because of puberty. Dad thought I should pace myself. He said I had plenty of time to be disappointed with life when I was his age.

"You can't fool God, Robin. God sees everything and He's worried about you."

"Tell him to take a number." I laid my head back down on my books and waited for her to go away.

"You know, sometimes you make me wonder if we're really friends."

"Yeah, well maybe you should stop wondering."

I buried my face in the crook of my arm. My cheeks were hot with shame. It still shocked me how mean I could be, how well I could imitate girls like Joyce if I wanted to.

When I woke again at the bell, there was a piece of paper in front of my nose, folded a million times into a small, fat square. My name was written on one side in purple pen, a heart over the *i*. Carol Closter might talk to God, but in some ways she was just like every other teenaged girl.

I shoved the note in my pocket and forgot about it. I'd had it with people who wouldn't speak up for themselves. If God had something to tell me, he could put some pants on and tell me himself.

I didn't see Carol again until Friday afternoon. The last bell had just rung and the hallways were like roiling rivers, everyone rushing to their lockers, groaning about homework, plotting their weekends. The scream tore through our clamour like a gunshot. It was an awful, injured sound, wide-mouthed and from the belly. We froze and pricked our ears. Even after it stopped, we stayed frozen, mute antelope waiting for a signal. Then the gym door flung open and someone tumbled into the hall as if she'd been spit out. She was in a towel, her hair a mat of white suds. She ran toward us, wiping at her face with one hand. Carol.

As she neared us, the crowd parted to let her through. We flattened against our lockers, made more room than necessary. Whatever had happened, it had nothing to do with us.

Carol slipped and landed against some kid's legs. Nobody laughed. It took her forever to stand. The floor was wet beneath her and she wouldn't let go of the towel. I closed my eyes. I couldn't bear it if she looked at me. At last she was up and running again, more slowly now, limping maybe. I couldn't watch, heard only the slap of wet feet on linoleum and the boom of a fire door slamming shut.

Two girls ran into the office. Seconds later, Mr. Galpin came out, a paper napkin tucked into his collar. "Which way?" he said. Kids pointed meekly. He tore the napkin from his collar and flew out the door.

We camped against our lockers. "Oh man," someone kept whispering. "Oh man. Oh man." Nobody wanted to go home yet. We were terrified and giddy, flooded with adrenaline and something else familiar that I couldn't quite name. Relief, maybe, though that didn't seem right.

The memory was just a feeling, then bits of light and sound. I was nine years old, lying down in the back seat of the car and counting streetlights as they flew across the rear windshield. My parents were up front, not talking as usual. Suddenly the car slowed and the windshield exploded with light. I reached up to touch the glass. Still cold. Dad pulled over to the side of the road. "She should see this," he said.

Mom said it was morbid, that I was too young, but she knew there was no use arguing. Dad got out of the car and left the engine running so she could listen to the radio, which she did loudly to drown out the noise of sirens and shouting. When I got out, Dad gave me his hand, so I knew something special was happening.

I felt it from across the street, hot as an August day. The flames were orange and red and blue. Firemen's voices barked over the roar of the fire, jets of water arcing gracefully to the sky. Around them, sparks snapped in the air, playful as fireflies. I squeezed Dad's hand. I'd heard stories about house fires, but I'd never seen one until then. When Dad talked about another poor sap who forgot to unplug the Christmas tree, I thought only about what I would save from my own burning house— how would I choose between beloved but aging toys and gift-wrapped boxes that may or may not contain socks? I hadn't realized a fire could be so beautiful, like a hundred sunrises set against a black velvet curtain. The night was electric with it.

"Are you scared?" Dad said.

"No," I said, thinking that maybe he was. He held my hand so tightly his school ring pinched my finger. Insurance men have tremendous respect for fire. They're a lot like arsonists that way.

"Well, you should be," he said. "Do you know why?"

"Because we're all one bad decision away from disaster?"

The light from the fire reflected in his smile. "That's right," he said. "That's my girl. Don't worry," he said, squeezing me tighter. "Nothing like this will ever happen to you."

But I wasn't scared, not even a bit. Dad's arm was around me, Mom was safe in the car, and the heat in the air made everything shimmer. That's when I noticed a family huddled together under wool blankets at the edge of the light. They had a daughter too, about my age. When she turned around and saw me smiling, I bit my lips so hard they bled.

I didn't yet have the experience to imagine what had happened to Carol Closter, but whatever it was, it hadn't happened to me. What I felt that day in the hallway was the same horrible, guilty relief I'd felt the night of the fire. I would never be that girl under the wool blanket.

At last the gym doors opened again. The gym teacher came through them with Allen Wendell, his arm around the boy's wet shoulders. Snot ran down Allen's trembling chin.

When Mr. Galpin returned, he was alone. "Go home," he said, barely looking at us. "Everyone just go home."

We shuffled outside. It was a bright day, but the sun gave off about as much warmth as a drama club prop. I didn't see Melanie anywhere. Moody Miller was sitting on the roof, still as a gargoyle. I wondered if he'd seen Carol run out the door. He probably saw the beginning and end of a lot of things up there. Nervous whispers were already turning into careful laughter, prickling at the back of my neck. Any relief I'd felt vanished. I hugged my books and hurried across the parking lot. For once, I was eager to get home.

Jamie Finley caught up with me at the edge of the football field. "What was that?" he said. "You think she's okay?"

I shrugged. I didn't want to think about it.

"Yeah," he said, nodding. "Shit." He raked his hand through his hair. I could smell his apple shampoo. His hair was long for a swimmer. Most of the guys on the team shaved their heads—among other things, Melanie said. A football player started skipping around the parking lot, flapping one arm and pinching his T-shirt under his chin like a towel. He had a white beret on his head, the kind the school majorettes wore, and the pompom bounced up and down. Troy Gainer leaned against his red Mustang, laughing. The hatless majorette beside him fluffed her hair and smiled.

Jamie shook his head. "Not cool, guys. Not cool."

I'd already started walking again. He caught up and settled into step. "My friends aren't always jerks," he said. "Just most of the time. Hey, you're really fast. Have you ever thought about trying out for track? Seriously, where's the fire?"

I stopped in the middle of the field, arms braced over my books. Laughter wafted across the field. Wherever Carol had run to, I hoped it was out of earshot.

"Who wants to know?" I said.

"What do you mean? I do. Didn't I just say the words?"

"I don't know," I said. "I don't even know if you're really saying what you're saying."

"Okay, I'm lost."

"Me too," I said, feeling tired again. My books weighed a hundred pounds. Being fourteen was turning out to be a lot more complicated than television had led me to believe.

I hitched up my bag and headed for home. This time Jamie let me go.

———

When I got home, Melanie was sitting on my front step. She chewed her hair when she was nervous or upset, and she was chewing it now like it was chocolate flavoured.

"What are you doing here?" I said.

Melanie pushed up the sleeves of her blouse. She'd rolled them up, but they were still soaked to her shoulders. Her jean skirt was dark in the places that hadn't dried yet. She'd walked half a mile like that. I wondered how far somebody could get in a towel.

"I can't come to my best friend's house?" She'd always been a bad liar. It was one of her better qualities. "What's wrong? Did something happen?"

When I didn't answer, Melanie reached down and plucked a mini daisy from the grass. They were weeds, really, but every little girl called them mini daisies. We used to braid them or stick them in each other's hair. She ran a finger down the flower's stalk, splitting it with her pink nail. She was making a friendship bracelet. You had to break one flower to thread another one through. Her legs were shiny below her skirt, shins greased with baby oil. She had tanned at lunch like it was just another day. And then this.

"You're starting to burn," I said. I poked her knee with my finger. Hard.

"Ouch," she said, and we watched the moon I'd made go from white to pink.

"Don't you want to know why I'm all wet?" she said.

"Not really."

Melanie poked her other knee and smiled. She hadn't come to confess, I realized. She'd come to gloat.

"I have to go in," I said, stepping past her to the door. I didn't know this Melanie. I wasn't sure I wanted to. But I was jealous too. Whoever this Melanie was, she would probably get everything she ever wanted. I pictured Jamie Finley in a grey tuxedo, pants flooded, a lavender rose limp at his lapel.

"Yeah, me too," she said and tossed the flowers in the grass.

Mom was smoking at the kitchen sink, staring out the window at the driveway. She'd been to the salon, and her hair was freshly bleached and curled. Anniversary diamonds glittered at her earlobes. Her cocktail dress pulled across her chest and puckered between the buttons, and the heels of her silver sandals needed new tips, but from the neck up she was a knockout.

"Was that Melanie out there?" she said. "She didn't come to the door."

"She had to go home."

Mom nodded and stubbed out her half-finished cigarette in a crystal ashtray. "I should probably quit," she said as she eased another from the pack on the counter. Beside it was a small white vase filled with flowers. Pink tulips and orange gerberas. A teddy bear hugged the vase, his paws handcuffed with yellow ribbon. It wasn't the kind of thing you send to someone you love. It was the kind of thing you send to someone in the hospital.

I poked around inside the fridge. She hadn't gone grocery shopping all week, but eating was a hard habit to break too.

"We're dining at the club tonight," she said.

"All of us?"

"Of course all of us."

"But why?" I groaned.

"Because we're a family, that's why. And don't frown. Once those wrinkles set in, they never come out." She pressed a thumb between her own eyebrows, then reached for the radio on the windowsill. A man was shouting about the grand opening of another car dealership. "These deals are groovy! Tune in, turn on, and drop by!"

"Mom?" I wanted to tell her about Carol and about Melanie, but I'd stopped telling her things by then and I didn't know how to start again. "You look really nice," I said.

The ad ended and Eddie Fisher started singing about the games that lovers play. Mom took a thick, wide-throated drag and held it for a long time before turning her face and letting the smoke stream over her shoulder.

"Thanks, kiddo," she said and turned off the radio.

If Golden was a town of mannequins, the Golden Country Club was its Macy's window. The parking lot was crammed with Cadillacs and Continentals. Evenings and weekends, valets in red vests and sycophantic smiles clogged the neighbouring streets with the overflow. Inside, men wore plaid jackets and ordered whiskey sours. The temperature was kept at a crisp fifteen degrees so the women could wear their stoles year-round. Whether they hailed from Sacramento or Sarasota, they spoke with a drawl particular to cotillions and tennis courts.

Dad looked smart in his navy blazer that night, hair combed back, white teeth bared, affecting the expression of a man enjoying himself. He was a member for the business connections and because it was what families like ours did. He went no more than was necessary. He didn't even like golf. Now and then, he'd wave across the room while mumbling that, Jesus Christ, he hoped So-and-So wouldn't come over. He gave people advice all week long, he didn't want to do it all weekend too. Mom made small talk for both of them while cutting her Salisbury steak into tiny slivers she didn't eat. I ate my hamburger in silence and made a list in my head of all the places I would rather be.

When the entrees were cleared, Dad ordered a bottle of champagne and poured me half a glass. "I guess we have something to tell you," he said and made a ceremony of smoothing his tie. Mom rearranged the napkin in her lap and gave me a smile as strained as her dress. They didn't notice Vera Miller until she was standing right behind them.

"Hello, Fishers." She held up her martini glass. "Looks as though we're all celebrating tonight."

Vera Miller was one of the professional Country Club Wives, women who were attractive without being pretty and had a way of laughing without smiling. Loud and glamorous, she was the kind of person everyone knew but few people liked, including her two ex-husbands and two sons, none of whom talked to her. Her oldest son was a senior at my school who wore skinny leather ties and sold his mother's prescriptions out of his Camaro in the parking lot. He liked to tell everyone how his mother had been a drive-in waitress before she got married, the kind who wears roller skates. He said it with a sneer, but I couldn't help admiring somebody who'd had what was possibly the world's greatest job. Her other son was Moody.

"No, no," Mom said, lowering her own glass. "Just felt like champagne. Hello, Vera. Congratulations. How was the wedding?"

"Another Vegas quickie. They give me a discount now."

"Well, you look happy," Mom said.

"You know what they say. Third one's the harm. I mean

charm." As Vera laughed, her martini glass flung forward. Cloudy liquid sloshed around the rim, but not a drop spilled. I pictured her on gleaming white roller skates, carrying trays of milkshakes.

Vera tossed an arm over Dad's shoulder and slumped forward, her breasts testing the integrity of her scooped neckline. "What I wouldn't do to find a man like this," she said. "You're a lucky woman, Elaine."

There was a long pause. "I'm the lucky one," Dad said, like a kid in a school play who's forgotten his lines.

"I guess you Fishers are just a bunch of lucky buggers," Vera said.

Mom smiled without teeth. I'd once heard her tell my dad that if he wanted a socialite wife, he should have married someone like Vera Miller. He'd said if he was going to have an ex-wife, he was glad it was her. She hadn't laughed.

A greying man in a white dinner jacket appeared at our table. "Here's *my* lucky bugger now. Darling, you know the Fishers."

"Podiatrist?"

"Insurance," Dad said, amping up his smile a few more watts. "We do your life and disability." He shook the man's liverspotted hand.

"Yes, right," the man said. "Small world. Well, Vera, that's probably enough fun for one evening."

He took hold of her elbow and, in the attempt to extract his new wife, sent half her martini down the front of Dad's shirt. "You'll have to forgive her," the man said. "Thirty-seven years old and she still can't hold her liquor."

While Dad dabbed at the vodka with a napkin and Mom talked about what a whiz their drycleaner was, Vera bent down to me and smiled.

"Don't listen to a word we say," she whispered. "We're all a bunch of fakes and phonies. Even the Fishers with their beautiful house and beautiful everything. Did you know that? Oh, you do know. I can see it in your eyes." She grinned, delighted. "Liar, liar, pants on fire." If she'd leaned in any closer I could've lit her breath with a match.

"All right. All right. Let's save it for the late show." Vera's husband tugged her away, her martini glass terrorizing the other diners as she stumbled along.

"What a piece of work," Dad said.

Mom poured herself another glass of champagne. "I actually feel sorry for her."

"I don't," I said, and they both looked over as if surprised to find me there.

"You would if you knew who the sole beneficiary of his will is," he said.

"Thirty-seven," Mom scoffed. "In dog years maybe."

Our cheesecake arrived. Nobody ate. Dad stabbed his slice with his fork and signalled for the bill. Five minutes later, we were on the road, Dad driving with the meticulous care of a drunk insurance man, Mom leaning her cheek against the passenger window and staring out at the dark. When we arrived safe and sound at our beautiful everything, she went to bed and he went to the pool house, and Vera Miller was forgotten, along with whatever it was they had wanted to tell me.

I got up in the night to use the bathroom. The window was open and my parents' soft voices drifted in, carried over the pool as clear as a telephone call.

"You don't want it," she said.

"I didn't mean that."

"What *did* you mean, then, Jim? Why don't you just say what you mean?"

They were standing at the back of the yard, still dressed for dinner, though Mom's feet were bare. It was a nice night, not too warm yet. Neil's stars studded the sky. I thought they were arguing about the yard, maybe that new tiling for the pool that she'd seen in some magazine but he'd said was too expensive, he had his limits. With the moonlight on their faces, they almost looked like a couple of kids sneaking out to fool around.

"I'm not getting rid of it," she said. "If that's what you meant."

"I didn't say that. I just meant—Well, Jesus Christ, Elaine, let's not go off the deep end here." Dad was holding a glass of something. He took a drink, tipping his head far back to get the last of it. "Don't you ever feel like, I don't know, you took the wrong bus one day and now you're living somebody else's life?"

"Whose life am I living?" she said.

Dad shook his head at his glass. "You can't want this either. That's all I meant."

"What, Jim? What can't I want? Why won't you say it?"

"All right, this. This!" He swept his arm over the grass, sent the ice cubes flying. "Thirteen more years of this."

"Fourteen," she corrected. "Fourteen years."

They didn't say anything after that. Dad stared at the nothing in the bottom of his glass. Mom hugged herself as if she felt a sudden chill. My own arms were covered in goosebumps. I stepped back from the window and saw them framed there, prettily, in the soft grey moments before dawn. Two actors waiting for the curtain to fall.

When I called Melanie on Saturday, Mrs. D'Angelo said she'd call me back, she was washing her hair. Mom wouldn't get out of bed. Migraine, she said. I thought I'd spend the day lying on the grass in the backyard, staring at the sun to see if I really could make myself go blind, but Dad had other plans. He stood over me with his hands on his tool-belted hips—never a good sign.

"Let's go, kiddo. Off your duff. We've got a lot to do."

"You're putting in the patio tiles?"

"What patio tiles?" He handed me our semi-annual earth-quake checklist.

"We just did this," I said.

Dad gave me one of his hundred-watt smiles. "It's never too soon to be safe."

Mom was still in bed, so he'd made breakfast. There was a stack of golden toast on the kitchen table, already buttered and jammed. It was strange to smell coffee that wasn't scorched.

The first thing on the list was the roof. I went out to the garage to get the ladder while Dad tied a rope around his waist. He double- and triple-knotted it, loop after endless twist. "Falls are the leading—"

"Cause of home injury deaths," I said.

He stared at me, trying to decide what kind of smart I was being. "That's right," he said.

For the next half an hour he shimmied around the roof, crouched down on all fours. He examined every shingle and rattled the base of the TV antenna. It was my job to hold the ladder and listen to his lecture. "One of these killed a fellow in Fresno last year," he shouted, gripping the weathervane. "Popped off and hit him on the head. Dead on the spot. Just like that."

"Lucky bugger," I said, Vera Miller's voice in my head like an echo.

After the gutters were cleared, wiggled, and tightened, Dad got started on the windows. Each pane of glass had to be tapped delicately, in a spiral pattern, with his knuckle. He patted down the frames as if he was frisking them for weapons. Next, the foundation. This was his favourite part. We circled the house for what felt like hours, Dad stopping every couple of feet to press his palms flat against the concrete like he was copping a feel.

"What am I doing?" he said.

"Embarrassing me?"

"What did you say?"

"Looking for cracks."

He shook his head. "By the time you see a crack, it's too late. You know that, Robin. What do you look for?"

"Irregularities?"

"That's right. You're checking for cracks, sure, but you're also on the lookout for smaller changes in the foundation, discoloration, bowing. See that?" He jabbed his finger at the concrete. I nodded dully. What was the point? We lived in

California. It was like digging a bomb shelter in the middle of a minefield.

"Wouldn't it be easier to not live over a fault line," I said.

"Without that fault line you wouldn't have a place to live. That fault line puts a roof over your head."

"Oh, that's logical."

"Look." He took my hand and pressed it against a ridge of concrete. "Feel that."

He was crouched down in the grass like a boiled crab. His face was red and wet with sweat. I twisted and pulled away, scraping my fingers on the wall's rough edge.

"What the hell is wrong with you?" he said, wiping his forehead with the back of one claw.

I didn't answer. He was ruining my Saturday, but it wasn't as if I had anything better to do. I could have blamed my sour mood on the heat, on being woken up in the middle of the night, on Joyce Peyton and her stupid capped teeth. But tallying up the offences didn't make me feel any better. The more I thought about it, the madder I got. I was furious suddenly. Dizzy with it.

"You think your old man doesn't know what he's talking about? You have no idea what's what, kiddo. Let me tell you. We're all just one—"

I clenched my fists and toes. At fourteen I wasn't above stomping my feet. "If you say it, I'll scream, I swear."

"Do you think I'm having fun out here? You think I like doing this? Who do you think I'm doing all this for? You know, you and your mother—"

I screamed anyway.

Mom came running outside in her nightgown. She looked from Dad to me, back and forth, up and down, searching for bleeding, contusions, broken limbs. "What happened? What on earth?"

"Nothing," Dad grumbled and disappeared inside the pool house.

Mom picked up the checklist. At some point, I'd thrown it on the ground.

"You know, your father does this because he loves you," she said.

I went to the kitchen to make a glass of iced tea. I slammed cupboard doors and rattled every dish I touched. When I saw that we were out of ice, I gripped the spoon so tightly it bent.

"It's too damned hot," Dad said, standing in the doorway. "We're all turning into a bunch of grouches. Good day for a swim."

"I guess," I mumbled. It wasn't yet noon and my T-shirt was already a second skin. But my anger clung to me just as fiercely, and I wasn't ready to let it go.

Dad forced a smile. He hooked his thumb under the metal

clip of his Rolex and cracked it open. "What do you say, sport? Think you still got it?"

From the time I could count, my dad had made me practise holding my breath underwater. Drowning was the second leading cause of death for young children and there was a gleaming turquoise deathtrap beckoning to me in our backyard. "Why do we have a pool, then?" Mom would say. "Why not just fill the thing in with concrete?" And he'd say, "Because we live in California, that's why." But I loved our drills. Some evenings, Dad would already be taking off his watch as he stepped through the door, saying "Let's see what you got," and I would run—run!—to get my suit on. I liked that first sharp plunge, how my small body could shatter the glassy surface, how the shock of cold made everything alive and bright. I liked the pull and push of the water, how weightless I felt as its fingers stroked my hair. Most of all I liked that above me Dad bent forward on the edge of a chair, watching his Rolex with the intensity of a bomb defuser. I would open my eyes and see him quivering over me like Jell-O, like liquid sapphires in the twinkling light, and I would want us to stay this way, a prince and his princess forever frozen in this fairy-tale world. When my lungs screamed for oxygen, I listened to the heartbeat of the pump, its thump a secret in my ear. For a while there was only this timeless blue place, only this me and that him. By the time I was twelve, I could hold my breath for almost two minutes.

The drills had stopped when he moved into the pool house. One day Mom found my Speedo in the garbage, folded carefully as a soldier's flag. "Maybe it's time to sign you up for diving," she'd said, placing it on my lap, freshly washed. I shook my head and shoved it in a bottom drawer, one more thing I'd unknowingly outgrown.

Now, Dad bounced the Rolex lightly in his hand. "Come on, champ. Humour your old man. Whad'ya say, sport?"

Watching us from the dining room, Mom gave me an encouraging smile. We both knew he was trying to hand me an olive branch, but it felt more like someone was tossing me an old bone.

"No thanks," I said and went to my room.

I'd had enough of counting the seconds to disaster, enough of holding my breath. I'd been doing it my whole life.

If he thought fourteen years was a long time, try being me.

That night I dreamed I was running down my street in my swimsuit. People lined the sidewalk to watch, faceless blobs and snorkelling masks. I didn't see Dad in the crowd, but Mom was on our front step, waving at me, her arm hinged at the elbow like a beauty queen. I called to her, but only sudsy water came out. I was drowning on the inside. When I woke up gasping, I tasted chlorine in my mouth.

I couldn't get back to sleep after that. Eventually I gave up and went to the backyard. Korea had made Dad an early riser. I thought he might want some help finishing off that list.

The day was crisp and bright, the sky so clear there was nothing for warmth to hold on to, the swimming pool as flat and shiny as glass. I found the checklist on a lounge chair, the paper warped with dew. I shivered and hurried across the lawn.

The pool house was shut up tight. *Pool house* is misleading. It was just a large shed, really, with a built-in bench, a small skylight that didn't open, air that tasted like dust. My dad had put it together years before from a kit he'd picked up at the hardware store. He'd said it would come in handy. He said it was on sale. Mom had eyed the plans suspiciously, then him. "Handy for what?" she'd said.

I listened for Dad's staccato snore. When I heard only the sound of birds in the trees, my dream slid over me cold as a wet sheet. I shivered again as I reached out to knock.

"Dad?"

All I heard was birds. I touched my fingers to the doorknob and turned slowly, holding my breath until the latch released.

"Daddy?"

Whenever I hear the phrase *clean getaway* on the evening news, I think of this moment, how the half-dozen paperbacks were lined up on the bench with a year's worth of *Life* magazines stacked neatly beside them, how for once his bathrobe hung on a hook. The pile of dirty shirts was gone, along with his contraband Cubans and the ashtray I'd made. He'd tidied up before he'd left. He'd even stripped the cot bare and bundled the sheets at the foot of the mattress, like a polite houseguest at the end of his stay.

3

Also gone: his Rolex, his shaving kit, his gold-plated pen. His golf clubs still leaned in the front closet, but his brown overcoat was missing. The maimed shoes were nowhere to be found, though they might have been in the garbage, or wherever tasselled loafers were laid to final rest. *Natural Disasters for Insurance Sellers*, taken. *Morbidity & Mortality*, not. Of course his favourite grey hat, of course his beloved '68 DeVille. These and other items are forever catalogued in my mind as Things Men Take When They Leave.

Mom didn't want to hear my list. "Your father and I had a disagreement, that's all," she said. "Sometimes married people need space from each other. It's not as though it's the first time."

"It's not?"

"Oh, now, let's not get dramatic."

She stood at the kitchen sink, staring out the window at the dark driveway, tapping cigarette ash into a souvenir mug from Reno I'd seen a million times but never thought about. Who had gone to Reno and when? What else didn't I know? Monday morning she was there again, or still there, in the same yellow nightgown, Reno mug now filled with coffee.

"Can I help you with something?" she said when she saw me, like I was next in line at the DMV. I went to school.

There, I discovered a bottomless mug of things I didn't know. When teachers called on me, I drew a blank. I answered math questions in gym class and history questions in biology. I was feeling pretty sorry for myself and miserable about humanity in general until I saw Carol coming down the same hallway where she'd run, half-naked, just days before. It was assumed Allen Wendell had been exiled, at last, to the special school on the other side of town. We never saw him again. But Carol Closter had come back.

Some said Allen and the Jesus Freak had been going at it in the shower when someone walked in. They said Bible-thumpers were all like that deep down. Some said the janitor had found her beneath the bleachers, praying on her knees among the cigarette butts and gum wrappers. Others claimed she'd thrown herself in the canal. Deer wandered down from the hills and fell in sometimes. Once, the waters had carried the lifeless body of a little boy to the next town. But I'd never heard anything about suicides, and Carol didn't seem like a girl who'd try to drown herself.

She walked quickly with her eyes fixed straight ahead, her arms wrapped so tightly around her purple binder that her knuckles were white, but there she was—either the bravest person I'd ever known or the craziest. Maybe there wasn't much difference between the two. Her hat that day was cotton-candy pink. Embroidered white butterflies fluttered around its rim.

One by one, kids saw her and froze. A teacher speared us with warning glances, but not a single whisper or snicker was heard. The silence was louder than any noise we could have made. She was a wraith haunting our halls, and nobody wants to see their sins illuminated by fluorescent lights. One by one, they turned their backs to her until only Carol and I faced each other. As she passed me she lowered her eyes, just as I had days before, as if there was something there she, too, would rather not see. I hugged my books and hurried the other way. I told myself I was lucky to be rid of her, that I should have listened to Melanie from the start. If I fanned through all my textbooks that day, searching for notes secreted in their pages, it was only out of habit. Carol Closter was not the sort of girl you wanted as a friend.

If Melanie had an opinion on Carol Closter's return she did not express it to me. Much as I tried to, I couldn't take it personally. Like Carol, Melanie didn't talk to anyone for days, not even Joyce. She kept her head down and her mouth full of hair. On Friday, she was waiting at my locker after school. I wasn't sure if this was a good thing, but I was still happy to see her.

"Do you want to go to the swings?" she said.

Carol had slipped and fallen a few feet from where we stood, but Melanie wouldn't know that. She hadn't stuck around to see how things ended. Maybe they hadn't yet. I nodded yes.

We walked to our old junior high without talking, got all the way to the field without a single word. Melanie chewed her hair while I tried not to think about my mom smoking at the kitchen sink, waiting for Dad's DeVille to pull into the driveway. The house was so quiet I could hear every dry suck of cigarette, the long sigh of each exhale. Silence wasn't so bad compared to that.

Up ahead I could see the playground, the familiar topography of logs and ropes and slides on an island of grey sand. It was empty except for a couple of little kids climbing on top of the jungle gym. There was nobody on the swings. I grinned at Melanie.

"What's so funny?" she said.

"You eating my dust," I said and shot off across the grass.

Running was another thing that high school kids didn't do, unless it was for gym class, and even then you could make a mile last an hour if you really put in the effort. It had been so long since I'd made my legs do more than shuffle, the ability to do so was a revelation. I'd forgotten how good it felt to know that you are strong and fast. Suddenly, Melanie was running beside me. We smiled at each other knowingly, then really kicked into gear. As I neared the sand, I held up my arms and aimed for the wide white ribbon in my mind.

We tagged the swings and threw ourselves at the sand, panting and laughing. It was hard to say who got there first, but it didn't really matter. The little kids sat on the rope ladder, clapping for both of us.

"You're crazy," Melanie said, smiling up at the sky.

The sun caught her gold cross. It glinted prettily at her throat. I'd asked for one for my twelfth birthday, but Mom said there was no way. Where she came from, those crosses hung from the necks of girls who got knocked up senior year and were married off before they could buy their own beer.

"Do you ever talk to God?" I said.

"You don't talk to God, Robin. You talk to a priest." She touched her fingers to the gold cross for a moment, then the tips of her collarbone, lips, and heart.

"What about when you pray?"

"Why are we talking about God?" she said and tucked the cross back inside her blouse. For her, religion was something you did in private, preferably behind a curtain.

I took a deep breath.

"I think my dad left."

"Left left?" Melanie said.

The weight of the word sunk in. I held my breath and waited for it to pass right through me. Somewhere inside me was a Dad-shaped hole.

"Where'd he go?"

"I don't know."

"Do you think he'll come back?"

"I don't know."

A cloud floated by. Cumulus or stratocumulus, or altocumulus maybe. We'd had a test on cloud types the week before, but I'd failed it. My eyes were heavy with waiting tears. I didn't know anything.

Melanie smiled encouragingly. "Joyce's dad left. But he came back. Now she's getting a car."

A car honked in the distance, as if on cue. Melanie sat up to look. A convertible full of kids idled across the field. Joyce Peyton popped up in the back seat, as if our words had conjured her. "Come on, Smellanie! Let's go!"

Melanie jumped up and ran her fingers through her hair, shaking out the sand. "Sorry," she said, starting back across the field. "I told her I'd meet them here. And sorry about your dad. Sorry!"

But she didn't look sorry as she climbed up beside Joyce on the top of the back seat and waved at me. She looked like she'd been voted homecoming queen. As the car peeled away, I tried to be happy for her. Melanie was living in a chewing gum commercial after all. I just wasn't in it.

The next day I woke to the smell of burnt toast and fresh paint. Old sheets were draped over the living room furniture. It was nine o'clock and Mom had already spackled. She angled the can so I could see the colour. "It's called *chartreuse!*"

She lost enthusiasm once she saw it on the wall.

"No problem! It's just paint!"

A flurry of doomed projects followed. It was just a lampshade, just wallpaper, just a rug. She attempted to recover the dining chairs with a bolt of white vinyl she'd found on sale, only to realize halfway through that she knew nothing about upholstery. She relined half the drawers in the kitchen before she decided they'd look nicer stripped back to wood. "If it's worth doing, it's worth doing well," she said, but I guess nothing was.

Projects were started and abandoned in hours, then minutes. But Mom was not discouraged. I could measure the days Dad had been gone by the miles of painter's tape and empty glue gun sticks. Mom used the kitchen calendar, hanging from a nail inside a cupboard door. Every day there was another black X in another square so small you had to look for it. I did.

Halfway through April the X's stopped, along with the projects.

I don't know what Mom did while I was at school in the days that followed, but when I was home she slept a lot. Between naps, she took baths that seemed to last hours. I would hear the gurgle of water down the drain now and then, followed by more hot water rushing from the tap. Meals were increasingly unpredictable. She'd forget to turn the oven on or forget to turn it off, the buzzer ringing not three feet from where she stood at the sink, staring at the driveway. One night she gave up altogether and halved a can of unheated tomato soup into two bowls. You could still see the grooves from the can in the gelatinous orange blob. She got down two spoonfuls before it sent her running to the bathroom.

"It's not that bad," I said through the door, swallowing hard to purge the film of vegetable mucus from my throat.

"Just a flu," she said on the other side, flushing the toilet again and again.

After that I made myself grilled cheese sandwiches while Mom nibbled Saltines and dry toast. She left money on the table so I could buy my lunch. If she forgot, I made peanut butter sandwiches and chewed them violently while I watched Melanie and Joyce giggle into each other's ears. It felt like watching someone playing me in the movie version of my life and having no say in the casting.

On weekends, I drifted on the air mattress, making eddies in the water with my fingertips, trying not to draw comparisons with the dead bugs that floated around me, destined for the great bottom vent of life. There wasn't anything else to do. If I played music or watched TV, Mom made me turn the volume so low it might as well have been off. She didn't have to tell me she was waiting for the phone to ring. Now and then she'd lift the receiver to her ear to make sure it still worked.

One night I heard her behind her bedroom door, talking on the phone. I picked up the extension, certain it had to be my dad. I only wanted to hear his voice, steady and solid as California rock. But it was some old woman. "Lainey, Lainey," she was saying. "What have you done now?"

It took me a few seconds to recognize the voice of my grandmother, a woman I spoke to only on holidays and birthdays. The one time my grandparents had come to California, they'd spent the week pointing out how fancy everything was.

Pimento loaf, eh? Fancy! On their last night, Dad cancelled our reservation at the club and drove everyone to the new Howard Johnson's. Mom had seemed both sad and relieved the morning they'd left, Gran with her grey ponytail and hand-rolled cigarettes, Grandpa in his ironed jeans.

"I'm sorry for you, Lainey. I really am. But I can't say I'm surprised by it. You made your bed with that one, my girl."

"I know, Ma. I know I did. It's just that—" She sniffled back tears. "What am I supposed to do, Ma? I wake up and I get dressed. But then I don't know what to do next."

Gran cleared her throat. "How far along are you, Lainey?"

There was a long, scratchy nothing, then Mom's voice sounding farther away than my grandmother's at the other end of the line. "A few weeks?"

I looked around, wondering which project they meant. From the kitchen, I could see the bolt of white vinyl folded on the dining table, beside it the crystal flower vase half-concealed now by decoupage. None of her attempts had lasted more than a few days, never mind weeks. Then I spied the calendar hanging from its nail. All those black X's. I lifted April, March, following the X's back to February. February 14, to be exact.

"You can always come home, Lainey. If that's what you need. Is that why you're calling? Do you need to come home again?"

"No, Ma," Mom said, her voice shrinking farther and farther away. "I don't need to come home."

"Well, all right, then."

I held on to the phone long after they'd hung up. I didn't know what to do next either. Eventually the phone beeped at me in protest. Fourteen, it seemed to count. Fourteen, fourteen, fourteen. *Fourteen more years of this.*

We're all just one bad decision away from disaster. I hadn't understood until that moment that, for my dad, I had been that one decision. Maybe Mom's too.

On the upside, I was finally getting that baby brother, like the family in the brochure.

I got back into bed and pulled the blankets over my head. My radio was under my pillow, John Fogerty wondering who stopped the rain. I pressed it against my ear. But once you hear something, you can't unhear it. Once you know something, it becomes part of who you are. I couldn't drown this out with a hundred radios. What I would've given right then to be lying on a beer-stained mattress, letting Troy Gainer feel me up.

Mom spent the whole of the next week at the kitchen sink again, staring out the window through a cloud of smoke. She stayed that way for hours. She was a foot from the fridge, but I never saw her eat. Sometimes she stood behind me while I watched TV. Planes glided silently across the screen. Beneath them, a rice paddy exploded, throwing up fireworks of dirt and smoke. You didn't need the volume up to know what it sounded like. Vietnam was the longest-running show on TV. "It's so awful," Mom said, looming over me. Suck, sigh, suck, sigh. Eventually she'd sit down and pull the afghan over her legs. When she tired of watching death and devastation, she'd go back to the kitchen window and stare at the empty driveway again. She did this all week, oscillating between the TV and the window, two channels that never ran any good news.

When I got home on Friday she was asleep on the sofa. I turned off the set and breathed in a moment of silence. No bombs, no cigarette.

Mom's eyes flickered open. "What time is it?" she said, rubbing them, searching around for her Salems. "I was watching that."

The phone rang. Her body jerked and stiffened, like an electric-shock patient. She leapt up and rushed at the phone. "Hello?" she shouted. "Hello? Hello?"

Her chest rose and fell. "One moment," she said and held out the receiver to me. "Don't be long."

"Hey," I said, hoping it was Melanie while trying to sound like I wasn't.

"Robin? Hi. It's Jamie."

"Who?"

"Jamie Finley. Skinny guy, slow walker?"

"Oh, hi."

Neither of us said anything for a few seconds. Mom waited in the middle of the kitchen, counting them out on the oven clock. I stretched the phone cord into the dining room.

"So anyway," Jamie said. "We're going to The Place tonight, me and some of the guys from the team. Gainer, Travis, Bowman . . ." He rattled off a list of names I didn't know. "Everyone'll be there. So, yeah, I thought you might want to come too."

"Why?"

"I've seen your friends there—Melanie and Joan? They're always hanging around."

She'd gone with Joyce. It wasn't a surprise, but it still sent blood to my ears.

"Joyce isn't my friend," I said.

"Well, I'm your friend, right?"

Mom tapped her wrist. Tick-tock.

"I have to get off the phone," I said.

"Oh, okay." Jamie gave me the address. "Just in case you change your mind."

The evening was endless. Mom smoked at the kitchen sink with one eye on the driveway and the other on the wall phone. I should have been studying my vocabulary homework—*koan*, *lassitude, myriad,* and other words nobody would ever need. Instead I parsed my mental transcript while I poked my eyes with a mascara wand, failed to brush the ponytail bump out of my hair, and faced the slim virtues of my closet with dread. There were a hundred reasons not to go—myriad reasons, you might say. What if I went and Melanie ignored me? What if Troy didn't? Melanie was usually the one who talked me into things. I knew what she'd say now. *Spread your wings, Robin! Spread your wings!* I ruined a can of SpaghettiOs just thinking about it. My stomach was too knotted up to eat anyway. Mom, wisely, stuck with dry toast.

"Do you want to watch some television?" she said as we scraped our plates into the garbage. "We can turn up the volume. We don't have to watch the news."

"You're a real party animal, Mom."

"Fine, fine. It's all brain rot anyway." She fished a cigarette out of the pack. She'd started leaving it and her silver lighter out on the counter. She didn't bother with the enamel box anymore.

"You look pretty," she said, turning her head as she exhaled. "Why are you all gussied up?"

"I'm going to Melanie's." I gnawed my lip. I had to say it before I could change my mind. "And I'm spending the night."

She looked at me one-eyed, like a bird. "You put on makeup to go to Melanie's?"

"Nobody says gussied up, by the way. Except country bumpkins. And Canadians, I guess."

The eye narrowed. Suck, sigh, suck, sigh.

"You tell me to dress nice all the time, and then when I do I get the third degree."

"All right, all right. I only said you look nice." She twisted at the waist. Her head was already halfway there. She wasn't going to stop me. She was going to look out the window. Suck, sigh, suck, sigh.

I breathed deeply, but it didn't help. She left no air in the house. I felt another scream coming. "You smoke too much," I said.

"Do I?" she said to the black glass. "I didn't know it bothered you."

"Well, it does. It's disgusting. You'll probably get cancer."

Her head snapped around, tears welling in her eyes. "That's enough. I'm still your mother."

Still, as in so far. As in count your lucky stars, kiddo. As in nobody ever wanted you. As in nobody wants you now. Except maybe Troy Gainer.

"No wonder Dad doesn't want to be married to you."

Mom pushed herself away from the counter slowly and straightened her spine. It was easy to forget how tall she was. Like many women of her generation, you could measure her self-confidence in inches. Or her anger. Her hand was so quick, it was seconds before I understood I'd been slapped.

She'd never hit me before, but you wouldn't have known it. My cheek hummed from nose to ear. As she dropped her cigarette in the sink, her hand was shaking. "I hope you have better manners at the D'Angelos'," she said and went to her room.

I waited a few minutes, then followed her there. Pressing my cheek against her door, I heard the faint pop and rattle of her Valium bottle, the rush of water from her ensuite tap. She'd be out cold in half an hour. I watched an episode of *All in the Family* with the volume off. I never got the jokes anyway. Gloria and Edith were getting worked up about something and making Archie miserable. When it was over, and everyone on TV loved each other again, I knocked on Mom's door just to be sure. I imagined a studio audience watching me with my ear against the wood, the laugh track kicking in as I grabbed a bottle of something from the liquor cabinet and sped off on my bike.

Dusk had always been my favourite time of day to ride, when lights glowed storybook yellow and everything else was a different shade of blue. The streets were quiet at that hour, all the cars tucked in their driveways where they belonged. Melanie and I used to ride our bikes everywhere, all the time, streamers and hair whipping the air. One more thing we were too old to do now. I let go of the handlebars, arms out, feet off the pedals, smiling at myself in the dark. I was free. The world was mine. Melanie didn't know everything.

For all its lore, The Place was just a small white bungalow in another development going the way of the bulldozer. Nothing lasted long in Golden. Last year's mini-malls were blasted to make way for stucco homes with built-in barbecues and two-car garages while homes were razed to make room for new mini-malls with movie theatres and rooftop parking. The bungalow sat at the end of a long row of identical bungalows, flanked on one side by a line of scrawny trees. A tricycle lay on its side on the overgrown lawn. A family had lived here once, before moving on to something with more closet space. Within the year it would probably be an Orange Julius. What did I care? I dumped my bike behind some bushes and went inside.

The front room was empty, except for a couple making out in the middle of the floor, their legs entwined double-lotus style. There was no mattress, just shag carpet and an old lumpy pillow squatting against a wall. Girl laughter and the scratch of a portable radio drifted in from another room. I stepped around the couple carefully and followed Jim Morrison down a hall.

It was your standard rec room—low ceiling, gloomy. Empties lined the windowsill, some swollen with cigarette butts, some choked with candles. There wasn't any furniture, just wooden crates pushed against the walls and a pile of mangy pillows on the floor. A dozen kids lounged or leaned around the room, their hands wrapped around beer bottles or stuffed in their pockets. Pot smoke camped around shoulders, like a gathering storm.

There was a wet bar on one wall and a brick fireplace on the other, painted black with soot, as if a bomb had gone off. Fireplaces weren't uncommon in Golden, just not intended for use, like guest soap and wedding china. Now it was the only source of heat against the looming desert night, and nobody knew how to work the flue. Someone had tried to burn a chair leg. It lay charred but whole amidst the cardboard boxes and yesterday's news. A guy knelt at the hearth, jabbing things with a poker. I could hear my dad drilling me. *Are your fire extinguishers in working order? Where are your exits? Stop, drop, and what?* I walked over to the fireplace, reached inside, and pushed the lever back. There was enough smoke in the air as it was.

Melanie and Joyce Peyton stood awkwardly in a corner, hiding behind plastic cups.

"I can't believe you're here," Melanie said when she saw me, more surprised than happy, I thought. But then she smiled and threw her arms around me and whispered in my ear, "Guess who else is here."

Right then Troy Gainer strode into the room, carrying a bag of sunflower seeds. He flopped down beside the fireplace and watched the guy poke at the fire. I was standing five feet away, but Troy didn't notice. I could have been a floor lamp for all he cared.

Jamie Finley was right behind Troy. When he saw me he smiled. "You came," he said, sounding as surprised as Melanie, but in a good way. There were dimples everywhere.

Troy flicked his eyes over me and away. He popped a seed in his mouth, turned and spat. Sunflower shrapnel stuck to blank wall. "This place is a real drag," he said. "Nobody ever brings any booze." Melanie and Joyce looked guiltily at their cups. "I brought something," I said and took the wine out of my bag.

Troy groaned. "Does this look like a dinner party?"

Jamie smiled again. "I think I saw a corkscrew somewhere," he said and led me out of the room.

The kitchen was in the back of the house, if you could still call it a kitchen. A tower of beer cases tottered where the stove and fridge had been. The linoleum was sticky under my Keds.

"This place could use a woman's touch," Jamie said.

"This place could use a blowtorch."

We held candles to cupboards and drawers, searching for a corkscrew, but all we found were mouse droppings. "Maybe in the sink?"

As I dug through the plastic cups and empties, my thumb grazed something sharp. I jerked back and brought my foot down on a broken beer bottle. I yelped and hopped around on my other foot, but I couldn't get away from the pain.

Jamie put his hands on my shoulders to stop me. "Just hold still for a sec. And maybe don't look down."

I did, of course. I hadn't expected to see my heel wedged inside the cylinder of brown glass, jagged tips cradling the laces. It made me think of the ships in a bottle that Melanie's father built in his garage.

Jamie looked at me gravely, dimple-free. "It's gotta come off," he said.

"I've actually grown kind of attached to it," I said. "Seriously, it's fine. I'm pretty sure I can walk like this." Mr. D'Angelo had shown us how the ships got in the bottles, but he'd never said anything about getting them out.

Jamie put his hands on my shoulders again. "Do you know how people walk on burning coals? They believe it won't hurt, so it doesn't. Mind over matter, right?"

I nodded, grateful. If it had been my dad in that kitchen, I'd be listening to a story about a girl who stepped on glass one day and dropped dead the next.

"Okay," Jamie said and hooked his hands under my arms. As he lifted me onto the counter, a giggle bubbled up from somewhere. I could feel myself blush. Jamie's cheeks had two permanent splashes of pink that made it look like he'd just stepped in from the cold. "Close your eyes and take a deep breath," he said. I followed his instructions. He smelled like apple shampoo again. I hoped my foot didn't smell like foot.

I heard the crack of glass and felt the bottle release its grip, then Jamie's hand warm around my ankle. He slipped off my shoe and peeled away my sock.

"You've got big feet," he said.

"Is it bad?"

"Nah, you'll grow into them. Does it hurt?"

"Only when you make me laugh."

"The good news is, I found the corkscrew." He laid it in my open palm. "I'll look for a Band-Aid. You open this. It'll help."

I'd never opened a bottle of wine before. I couldn't get the screw to go in straight. I tried using the tiny knife to carve out the cork instead. Troy came into the kitchen and watched me making a mess.

"You're doing it wrong," he said, taking over. "You really screwed it up." Eventually he gave up and pushed the cork in. He smiled and held up his hand. It took me a while to understand that I was supposed to slap it.

Troy was shorter than Jamie but wider and thicker. The muscles on his neck flexed when he drank. "Not bad," he said, leaning against the counter beside me and taking a second long pull. He handed me the bottle. I took a sip and fought back a grimace. The wine was sour and warm.

"Your foot's bleeding," he said.

"Uh, yeah." I took another drink to stop myself from talking any more.

Troy saw my sock on the counter, dotted with blood. He picked it up and bit into the cotton, making a small hole with his teeth. Then he tore the sock in two and slid the elastic cuff over the arch of my foot. "I guess Boy Scouts wasn't a total waste of time," he said. He wrapped his lips around the bottle and sucked. I watched, amazed, this boy who'd put my sock in his mouth.

Between swigs, Troy moved around the room. He was one of those guys who can't sit still, all fast-twitch muscle and new testosterone. He ran his hands over his half-inch of hair. He did a drum solo on the counter, hummed something I didn't recognize. Melanie said boys liked getting compliments, so I told him he had a nice voice.

"You like the Eagles? I took you for one of those Carpenters chicks."

"Yeah right," I said, feeling bad for Richard and Karen.

He really got into it then, singing and strumming his stomach. When he bent into the bridge, I could see his scalp through his buzz cut, white and vulnerable. Dog tags were tucked inside his T-shirt. You could buy them in the city, where broke vets traded them for a few bucks at the army surplus. Half the guys at school wore them. *Nam*, they called it, staring off at the horizon as if they were remembering the jungle and, man, the shit they'd seen.

Troy sang, swaying toward me until his thighs pressed against my knees. "You ever make out underwater?" he said. I shook my head. He took a big swig and mashed his lips against mine. Bordeaux flooded my mouth. He laughed while I coughed.

Melanie watched from the doorway, grinning at me as if I'd won the lottery—or she had. Jamie stood behind her, looking like he'd lost.

"I guess you don't need these anymore." He dropped a wad of napkins on the counter.

Troy took one and wiped his mouth. "You were right," he said. "She does have cock-sucking lips."

"I never said that."

"Yeah, sure. Finley here's a real gentleman."

Troy pointed the bottle at Melanie. She stepped into the room and held out her cup. When he pointed the bottle at Jamie, he shook his head. It was my turn again. Fine by me. Jamie settled against the doorframe and watched me dribble wine down my shirt, me and my cock-sucking lips.

The wine swished between me and Troy. I took small sips, trying to get used to it. Melanie sipped delicately from her cup. Nobody had much to say, but I was used to couples that didn't talk. Troy and Robin and Jamie and Melanie. I saw the four of us riding around in Troy's red Mustang, happily ever after.

Troy wasn't exactly Prince Charming, but then I was no Cinderella either. Selling is believing, my dad always said. When he told clients they could step outside his office and be hit by a bus, he believed it one hundred per cent even though his office wasn't anywhere near a bus route. I could do this, I told myself, taking a bigger sip this time. Falling in love with Troy Gainer wouldn't be nearly as bad as getting hit by a bus.

"Jamie made varsity," Melanie said.

I tipped back the bottle, gulped. The wine was starting to taste pretty good.

"It's no big deal," Jamie said.

"He almost broke the two hundred last week," Troy said. "Not bad for a beanpole. Tell her, Thinly."

"Tell her yourself."

"What's your problem?"

"I don't know, Gainer. Why don't you tell me what my problem is?"

"Two hundred what?" Melanie asked, but nobody answered.

"Hey, Jamie," I said. "If you're so great, can you do this?" I grabbed the eyelashes of my left eye and flipped my lid inside out. Jamie was the only one who didn't laugh.

He crossed to the window and stared out at the dark. The frilled curtains had pieces of fruit all over them. In some past incarnation of our kitchen, we'd had the same ones. Now they were plaid. Why have curtains at all when you never shut them? But I liked the fruit, which had begun to swirl pleasantly. My foot didn't hurt at all anymore. I felt good. I was swirling pleasantly too. It was the right decision to come, maybe the best decision I'd ever made. When Troy and I were a couple, we'd come back every weekend, maybe every night. Music trickled in from the rec room. I wished they'd turn it up so we could dance. Everything was wonderful and everyone was happy. Everyone but Jamie.

"Why don't you have a drink, Mr. Finley. Loosen your tie." I held out the bottle. "Don't make me limp all the way over there."

"If I drink, will you stop whatever it is you're doing?"

"I'm just having fun, Thinly. Is that a crime?"

Joyce appeared in the doorway. "Is what a crime?" When nobody answered, she crossed her arms and pursed her lips.

The fireplace guy came up behind her, using the poker as a cane. "Keg party. You jackasses coming with us, or are you staying here and babysitting?"

Jamie kicked at the empties on the floor. They scattered noisily across the linoleum. "I hate this fucking town. Drink here, drink there. Who the fuck cares? The day I turn eighteen, I'm out of here."

"Me too," Melanie said, though like most of us she'd never gone farther than Anaheim. There were only three reasons people left Golden: divorce, draft, and death.

The guy with the poker picked up an empty plastic cup and flung it at the pile on the other side of the room. "Babysitting it is," he said. Melanie put her plastic cup on the counter. Nobody else moved.

"Well, I'm going," Joyce said and followed him out.

"Aren't you guys coming?" Melanie said.

Troy put his arm around my shoulder. "Maybe later," he said. I took another drink.

Jamie grabbed the bottle from me, swallowed the last of the wine, and tossed it in the sink. "No point hanging around this dump." Then he pivoted on one of his own big feet, crossed to the doorway, and was gone.

"Are you sure?" Melanie said nervously.

Now who's the brave one? I thought. Now who's spreading her wings? I stuck my hands under my armpits and flapped. Melanie rolled her eyes and followed the others out.

We heard the front door open, kids talking, shuffling

outside. "Don't do anything I wouldn't do," someone yelled from the living room. A door slammed shut.

"So," Troy said.

He took my hand and led me slowly through swaying halls to a small room at the back of the house. There was no candle, only moonlight and not enough of it. As my eyes adjusted, I was relieved to see the rumours about mattresses weren't true. It was just an empty second bedroom with cowboys on horses leaping across the walls. A child's room, a little boy's.

Troy moved closer, lips parted. I did the same. Our first real kiss.

"You know, I don't usually go for freshmen," he said.

"Thanks," I said, hoping he meant I was special.

Kyle Lincoln had given me a hickey at the winter dance. When Dad saw it, he told me the human mouth was dirtier than a dog's. Mom brought home a bunch of pamphlets on venereal diseases and left them in my room. For weeks I'd thought I had syphilis on my neck. I hadn't even wanted the hickey. The junior boys, I found out later, had a bet going over who could mark more freshman girls that night. I guess Kyle really wanted that ten bucks because he went for the jugular the second the spinning lights hit our faces. Troy's mouth was no less startling. His lips and tongue were everywhere, as if he was trying to eat me. Somewhere in the middle of all this, he pulled me to the floor. I tried to feel good about the way things were turning out.

The carpet stunk vaguely of vomit. Troy smelled of chlorine and aftershave. He lay on top of me, crushing me with his weight. I didn't know what to do with my hands. His hands slipped under my top and to the back of my bra, groping around like he'd lost his keys.

My bra sprung open.

"You're smaller than I thought," he said.

"Sorry," I said, crossing my arm over my chest.

"It doesn't matter," he said and moved on to my jeans.

I felt his fingers on my zipper.

"Wait," I said. "Just wait."

"What's wrong?"

Everything was wrong. Everything was wonderful. I just needed a second to realize that this was what I wanted. Troy and Robin, sitting in a tree.

"I've never done this before."

"Come on," he moaned. "You like me, right?"

"Yes?"

"Well, I like you too, so shut up for a minute."

I felt the zipper release and closed my eyes, horrified. Caught in my old day-of-the-week underwear. They weren't even the right day.

There was a noise outside the window, the swish of long, dry grass. Then a metal twang and someone swearing under his breath. Troy stopped moving. I heard the tick-tick-tick of a bicycle wheel spinning in the air, the front door creaking open.

"Hello?" Jamie said. "Are you here?"

Troy's hand slipped over my mouth.

We could hear Jamie's footsteps on the carpet, back and forth, back and forth, like something was being worked out. I couldn't decide either. Go away, please don't go—with every step, I changed my mind. Go, I thought finally. Please, please go. I definitely didn't want him to see me on the floor with my jeans around my knees. I didn't want anyone to see me this way.

At last the front door slammed shut. Troy's hand slipped from my mouth. "That was weird," he said and got to work again. He tugged on my underwear, in a hurry now, the elastic sharp on my skin until it snapped. "Shit," he said.

"It's okay," I said.

Looking back, that was probably the wrong word to use.

He pushed himself between my thighs and tore inside.

I gasped. Girls at school talked about how it hurt at first and then it didn't. But this couldn't be right. The pain was too deep, too wrenching, like something inside me was breaking that couldn't be fixed. I felt other things, his head stubble against my cheek, the carpet rubbing parts of me raw.

I remembered Jamie's hand on my foot, warm and gentle. What had happened between then and now? I turned my face away. It wasn't a bad house, really. It just needed a bit of sprucing. Maybe they wouldn't knock it down. Maybe Troy and I would buy it after we got married. This is where the bed will go, I thought. That's where we'll put the dresser.

"I love you," I said. Troy didn't answer. To be fair, he probably didn't hear me. There was a lot of grunting going on. His dog tags jangled against my collarbone. Troy loves you very much, I told myself.

Troy groaned one last time and collapsed against me, his swimmer's weight knocking the air from my lungs. The feeling of him slipping out of me was worst of all. He stood up and tugged at his pants, so I knew it was over. I sat up and cradled my knees.

"So I'm gonna go to that party," he said. "Do you want a ride home or something?"

I shook my head.

"I won't tell anyone," he said, zipping up.

I nodded, grateful. It never occurred to me that I was the one who should do the telling.

"You know, I thought you were lying about the virgin thing," he said. And then he was gone.

I pressed my fingers against my eyelids. If I didn't cry, then maybe it hadn't really happened. What had happened? I wasn't sure. Troy Gainer was good-looking and popular. He said he liked me. He was the second boy I'd ever kissed.

It took forever to get into my jeans. They didn't seem to fit anymore. I groped around for my underwear. I didn't want them, but I couldn't leave them either. I tried pushing them into my front pocket, but something was already in there. A piece of paper folded into a small, fat square, my name on one side in purple pen. I took it to the rec room where the chair leg still glowed orange in the fireplace. Nobody in Golden knew how to put fires out properly either. I unfolded the paper and smoothed it flat.

Dear Robin, I'm sorry that you're sad but you shouldn't be because <u>God loves you very much</u>. He has special plans for you Robin just like He has special plans for me. So whatever happens try to remember that you are His SPECIAL LAMB. We both are. Those other girls aren't anybody's special anything.

Sincerely, your one and only <u>TRUE</u> friend forever and ever,

Carol Closter

PS I forgive you for not talking to me in the library AGAIN even though it is <u>RUDE</u>.

I wiped the tears from my eyes, folded the note back up, and put it in my pocket. Then I rolled up pieces of newsprint and arranged them around the chair leg like a teepee. I laid the underwear on top. When the flames caught, I blew on them gently, coaxing them toward the cloth. The polyester-cotton blend didn't burn so much as melt, the black spreading slowly like gangrene. T . . . U . . . E . . . This would take a while.

I went to the window and pulled back the curtain. Shadowed houses and scrawny trees. Dead geraniums slumbered in the window box. The tricycle was still missing one of its back wheels. Nothing had changed, but everything had. Beneath my thoughts was a quiet roar, a familiar sound but too far away to name. When light flared orange in the window, I touched my fingers to the cold glass, lost memories tugging at my whirring mind. The wine, I thought. I'm just drunk. By the time I turned around to check the fire, the mantel was engulfed.

I ran to the kitchen and filled a plastic cup with water, but it was too little and I was too late. Fire crawled up the wallpaper. It peeled away from the walls like sunburned skin. I stood there, mouth open, cup in hand, as though I was making a toast and couldn't think what to say.

When the house fire I'd watched with my dad looked extinguished, the firemen had attacked the charred remains with their axes. With every blow that poor family had squeezed closer together under their blankets, but it had to be done. "The fire looks dead," Dad had said, "but it's in there, it's alive. It's just waiting for oxygen—and boom." As if to prove him right, the front bay window belched flames that sent everyone reeling back several feet. "What'd I tell ya?" he'd said. "What'd I tell ya."

I knew it was hopeless. I could already feel the heat on my face. The flames would be everywhere soon, in the walls, under the floorboards, between the joists. Black smoke would choke the room until the windows burst. The walls would crumble like gingerbread. Then the beams would snap, the roof would collapse, and this fire would swallow everything inside in one bright gulp.

I wanted it to. I wanted to see it gone. Jim Fisher's little girl. A walking bad decision.

Only when I heard the sirens did I drop the cup and run.

The ride home was endless. A million dark streets and sleeping houses, their windows like eyes. My heart banged against my ribs. Blood thumped in my ears. I pedalled as hard as I could, but my legs were heavy and my bare foot was aching again. When I reached my street at last, every house was on fire, their windows dazzling with orange light. But it was just the sun coming up over the hills. The world had not stopped spinning.

Mom was asleep on the sofa. The TV was on. Station identification, no volume. As I crept past her to turn it off, she stirred awake.

"What are you doing home? Did you and Melanie have a fight?"

I opened my mouth and shut it again. I wanted to tell her, but I couldn't say the words. I needed her to know just by looking at me.

Mom held up a hand. "Earthquake," she said, as if announcing the time.

The floor shook. I stumbled against Dad's armchair. I couldn't remember what I was supposed to do. Put my head between my legs? Breathe into a paper bag? What was it that never strikes the same spot twice? Mom jumped up, grabbed my arm, and pulled me under the sofa table. We knelt together, holding hands. She smelled of dirty laundry and unwashed hair. Where was the Chanel No. 5? The Final Net? I shifted away from her, worried she'd smell the wine on me, other things. All the smells in the world were wrong.

We listened to things falling around us, calling the sounds like bingo numbers. "Pictures," I said. "Crystal," she sighed. It lasted less than a minute. Dad always said you had to be impressed by an earthquake's efficiency, among other things.

We stayed where we were for another minute, waiting for

aftershocks. When none came, Mom crawled to the kitchen for her cigarettes. She sat on the floor, back against a cupboard, and lit her Salem.

The phone rang, no doubt one of Dad's customers. The important ones had his home number, though it was Mom who would usually talk to them, sitting on a kitchen stool, long frame hunched, offering what encouragements she could muster before the pot roast set off the smoke detector. "I supply the *in*surance," Dad liked to joke. "Elaine supplies the *re*assurance." For once Mom didn't answer. The sound seemed to get shriller with every ring. Soon the phone was joined by the doorbell. Our house thundered like the inside of a belfry. "Where's your shoe?" Mom shouted over the noise.

"Hello? Mr. Fisher? Mrs. Fisher?" The knocking wouldn't stop. Finally, Mom got up and went to the door.

"Well, now," she said. "Wasn't that a lively way to wake up!" Mom had her country club voice on, cheerful but impersonal. Whoever it was, they weren't getting through the door. "Oh, we're fine, just fine. It was barely an earthquake at all."

From what I could see, she was right. Leather-bound volumes prayed at the feet of naked bookshelves. Glass had been broken, a ceramic lamp, a potted fern. Nothing that couldn't be fixed with a glue gun and a bit of prairie ingenuity. Family photos lay supine on the floor, the three of us still smiling our phony smiles. Outside, the sun was sharp against a powder-blue sky, not a cloud reflected in the crystal pool. And behind that, of course, the pool house, empty but still there.

"That's kind of you, but as I said, we're fine. My husband's in the insurance business so—"

Mom swayed back a step. I thought it was an aftershock, but she was the only one moving.

"Are you all right, ma'am?"

"Of course." She touched her fingertips to her forehead. She stepped back again and clutched at the wall. "Now if you'll excuse me, I don't seem to be feeling very well at the moment."

The door swung open wide, and I saw the uniform, the walkie-talkie.

"Ma'am? Oh jeez." He barked into the walkie-talkie, something about *ambulance* and *shock*. "We got us another one," he said just as Mom's knees buckled and bowed.

I tucked farther under the sofa table and closed my eyes like some dumb scared kid. Please, please, please just make it all just go away, I whispered. I won't touch another boy, bottle, or fireplace as long as I live. I'll be a better daughter. I'll study hard and get good grades. I'll sit in one of Carol Closter's bean-bag chairs if I have to. I didn't have a cross on a necklace, so I reached into my pocket and touched the square of folded paper.

When I opened my eyes again, the man with the walkie-talkie was in our foyer, with both arms around my mom. Not a police officer, I realized, but a neighbourhood security guard, one of the men who did crosswords in their cars by flashlight. He wasn't there to arrest anybody. He looked barely old enough to drive. His arms shook trying to hold her without touching the breasts that spilled out from her gauze-thin slip. One of her hands was flung toward me, lit cigarette still dangling between her fingers. If you didn't know better, you'd think they were dancing. You'd think we were all having the most marvellous time.

4

Early in the morning of April 1906, on what began as a calm spring day, an earthquake shook San Francisco awake. It didn't last longer than a minute, but the fires that followed burned for three days. Some were set by green firemen unskilled in the nuances of dynamite. Some were set by property owners who, having built their dreams directly over the San Andreas Fault, couldn't get coverage for quakes but had come by fire insurance easily enough. When the smoke cleared, more than three thousand people were dead and three-quarters of the city was destroyed. One of the worst fires was started by a woman cooking breakfast for her family. It was known as the Ham and Eggs Fire, which was also the punchline of many mornings in the Fisher household.

This is one of the stories my dad liked to tell.

My mom told different kinds of stories.

She told the security guard that she was prone to fainting,

that the earthquake had upset an old inner ear problem, but everything was fine now, really, thank you so much. She told Dad's client that the damage always looked worse than it was, that there was probably nothing to worry about, and if there was, weren't we all lucky to be so well insured. She told me we'd sweep up later, she didn't feel quite up to it, she probably had an iron deficiency, she should take vitamins, cut back on coffee, get more sleep. And just like that, all questions and possible answers were swept under the rug. The actual shards of porcelain and glass we would just have to step around.

If lack of sleep was Mom's problem, she seemed determined to make up for it. After she waved off the security guard and said goodbye to the client, she unplugged all three phones, kissed my cheek, and went to bed for twenty-four hours.

While Mom slept, I undressed, carefully, with my back to the mirror. Even with the curtains drawn and the lights off, I still saw the blood on the crotch of my jeans and the thin purple bruise on my hip where my underwear had dug in. I scrubbed the jeans with a bar of soap in the shower, then put them in a paper bag and shoved them under my bed until garbage day. The bruise wouldn't come out no matter how hard I scrubbed. It was too warm for pyjamas, but I dug out a pair from the bottom of my dresser and put them on. I wanted every part of me covered. I would've worn a hat if I'd owned one. Scoured pink and wet-haired, I got under the covers and stared at the ceiling. Every sound through my window was a siren, every headlight a police car. At some point I fell asleep. When I woke again it was dark outside, and my hair had dried flat against the left side of my head. I knew I should get dressed, but that would involve getting out of bed. If they came to arrest me, it would have to be in my pink bunny slippers.

Sunday, tired of sleeping, I flipped between the religious shows with the telephone on my lap, waiting for Melanie to get home from church. She said all TV preachers were phonies. When the Pope wore jewels, at least you knew they were real. But I liked the one in the silver suit and the bolero tie. His mascara ran as he cried for the lost souls watching at home. I figured you had to be pretty sincere to let yourself go like that in front of a live studio audience. Plus, there was nothing else on.

The D'Angelos usually got home at one o'clock, then ate a late lunch. I called at two. "She's in her room with Joyce," her sister Claire said. "But she told me to tell you she's not here. Aren't you friends anymore?"

Joyce had gone to church with them, Claire said, and she and Melanie had spent the whole hour whispering and making faces at the boys in the next pew. "They were whispering about you too," she said. "But I couldn't hear what they were saying."

I was only half listening. Over her, I heard the clock in the hallway ticking down to Monday morning. If they arrested me, at least I wouldn't have to go to school.

"I don't think I want to be a teenager," Claire said.

"Me neither," I said and hung up.

The preacher in the bolero tie said there were operators standing by to hear my troubles and take my generous donation. I was dialling the toll-free number when Mom came into the room.

"I must've caught that flu," she said.

"Me too," I said and coughed like a Victorian heroine. "I should probably stay home tomorrow."

Mom lifted a hand and I leaned forward. Her palm was hot from sleep. My forehead must have felt ice cold in comparison.

"You do feel warm." She sat down beside me and pulled her legs up under her nightgown the way I used to when I was little. It billowed around her knees in soft blue waves. "All right," she said, frowning at the set. "But for God's sake, change that channel."

My dad always said earthquakes had a way of getting inside people, that there's a kind of damage that even Richter couldn't measure. He'd had customers who survived the mildest of shakers only to quit their jobs, sell their homes, leave their wives. Not Mom and me. We battened down the hatches. We weren't going anywhere.

We traded the news for game shows. You can lose yourself far more easily in the splendour of someone's brand-new dinette. We clapped our hands and bit our nails. We shouted out heartfelt advice. If our eyes teared up, it was only because we really wanted Marlene to get that snowmobile. "I never knew how wonderful these shows are," Mom said. "That new car is going to change her life."

Whenever I hear the phrase *mutually assured destruction*, I think of this time. *Plausible deniability* is another good one. When they came up with *Don't ask, don't tell*, it made me laugh. As if being gay were the worst thing you could admit to someone. It would make a great name for a game show, though. For two weeks that spring, we were the stars of our own game show. It was called *Let's Pretend the Rest of the World Doesn't Exist*.

We kept the phones unplugged and let the doorbell go unanswered. The delivery boy from Lucky's eventually gave up and left our standing grocery order melting on the front step. Three lamb chops, three pork chops, three sirloins. I packed these things into the fridge, where they rotted in triplicate, and burned endless cheese sandwiches instead. Mom had no appetite anyway. She sipped coffee with lots of milk and nibbled at Saltines. When Mrs. Houston called "Halloo! Halloo!" over the fence, we buried ourselves under the afghan, eyes wide behind the holes in the knit, as if we expected the old woman to hurdle the fence and throw herself at the sliding door.

Vera Miller had a logistical advantage the afternoon she called to us through the mail slot. Mom had been standing at the front door, staring at the Lucky's bill. Instead of pork chops, the delivery boy had left notice of our overdue account. Apparently we hadn't been paying for all that food we hadn't been eating.

The mail slot creaked open. "I just came by to make sure you're all right," Vera said through it.

"Why wouldn't we be all right?" Mom said, bending down to answer.

"Oh, honey. Never kid a kidder. Look, can I come in? I brought you a casserole and it's about to turn in this heat."

Mom straightened up, pushed a fist against her lips, and burped. Her other hand pressed the curve of her stomach. She did this a lot lately, but not usually at the same time. She reminded me of those women in the Midol ads.

"Is that a yes?" Vera said.

"You can come in," Mom said, burping again. "But the casserole stays outside."

Vera entered, slowly, careful of her step. My mom had never been much of a housekeeper, but she'd managed to keep the important surfaces clear. Now our house looked like it had been lifted off the ground, held upside down, and shaken. We kept putting off cleaning up the mess the earthquake had left. "Aftershocks," Mom had said. "Might as well wait." For two weeks we had applied this logic to everything, including bathing and getting dressed. All other rules were suspended until further notice. There were plates of half-eaten grilled cheese all over the place. Wet towels sprawled on the backs of seatless dining room chairs. Behind Vera, newspapers were piled against the front step like a snowdrift. The grass was so high we could have sheltered Viet Cong out there.

"Go ahead and say it," Mom said.

But Vera only fixed her smile and said, "I don't suppose you have a pot of coffee on?" Which told me things were even worse than I'd thought.

Mom led Vera to the kitchen and poured two cups of coffee from a lukewarm pot. Vera scanned the table. There was no room for a cup among the paint chips and bread crusts. She gave up and held hers with both hands, suspended above her lap. I stood in the doorway watching her, worried for her white slacks.

Mom balanced her own cup on her knees. On her better days she changed into an old work shirt she used to garden in, paired with a shapeless skirt, and talked about doing laundry or maybe running the dishwasher. Other days, she was less ambitious. Today was a nightgown day.

"How are you?" Vera said. She reached out a manicured hand and patted Mom's knee. Mom covered her flinch with a tight smile. "I'm fine. We're fine. Everything's fine."

"So long as everything's fine," Vera said, one sculpted eyebrow arching to the ceiling.

After a silent moment, she turned to me. "Are you fine too?"

"Robin's not feeling well," Mom said.

"So why are you the one turning green?" Vera said. "Must be one of those spring flus."

Mom was at her worst in the mornings, when the plastic smell of processed cheese would send her running for the bathroom. She'd stopped burping, but her face was waxy. She squeezed her coffee cup like it was the only thing keeping her upright in the chair.

"You shouldn't stay too long," she told Vera. "I'd hate for you to catch it."

"If the bubonic plague couldn't kill me," Vera said.

They stirred sugar into their coffees but didn't drink. I could see they weren't going to say much with me hanging around. "I think I'll go to my room," I said, then slipped out the sliding doors, went around the front of the house, and sat under the open kitchen window.

"How did you hear?" Mom was saying as I wedged myself into the weedy flowerbed.

"Let's just say I have a sixth sense about these things," Vera said.

"I guess everyone at the club knows."

"All they know is that he's missed four tee times and nobody's seen the two of you in a month. They think you've gone bankrupt. It's their explanation for everything. Those people have the imagination of a golf club. You *are* all right that way, aren't you? Jim might be a lot of things, but he wouldn't do *that*."

Mom didn't say anything. I thought of the Lucky's notice, all that rotting meat on the other side of the wall. I could almost smell it.

"No," Vera said. "You're right. Don't tell me. It's none of my business. How about I tell you something. Gwen Ryan got one of those Pomeranians. She dresses it up and calls it Baby. It's too cute to be one of her kids, but it does shit on everything, so I suppose there is some family resemblance."

"Vera!" Mom said, a smile in her voice.

I heard the scratch of her silver lighter opening, teaspoons tinkling against porcelain. The sounds of women in a kitchen. Relaxing a little, I leaned back against the warm siding and closed my eyes.

"You know Kathy Armstrong moved back with her parents in Anaheim," Vera said. "Tom will have to drive all that way if he wants to see those kids, I guess. Serves him right. Where are your people from? Somewhere in Ontario? Wouldn't that put a knot in Jim's shorts."

"We're not going anywhere," Mom said.

"Good for you. Why should you?"

"I might redecorate the den. Maybe I'll turn it into an arts and crafts room."

"That's right. Keep busy. My cousin Becky sat around crying and watching game shows for three months. She sees a therapist in the city now. Pops Seconal like antacids. Redecorate. Get your hair done. Buy new clothes. You'll feel like your old self before you know it—better. When Jim comes back, he won't remember why he left."

Mom didn't say anything.

"Oh, don't you worry. They always come back. They're like dogs. They see a cat and they chase, but eventually they come home."

"Jim's not like that."

"They're all like that, honey. I loved all my husbands to bits, I did, but I still fantasized that they'd choke to death on a plate of ribs. Even the new one."

"Then why do you marry them?"

"What else am I going to do? Take up macramé? They keep things interesting. My point is, I'm on your side, Elaine. You don't deserve it. And your girl, what they're saying—" Vera's voice dropped. I had to stand up and flatten myself against the siding to hear. "Well, that's all on Jim."

"What are you talking about?" Mom said.

"Don't you—Oh, well, nothing. Nothing at all."

I heard chair legs scraping, heels clicking. "You know, I've got a lot to do today, Vera. But thanks for stopping by."

"All right, I'm going. You don't have to shove."

The front door opened and Vera Miller stumbled backwards onto the step, one white pump sinking into her hamburger surprise. The door slammed shut. "Don't be a stranger!" Mom shouted through the mail slot.

Vera lifted her foot out of the dish. Her pump stayed put. She bent over to examine the damage. The white leather was coated in thick beige sludge. My mom always said the two key ingredients to any casserole were cream of mushroom soup and pity. Two things made to stick to your ribs like glue.

"Do you really think my dad's coming back?" I said.

If I'd startled Vera, she didn't show it. "Moody says he hasn't seen you in school much," she said. I was about to point out that Moody Miller probably hadn't seen the inside of school much either, but I didn't want to push it. Vera set the pump on the concrete, pointed her toes like a dancer, and slid her foot inside.

"If he comes back it's only because he has to," I said. "Not because he wants to."

"Oh, honey. That's women you're thinking of. Men don't have to do anything they don't want to."

I surveyed the driveway. The oil stain spread out in four directions, like a cross or compass rose, depending on how you looked at it.

"But don't listen to me," Vera said, holding my gaze. "In fact, don't listen to anybody except yourself."

"You're all a bunch of liars," I said.

Vera grinned. "I think you girls are going to be just fine." She picked up the casserole dish, balanced it on an open palm like a tray, and strutted down the stone walk like it was a red carpet.

I went back inside. Mom was smoking at the kitchen sink, watching Vera scrape her pump on the grass beside her car.

"Is there anything you want to tell me?" she said.

"Is there anything you want to tell *me*?" I said.

Mom turned slowly. The colour had returned to her face. We heard Vera's station wagon start up and drive away. "Forget it," Mom said, which was exactly what I was trying to do.

Unlike me, she would have to say the words sooner or later. Later was fine by me.

Mom was up early the next day, slamming cupboards and drawers, looking for things—the chequebook, her car keys, a sleeve of Saltines to eat in the car. She didn't say where she was going, but she had changed out of her nightgown into the work shirt and another shapeless skirt. She came back two hours later and dropped a brown folder onto the dining table. *Jim* had been crossed out on the tab and *Elaine* written over top. *FISHER* remained in faded black capitals.

"Go ahead," she said, nodding at the folder as she dug her cigarettes out of her purse. "Maybe you can make sense of it, because I sure can't."

I opened the folder shyly and scanned the contents. There were deeds and bank statements, mortgage papers and car leases, receipts, invoices, bills, bills, bills.

"What does it mean?" I said.

"It means I have to get a job."

Dad's accountant had told her there was enough in the joint account for us to eat or pay the mortgage for about six months, but not both. It was either get a job or sell the house, which was not, technically, hers to sell.

"But you can't work," I said. "Can you?"

"I'm not completely hopeless. I had a job once." She flicked the lighter, but it wouldn't catch. She tried again and again until her thumb was red. "Goddamn it." She slammed the lighter down on the glossy oak.

I took the lighter and got it going for her. She lifted the cigarette, trembling, to her lips, breathed in and out. With her other hand she rubbed the groove she'd made in the wood. "I'll have to sand the whole thing," she said. A tear cut a path through her rouge. My hand closed around the lighter, making a fist.

"You hate this table," I reminded her.

"I do?" She studied it for a minute, then sniffed and wiped her eyes. "You're right, I do. I really do."

5

Mom said she was sorry, but I had to go to school tomorrow. Dad's accountant had a client who needed a secretary and he'd recommended her for the job. Starting next week she'd be getting coffee for lawyers. "It only seems fair that we're both miserable," she said.

"But you don't have to go until Monday."

"No point putting off the inevitable," she said and burst into tears.

She'd been like that all week—crying when contestants overbid their showcase, or we ran out of milk—but that didn't make me feel any better about going back to school. I lay awake that night wishing for another earthquake. Better that the ground open up and swallow me whole. But when dawn broke, the house was still, the sky through my window clear and blue. Birds swooped between the budding lemon trees. A neighbour's cat stalked them from a fence. It felt like we'd been holed up for months, but it had only been a few weeks. The seasons hadn't even changed. It was by all accounts a beautiful spring day. But nature is deceptive that way. The Grand Canyon looks glorious until you realize it's really just the world's biggest hole.

I declined Mom's offer of pancakes. "They're only burnt on one side," she said. I couldn't have kept them down anyway. I swung my book bag over my shoulder, took a breath, and went to school.

I was barely in my seat when the whispers began. They buzzed around the room like horseflies you couldn't swat. Notes sailed from hand to hand. The teacher had to hit the board with his pointer to get their attention. "What's so exciting?" he said. "No, really. I'd love to know." I put my head on my desk and shut my eyes. I didn't realize this would be the easy part.

As I walked to my next class, boys' taunts trailed me. *Hot stuff. Hot to trot. Too hot to handle. Oh man, my burning loins.* Girls whispered and coiled away, built fortresses with their bodies. The only one who left me alone was Troy Gainer. When he saw me, he stuck his tongue under his lip like he was trying to wedge something out of his teeth. I ducked into a bathroom and waited for the bell.

Girls came in and I pulled up my feet. They left and I put them down again. Except for the accompanying smells, it wasn't so bad. I figured I could stay there until the end of the day or maybe graduation. But my legs cramped after a while and my stomach wasn't much better. When the lunch bell rang, I stood up and unlatched the door. If I didn't go now, there was a good chance I never would.

Melanie sat with Joyce Peyton and Amanda Clemens in the middle of the lunch yard, bright sun on their smiling faces. They were laughing and dipping french fries into a puddle of ketchup. They were having a wonderful time. Watching them from the other side of the lunch yard, I saw it clear as glass, how difficult I'd made things for myself, how easy it all could be. I would go to pep rallies and prom. I would pad my bra and learn how to feather my hair. I'd do whatever they wanted me to. My eyes welled with relief as I walked toward them. That's how stupid I was.

When Joyce saw me coming, she stood up and crossed her arms. "You can't sit with us."

"Melanie?" I said.

Melanie stared hard at her lunch. She wouldn't even look at me.

"You can sit here, Robin." Carol Closter was at the next table. She moved her books over to make room for me, as if the table wasn't empty around her. Everyone ignored her, including me.

"Troy told everyone," Joyce said.

"What? That you're a bitch?"

Amanda Clemens chuckled. Joyce shut her up with a glance.

Melanie mumbled something into her mashed potatoes.

"You know she did," Joyce answered.

"Did what?"

Melanie looked up at last, her eyes crinkled with worry. "Did you really burn down that house?" she said.

I wiped roughly at my eyes, sniffed back a trickle of snot. "So what if I did?"

Melanie's eyes widened. Her hand went to the cross at her neck. Joyce laughed, delighted. "Oh my God, Fisher. You're as big a freak as Cloister."

Carol dropped her head, put her elbows on her tray, and folded her hands. It was infuriating.

"What is your problem?" I snapped. "Why are you even sitting here? Take a hint, would you? Get a clue. What's wrong with you, anyway?"

Carol didn't so much as flinch. But her eyes were squeezed tight, so it's possible she didn't know she was the one I was shouting at. Maybe she wasn't.

I could feel the tears coming, that and the end of the world. I scanned the yard for the fastest way out and met dozens of gaping stares. A few tables over, Jamie Finley stood up, holding his empty tray. When our eyes met, he froze, then spun around so fast he sent fries flying over the heads of several squealing cheerleaders. A bunch of guys stood up to applaud the move. "Smooth move, ex-lax. Looking good!" Jamie chucked the tray to the ground and pushed through the clapping crowd.

Carol, oblivious, kept her eyes closed, her lips moving quickly over her Wonder Bread.

"What's she doing?" Amanda said, nose wrinkled like she smelled something bad.

"She's praying," Melanie said to her plate.

"Yeah, for Robin's cherry!" Joyce shouted as I bolted across the yard. "Too late, freak."

There are several options for dealing with graffiti on a locker. You can repaint, obviously, but not without some expense. A chemical remover can be applied to affected surfaces, but the smell is noxious and not recommended in high-traffic areas. If these options are not readily available, scrub at it with steel wool pilfered from the home ec cleaning closet, making it worse, scratching the metal, adding insult to injury that only the kind janitor with his callused hands and weary smile can fix. When he promises that it will be erased, take him at his word. A school janitor is someone who knows about dirt.

Kids gathered as he worked, scrubbing small circles with his rag, the hall filling with the sharp smell of gasoline. It lifted the marker with surprising ease.

"*Pyro lut?*" someone read.

"*Slut*, bonehead," someone else said. "*Pyro Slut.*"

Missy Carter, president of the Civil Liberties Club, stood beside me with her arms crossed. "This is a defamation of character," she said. "They've created a hostile learning environment. They've violated your right to freedom from oppression." Someone joked that she could violate him anytime.

"You could sue," Missy said, ignoring him.

"I don't want to sue," I said. "I just want my book bag."

"That can wait." When I turned around, Mr. Boyd, the freshman counsellor, was frowning at me beneath his toupee. He curled his finger at me like a worm. "The vice-principal would like to see you. Now."

I followed him to Mr. Galpin's office, where he knocked twice on the rippled glass door and left me to wait outside. There were chairs lined up against the wall. Moody Miller slouched in one of them, carving something into the arm with a thumbtack. He glanced up from his artwork. "Troy Gainer's a real shit. You want me to key his car for you?"

"That's okay," I said, tearing up again. It was the nicest thing anyone had said to me all day.

Mr. Galpin's door swung open. He looked about as miserable as I felt. He wore a crisp white shirt, but he hadn't shaved at all that morning. His stubble was white around his mouth like the muzzle of an old dog.

"How are you, Miss Fisher?" he said.

"I'm fine," I said. "How are *you*?"

Mr. Galpin smiled sadly. "I'm fine. Thank you for asking. Come on in."

I'd never been in a vice-principal's office before. There were stacks of paperwork, file folders filled with failure. One wall was covered in photographs of the teams he coached and clubs he sponsored. Mr. Galpin had been marked long ago as a soft touch who'd say yes to pretty much any extracurricular request. I couldn't see the one photo on his desk, but I knew it was probably of his dead wife and daughter. Even supervising the chess club had to be better than going home to an empty house.

There were two wooden chairs for visitors. I didn't sit down. A visit to the vice-principal's office meant your parents were divorcing, somebody was dying, or they'd found a bag of pot in your locker the size of a bread loaf. Basically, your life was over. I thought I should be standing when that happened. Mr. Galpin sat on the edge of his desk. It was supposed to make me feel better, but had the opposite effect.

"Miss Fisher, maybe you know why you're here. Then again, maybe you don't." I said nothing. He cleared his throat. "Well, it's come to the administration's attention that students have been using an abandoned house for drinking. Now this is nothing unusual, I'm afraid. If I had a nickel for every one of these places—" He stuck his hand in his pants pocket, palmed the change, then put it back in his pocket. "Well, there was a fire at this abandoned house a few weeks ago. I've spoken to the police and from what I understand, what with the nature of these sorts of places, the candles and whatnot, and then the earthquake—well, things are inconclusive at best and nobody's all too sure it's even worth the bother. Things like this happen. As far as the developer is concerned he'd rather it go away, insurance premiums and whatnot. Between you and me, he has a son at another high school who doesn't have an exemplary record and, well, really, it isn't any of our business what happens or doesn't happen off school property."

The intercom on his desk buzzed. He reached over and pressed one of the buttons on top.

"Not now, Bev," he said and let the button go.

"Am I in trouble?" I said.

"Well, that isn't always a question someone else can answer, Miss Fisher. Do you think you're in trouble?"

"Am I getting suspended?" I tried, maybe too hopefully.

Mr. Galpin shook his head. "It's not quite like that, Miss Fisher. It's not that sort of situation. But . . ." He looked at the photo on his desk, then turned it to face the wall, as if he didn't want them to hear. "Is there anything you'd like to tell me, Miss Fisher?"

I thought about it for a minute. "Does anyone answer yes to that question?"

Mr. Galpin chuckled softly. "No, I suppose they don't. Look, I don't know what did or didn't happen. I don't give credence to rumours, and rumours are pretty much the currency of secondary education as I'm sure you are well aware, so I just have to be content with not knowing. That's part of my job. Do we ever really know anything anyway? Now there's a question." He looked at me like he expected an answer.

"No?" I said.

"No, indeed. What I will say is that it seems to me that you've hit a rough patch, Miss Fisher. A very rough patch. I'm guessing that right now you're probably wondering how many ways out of this school there are. Twenty-six, in fact. But in my experience, these things tend to have a short shelf life. This will blow over. Whatever has or hasn't happened is now in the past. The school year is almost over. Keep your head down and your eye on the prize."

As he walked to the door, I saw that the back of his shirt was badly wrinkled, as if he'd pulled it straight out of the hamper. Or slept in it.

"And if you ever do feel like talking about anything—anything at all—well, now you know where to find me. In the meantime, we'll get you a new locker. How does that sound?"

He held out his hand and I shook it.

"Okay," I lied. Much as I liked Mr. Galpin, I didn't believe him for a second. The man wasn't optimistic enough to iron both sides of his shirt.

The crowd around my locker had cleared. Only Carol Closter stood there now, clutching her purple binder and shaking her hat at the mess. I left my books and made for the side door. Twenty-six exits. I only needed one.

I heard the door slam twice behind me, then quick, light steps. Carol chased me halfway down the sidewalk.

"I'm not supposed to run outside," she said, wheezing.

"So don't," I said, but stopped anyway so she could catch her breath. She pulled an inhaler out of her pocket.

"I told you those girls weren't really your friends," she said. "But I'm your friend, Robin, and I know those disgusting things they're saying are lies. You just have to suffer their persecution with immaculate devotion, that's all. That's what I'd do."

"Great. Thanks." As usual, I had no idea what she was talking about. "Can I go now?"

She squinted at me from under the brim of her hat. "Do you know the story of Saint Lucy?" she said. "They were going to take her to a brothel and defile her, but a team of oxen couldn't even move her. Then they tried to burn her at the stake, but that didn't work either. She couldn't be burned."

"So, what? She lived?"

"Nah. They stabbed her to death instead." Carol jabbed at the air between us with her purple pen to demonstrate. I started walking.

"I know it doesn't seem like it right now," she shouted after me, "but it's sort of a happy ending, if you really think about."

Mom was in bed when I got home. It was two o'clock in the afternoon but she was bundled under the covers. Her eyes were red and puffy. I saw the Valium on her nightstand beside a bottle of unknown pills the size of Brazil nuts.

"Are you sick again?"

"Just tired," she said, closing her eyes.

"You need to eat more," I said.

"You're right. I will. How was school?"

"Fine."

"Good."

The air was stale with old coffee and cigarettes. Dirty clothes and towels were strewn across the floor. She'd probably slept all day again. I opened a window and walked around angrily, picking things up. "I'll do it," Mom said, hugging her pillow, drifting off into her Valium cocoon. I ignored her and stomped around the room, mad at the carpeting, wanting to make more noise. She couldn't even do laundry. How was she going to have a baby and keep a job and pay the bills? She should marry Mr. Galpin, I thought. Then the four of us could all be sad together.

As I stuffed a towel into the hamper, my hand touched something wet. I dumped out the hamper and there it was. One of Mom's shapeless skirts bundled haphazardly with her underthings, everything heavy and wet, almost black with all that blood. My hands were red with it.

I knew plenty about periods, some about miscarriages. I also knew there was a doctor in Golden who took cash and didn't ask questions. Melanie had once lit a candle in church for all the unborn souls.

"Mom?" I whispered. There were a hundred questions I couldn't say out loud.

"I need to sleep," she mumbled. "Okay, sweetie? Okay?"

I bundled the skirt in a towel, put everything back in the hamper, and backed away. I needed to wash my hands, and maybe throw up.

"Okay," I said, unsure of what I was agreeing to. What a slippery thing that word had turned out to be.

Mom stayed in her room for the rest of the week, or so I assumed. I still had to go to school and wait for everything to blow over, as Mr. Galpin had promised. I was assigned a new locker near the ESL students, which suited me fine. I ate lunch on the gym bleachers, watching the square dancing team allemande all over the place.

At home, I camped out on the sofa in front of the TV's comforting glow, watching with the sound down. I was starting to like it better that way. I brought Mom dry toast, bottomless cups of tea, bowls of mashed potatoes I made from a box, cellophane bags of black licorice pipes from the corner store. She could not be tempted. She didn't even want her cigarettes, which sat with her silver lighter on the window ledge above the kitchen sink. I didn't eat much either. Food was too fleshy, too viscous, too red. I preferred the hole that hunger was gnawing inside me. I felt hollowed out, which seemed about right.

When Mom finally got out of bed, it was the middle of the night. She was slamming cupboards and drawers again, this time in the den. She pulled things out and dropped them on the floor. I yawned and rubbed my eyes, tried to make sense of the mess at her feet. Black umbrella, crime novels, two boxes of Puerto Rican cigars, imitation silver plaque from the Golden Business Association, real silver business card case.

"It all has to go," she said, climbing a chair to reach the top shelf.

"Even stationery?" I said, holding up a black Swingline stapler.

A dozen old *Time* magazines went crashing to the floor.

"Everything."

You'd think she'd been planning it for years, she moved so deftly. There were no decisions to be made. If it was his, it went into waiting cardboard boxes. When one filled, she labelled it with his initials and sealed it with packing tape. When she ran out of boxes, she used garbage bags. His armchair was dragged across the yard to the pool house, Mom heaving and panting as it dug its feet stubbornly into the grass. She piled the bags on top of it. The boxes she stacked on the little cot and on the floor. When she was done, she stood over the pile, glowing with sweat. It was the healthiest she'd looked in weeks. "Okay, then," she said and went back to bed.

While Mom slept, I cleaned, or tried to. I didn't dust so much as move the dust from one surface to another. I broke two plates and left exuberant scour marks on the aluminum pots. My beds were lumpy, my windows streaked. I swore at the fitted sheets and cursed whoever had invented grout. I didn't want to wake Mom with the vacuum, so I swept small squalls of grit into the dark. When there was nothing left to wax, bleach, or break, I went out to the pool house and took the first thing I saw that could be pocketed. Mom's silver lighter. Dad had given it to her as an anniversary present.

I got my bike from the garage and rode around for a while. I ended up at a vacant lot where weeks before a dozen houses had stood. You could still see the tracks the bulldozers had made, wide scars in the hard brown earth. Some kid's teddy bear was lying half buried under a bunch of concrete blocks. They formed a sort of pit. I took out the lighter, flicked back the lid, and thumbed the wheel. The flame sprang to life, hungry, ready. I gave it a furry ear, stepped back, and let it do its work. It took longer than I expected, but I didn't have anywhere else to be. When it was over, I kicked a concrete block over what remained. I didn't feel better exactly. But then again, I didn't feel worse.

The next morning, Mom was up before I was. I found her sitting at the edge of the pool with her feet in the water, a cigarette on a plate beside a pack of matches. She wore her oversized work shirt and a pair of fraying jean shorts. She was thirty-five then, plenty old by the day's standards, ancient by mine, but she looked like a kid sitting there, kicking her toes in the water and watching the waves ripple across the surface. The pool was fuzzy with dead leaves and bugs. They bobbed and flittered in her wake. It was my job to clean it, but I didn't want to swim anymore. Some nights as I drifted to sleep, I would catch the hot scent of chlorine in the air and have to rise and shower, with the moon through the bathroom window blue on my skin.

Mom reached for my hand. We used to hold hands all the time when I was younger, walking down the street, in the grocery store, watching TV—and then one day we didn't. I let go of her hand now. I didn't know how to be that girl anymore. Mom nodded and took a drag from her cigarette. Maybe she didn't know how to be that mother anymore either.

"I was a lifeguard," she said. "That was the job I had. Two summers at the lake. They didn't like to hire girls, but I passed the test and beat out three boys. The second summer I beat out five."

"But you never swim," I said.

"Don't I?"

"It wrecks your hair."

She leaned over the water and peered at her reflection. Unwashed for days, her hair fell limp and stringy around her face. Mom reached a hand toward her watery image and swatted it away. "That ship has sailed, I think."

She stood up and shed the work shirt. She had her swimsuit on underneath. "Here we go," she said, like someone about to jump off a cliff. Instead, she eased down the ladder until the water lapped her chin, and pushed off on her back. Her arms windmilled through the air, water sluicing from her fingers as she glided along. I wasn't a fan of the backstroke. Swimming backwards meant trusting what you couldn't see. But Mom didn't seem to mind that. "What a beautiful day," she said, face turned up to the sky.

It was the slowest backstroke in the history of the world. It was like watching somebody dream of swimming. When she finally reached the other end of the pool, she stayed there for a minute, clutching the edge. I put my hand in my pocket and felt the lighter. Dad had had it engraved with her initials. The letters were barely visible now, the silver rubbed clean from so much use, but they were still there. You just had to feel for them. At last Mom took a breath, large and extravagant, the new air preparing her, readying her muscles for what came next. I took it with her and watched her push off, held it until she came back.

Here we go.

6

A high school rumour has its own bell curve. It starts slowly, then picks up steam, climbs to an impossible fervour, and crests in a heady flurry before tipping over the edge and crashing to a dead stop. Which is to say that the looks and whispers at school dwindled until finally nobody looked at or spoke to me at all. Some days Carol Closter was the only person I talked to who didn't have crow's feet. That was fine by me, or so I told myself. Of course, I couldn't listen to "Rainy Days and Mondays" without bawling into my pillow, but wasn't that the point of sad songs?

You'd think with all that time on my hands, I'd have caught up on the weeks of schoolwork I'd missed. It's not that I didn't try, but it was hard to focus on anything through the fog that followed me around. Keeping my head down, as Mr. Galpin had suggested, didn't help. I couldn't find the track, never mind get back on it. The rest of freshman year was the real-life version of one of those nightmares you have in middle age, when you're sitting down for a big test and realize you haven't studied. Carol Closter left encouraging notes in my locker addressed to "Lucy," inspirational drawings done with her signature purple pen. There was one of Jesus playing volleyball that was actually pretty good. *You're God's MVP*, she'd written underneath in bubble letters. Unfortunately, God wasn't the one doing the grading. While other kids set out for lakeside camps and beach vacations, I'd be spending six glorious weeks in summer school.

"It won't be so bad," Mom said, dropping me off on her way to her new job. "Maybe you'll even have fun, make some new friends." She was enjoying getting coffee for lawyers more than she'd expected and sometimes it made her impossible to be around. She'd started watching *The Mary Tyler Moore Show*. While I admired Mary's swishy pantsuits, Mom admired her plucky spirit. She didn't get it at all.

"It's only a junior secretarial position," Mom said. "But Mr. Grant says there's a lot of potential for someone who applies herself."

"You have your own Mr. Grant," I said.

She clasped her hands together, smiling dreamily. "My own Mr. Grant."

My own prospects were less encouraging. Summer school was held at a junior high that looked a lot like my old junior high, which looked a lot like a prison for short people. I already knew the classrooms would wrap around a square gravel courtyard where I would eat Kraft slices or peanut butter on white bread for the next six weeks. When Indonesia's Mount Tambora erupted in 1815, the plumes of ash were so thick they blocked out the sun. The atmosphere choked with sulphur for months, and the average global temperature fell several degrees the following year. Parts of Europe and North America saw frost from June through August. It was known as the Year Without a Summer. Looking at the painted concrete structure curing in the morning sun, I could already feel my throat constricting.

Mom had dropped me off a half-hour early. I sat on the field picking mini daisies and waited for nine o'clock. I didn't feel like making a bracelet—I wouldn't have had anyone to give it to anyway—so I just ripped off their tiny heads by the handfuls and scattered them over the browning grass while I hummed Mary's theme song. *You're gonna make it after all.*

Slowly, other kids arrived, dragging their feet across the baseball field, kicking up dust devils with every begrudging step. Hooligans, petty criminals, and general malingerers from across the Golden school system. I searched for familiar faces and relaxed when I found none.

Eventually, Moody Miller arrived in his brother's car, smoke billowing. The passenger door opened and Moody spilled onto the ground, laughing. I laughed too until I noticed someone standing against the sun, light bursting all around them. I shielded my eyes. Carol Closter in a kaleidoscope of acid-coloured paisley topped with a bright green hat. It looked like a strawberry stem pulled down tight over her orange curls.

I squinted at her. "You're in summer school?"

"Isn't it great?"

"Weren't you on the honour roll?"

"Oh, I don't have to be here. My parents think the structure is good for me. I prayed to God that you'd be here too, and now here you are!"

"Thanks a lot," I said.

Carol put her hands on her hips and smiled. "Do you believe in signs, Robin? Because I sure do. God sends us signs all the time. Most people are just too dumb to notice." She squatted down and threw her arms around me, knocking us both over onto the grass. Her arms vise-gripped my neck. "This is going to be the best summer ever!"

"You really need to get out more," I said.

As I peeled her arms off, I saw Jamie Finley standing beside an old ten-speed, staring at me. Before I could stop myself, I smiled. I almost waved. Jamie dropped his eyes and pushed his bike toward the school.

"What's *he* doing here?" Carol said, squinting after him suspiciously.

I didn't know, but I took it as a sign that if there was indeed a God, he had a strange sense of humour.

Summer school was, in practice as in appearance, prison-like. We were permitted in the hall to use the bathroom, with a pass, for exactly three minutes. Otherwise, we were to remain in our seats, with our hands visible at all times. During class, we took turns reading out loud from our remedial textbook while our teacher dug under his nails with an uncoiled paper clip. Between chapters, we filled out multiple-choice exercise sheets. If someone tapped you on the shoulder, you shifted in your seat so he or she could see your answers. We didn't know each other, except in the vague way kids in a town with four highs schools do, but we would be shackled to one another for the next two months, so we made the best of it. If the kids from other schools knew about the fire, they kept it to themselves. Among us were girls who puked up their lunches every day, guys who stole cars, kids who'd been to foster homes and juvie and worse. What was it to them?

Moody Miller came in late every day reeking of pot. He sat at the back of my row and slept until lunch. Carol sat beside me, of course, reading her Bible or doodling in her notebook.

Being in summer school voluntarily, she wasn't made to read out loud or do much of anything. She'd pass me notes, drawings of Jesus at the beach, Jesus getting ice cream, Jesus snoozing at the back of a classroom, wearing a crown of z's. Now and then, we'd read something that made her lift her head and glare at our teacher. "A question, Miss Closter?" he'd asked her once. "No, no, Mr. Ford. Please continue. I'm enraptured."

At lunchtime, we were locked in the gravel courtyard with our brown paper bags. Moody and the other career stoners usually huddled in a shadowy corner with a joint. Jamie always sat by himself, doing homework or reading a dog-eared copy of *On the Road*. But most of us just sat wherever there was a free space. There were no cliques in that particular lunch yard. We were all equally lame. For a half an hour Carol had a captive audience and she did not intend to waste it. "What a load of malarkey," she'd say loudly the moment the door clicked shut. "If you believe what that guy's selling, I've got a bridge you can buy."

Carol, as we learned, thought most things were malarkey—rock music, science, canned pie filling, Dick Cavett. The moon landing had been faked, she insisted, and Kennedy was still alive on a tropical island somewhere. "Think about it," she said, tapping her head through her hat.

"I like Dick Cavett," someone said.

"You think you like him," Carol said. "You've been brain-washed like everybody else."

"What shows do *you* watch?"

"I don't watch TV. It's an instrument of Beelzebub. I prefer to read. Not that junk they think they're teaching us. The Good Book is the only book I need." She placed her hand on the little white Bible sitting beside her sandwich. She carried it everywhere. You never knew when you might need one, she told us. A kid nodded and said he felt the same way about his bong.

It would be a good while before many of those kids realized that Carol's friends Paul and Luke weren't kids who went to Reagan. But they seemed to genuinely like Carol, or at least get a kick out of her. Nobody in that dusty lunch yard ever called her a Jesus Freak or a Bible-thumper. They left her hats alone. Later, when the reporters came knocking, when everyone and their cousin tried to make a few bucks hawking their cafeteria memories to tabloid rags, not one of those burnouts spilled the beans on the girl with the wild stories they'd known one summer or her quiet, skinny friend. In that way, too, summer school was like prison. On the inside we were all innocent, and nobody likes a rat.

"Hey, Carol," they'd say. "Tell that one again about the guy who had to kill his kid."

"Abraham."

"Yeah, Abraham." And they'd lift their heavy heads from the warm stone table to hear the story again.

While Carol had everyone's attention, I'd keep an eye on Jamie on the other side of the yard. Usually his face would be deep in a book, his summer-long hair dusting the page. But sometimes when I glanced over he'd be staring at me. I'd cover my embarrassment with a whopping laugh, slapping the table like I'd just heard something hilarious. *Oh, that Abraham! What a card!*

The weeks found their rhythm. Days were hot and endless, evenings lonely but quick. After dinner, I did my homework on the dining room table while Mom practised her typing on an old IBM Selectric that her Mr. Grant had let her take home.

She showed real promise, Mr. Grant had told her. He admired her initiative.

"*Admired,*" she said. "That's the word he used."

Some nights he admired her on the phone. The first time he called I'd thought he was one of Dad's old clients. A few of them still called now and then, widowed women in empty houses or young mothers left alone all day. Mom could have had the number changed, but she didn't. They needed someone to talk to, she said. I guess Mr. Grant did too.

Weekends, I lay in the overgrown grass, head on top of the books I was supposed to be rereading, and plotted our move to Minneapolis, where I'd help Mom pursue a career in broadcast journalism. I pictured us on a city street, twirling around in our pantsuits, tossing our berets in the air. After a while, the grass held the shape of me, as if it was waiting for my return. I preferred it this way. I could almost lose my legs in it. I could almost disappear. If Mrs. Houston was gardening, she'd wave hello from her side of the fence, but she never commented on the lawn or asked where my dad was. Being a widow, she was probably used to men being there one day and gone the next.

On Sundays, Mom made a lasagna that we'd reheat night after night until the layers were as dry and crispy as winter skin. She was a career woman. She didn't have time to burn something every night. She didn't have time for TV either, but she always managed a half-hour to watch *Mary Tyler Moore*. She looked more like Mary every day. Her hair was back to its usual ambiguous blond, but she teased it on top now and flipped the ends. She'd traded her cotton blouses and slacks for smart shifts and black pumps and did her eyeliner the way the other secretaries had shown her in the bathroom at work. They were loads of fun, she said, a real hoot. The Girls, she called them, as in, "The Girls swear by this new cabbage diet" and "Well, the Girls thought it was funny." Mom switched to Virginia Slims, because that's what the Girls smoked.

"You've come a long way, baby," I said, but she only grinned vaguely, missing the joke.

They appeared at our front door one Saturday in July, big-haired, short-skirted, holding a deck of cards and a bottle of gin. The Girls—Lorna and Suzanne. They didn't huddle around the kitchen table like the neighbourhood women used to. No, the Girls lounged by the pool or reclined in the living room, their sweet cocktails leaving sweaty rings everywhere. They drank Dad's good hooch and fanned themselves with Mom's magazines. They wore nail polish on their toes called Deep Kiss and Marilyn Mauve. Suzanne read romance novels. Lorna preferred true crime. She said, "Don't you think?" after everything. *Robert Redford is scrumptious. Don't you think?* Suzanne thought everything was a riot. *Oh yeah, Redford's a riot.* When they wanted a refill, they'd jingle their ice cubes at me and say, "Would you, pet?"

The Girls gossiped about their bosses, the men who drank so much at lunch they slept at their desks all afternoon, the yellers whose tantrums sent secretaries to the bathroom to cry. They all had nicknames. Mr. Fingers. Pants McPatterson. All except Mr. Grant. He was heads above the rest of them, Mom said, and he deserved their respect. When she talked about him, Lorna and Suzanne would grin at each other, like they'd swallowed something tasty.

Mostly they talked about sex, more than kids at my school did, even more than Carol, whose little white Bible was filled with it and all the ways it could get you a one-way ticket to hell. The Girls compared notes on chest hair and back hair, who was a good kisser, who knew what to do with his hands. They swapped notes on emergency contraception like cake recipes, the things you could do with Coca-Cola, orange juice, and baking soda. They assumed they would shock me and were disappointed when they didn't, though it's true I'd never look at the contents of a pantry the same way again.

If anyone was shocked it was Mom. Lorna would be telling a story about getting felt up outside a ladies' room and Mom would start running around putting coasters under everything. "Who needs a refill! Who needs a snack!"

"Why so shy?" Suzanne said.

"I guess I was brought up to think that kind of talk was beneath a girl," Mom said.

"That's one way to do it," Lorna laughed. "Don't you think?"

"You are a riot!" Suzanne screamed.

But nothing the Girls said or did could convince Mom that they were anything but a breath of fresh air. "You girls are a breath of fresh air!" she'd tell them, inhaling deeply and letting it out in one big whoosh to prove the point. I would've plucked all my eyebrows out before I'd admit it, but she was right. The Girls were single and broke. They lived on the other side of the canal in a shared one-bedroom apartment. They had hotplates instead of ovens and roommates instead of families. They were no Phyllis and Rhoda, that's for sure. But they got a kick out of everything. The world for them was a big juicy peach. They did things and went places. There were beaches in Florida, they told us, where the women went topless, and whole neighbourhoods where nobody spoke a word of English.

"Imagine that," Mom kept saying. "Just imagine that."

I'd never been out of California. Imagine was pretty much all I could do.

7

Some days Carol showed up at summer school in a bright yellow T-shirt with *UP WITH JESUS* silkscreened on the front. Those afternoons, Mrs. Closter would collect her in a brown station wagon at lunch and ferry her away. Carol was not, after all, really one of us. She could come and go as she pleased, and twice a week it pleased her to volunteer with her church group.

With Carol gone, the yard was quiet as dust. You could hear girls' sticky thighs pulling apart and mouths being sucked dry as the stoners and rejects and misfits paired off, making out lazily against the walls, where the overhang provided shade if not privacy. Inspired by Jamie, who'd finished Kerouac and taken up Faulkner, I used the time to get a jump-start on my homework. American history was even more boring the second time around. I didn't want to try for a third. There was a daycare across the street, and sometimes the kids would get walked over in a line like little soldiers to use the playground. We could see them running around through the fence. *Let's pretend*, they'd shout to each other. *Let's pretend this is our castle. Let's pretend we're on a desert island.* It was nice to sit there listening to them, remembering when the whole world could be whatever you wanted so long as you believed it so. Those days, when I glanced over at Jamie, I'd often catch him grinning to himself and I knew he was listening to them too. I can't name more than twenty presidents, but I still remember the way his dimple looked when he lifted his face to watch them.

Now and then older guys cruised by the junior high, circling the block in their waxed trucks and deep July tans. They were older versions of us, dropouts waiting out the weeks until they shipped off. "Hey, losers!" they'd yell. "What's two plus two? What state's California in? Anyone know how to spell PBR?" A couple times, they threw empty beer bottles at our windows, but they were too lazy to hit anything. We'd even laugh at their jokes sometimes. The same guys would come back later, half-cut, and offer the girls rides home.

One Friday they were waiting for us after school with cartons of eggs. We were easy marks, half-blinded by the bright sun, and they took us out one by one as we came out the front doors. A few kids made a run for it. The rest of us crouched inside. There were no teachers in sight, and this was some relief. Their presence would have only embarrassed us.

Carol stood on her toes to peer out the small window in the door. "There are four of them and forty of us."

"They'll still kick our ass," Moody said.

We would just have to wait for them to get bored and leave. The boys mumbled fake bravery under their breath. The girls reapplied their lip gloss. Nobody seemed too surprised by any of it. Outside, the truck was idling. "Come on out and play," they called.

Some older kids filtered out of a classroom at the end of the hall, Jamie Finley among them. Seeing us huddled at the doors, he came over, curious, and stood beside me. It was the closest we'd been since he'd held my foot in his hand. He was taller now, but just as skinny. I waited for him to turn and give me his usual stony glare, but he only stared out the door's window as though he didn't know I was inches away, or didn't care. "What the fuck?" he said.

He opened the door a few inches and began to ease his long body through the gap. A bottle exploded at his feet, glass shooting across the linoleum, beer gushing everywhere. He pulled back, breathing hard. One leg of his jeans was soaked. "There's two more in the back," he said.

"Isn't anybody going to do something?" Carol said. "What is everyone so afraid of? When the Romans threw the Christians to the lions, they went to their death singing."

Jamie swallowed hard and curled his hands into fists. In a month, he'd be a senior, a year after that, gone. I reached out and touched the tip of one finger to his arm. I didn't mean to. My finger had a mind of its own. When Jamie turned his face to me, his green eyes were dark and worried. He didn't want to go out there any more than I wanted him to.

Moody made himself comfortable against a wall and drew a joint from behind his ear. "Make love, not war," he said. Jamie uncurled his fists and we both smiled, embarrassed, at the floor.

"Oh, forget it," Carol said. She clutched her little white Bible to her chest with one hand and threw open the door.

We watched through the window as she charged across the gravel in her pink hat, Good Book thrust in the air. The guys in the truck didn't throw anything. They just sat there, dumbfounded, as she flung herself toward them, belting out the "Star-Spangled Banner." Halfway between us and them, she skidded to a stop and chucked her Bible. It got about twenty-five feet before dropping in the dirt nowhere near their truck. Then one of them yelled, "Incoming!" and they all fired at once. When they ran out of eggs, they hurled a few more insults and sped away, howling with laughter.

Carol stood for a minute, back heaving, clothes dripping. But when she turned around she was laughing. She held up her arms like a gymnast who'd stuck her landing. "They didn't even knock off my hat!"

I smiled at Jamie, but he wasn't smiling anymore. He turned and started back down the hall, stopped at the first classroom door, made a fist, and punched it. We stared, slack-jawed, at the dent he'd made. Nobody seemed more surprised by it than Jamie.

"Far out," Moody said. "I am really starting to dig this summer school thing."

That weekend, the Girls talked Mom into going to the public pool across town. "But we have a perfectly good pool here," she said. "And they have perfectly good men there," they said.

They called it the "town pool," as if this made it something other than the tepid outdoor facility crawling with diapered toddlers that it was. It was as I remembered it. There were diving boards, lap lanes, and a small concession stand that served soft ice cream and limp fries. I was relieved to see I didn't know any of the boys who hurled themselves into the water, ignoring the lifeguard and the laws of physics, or the girls in crocheted bikinis and silver toe rings who lay on their backs, bellies exposed like contented cats. The rest were heat-dogged families making the most of another scorching Golden day.

Lorna and Suzanne laid their towels on the pokey grass where the young mothers watched their babies loll around on blankets. Babies left, babies right. Everywhere we looked—babies.

Two wiggled around on a blanket beside us.

"Let's swim," Mom said, looking at the Girls and not sitting down.

"You're a riot," Lorna said, taking a bottle of baby oil and a square of cardboard wrapped in aluminum foil out of her bag. They'd washed their hair that morning. Their bikinis weren't designed to go anywhere near actual water. Mom and I both wore Speedos, piling across the bums and sagging every which way. I wore a long T-shirt over mine.

"What about you?" Mom said, trying to sound cheerful. "Want to do a bit of diving with your old mom?"

"No thanks," I said.

"I haven't seen you swim in a while."

"Define a while."

She gave up, spread her towel, and sat. The babies gurgled and cooed at her. They squirmed and giggled. They wiggled their fingers and toes. Mom tried to ignore them, but the babies wouldn't have it. One climbed over her ankle and clutched her knee. She watched, horrified, as he got closer. He grabbed on to her thigh with one hand, the other reaching up, fingers squeezing. He moved his mouth at her, a little fish sucking the air. I found other things to look at. The state of my toenails was revolting. Something must be done.

"He's hungry," Mom said loudly. She was almost shouting. "Somebody needs to feed this baby."

"They've been fed," the mother said. She lay on a towel behind us, her face stuffed in a romance novel. She glared at me from behind her sunglasses, as if I'd been the one who'd spoken. She couldn't have been more than twenty.

"What happy babies," Lorna said.

What did they have to be sad about? I wondered.

"Twins?" Suzanne said.

"Fraternal."

"They must be a riot."

"That's one way to put it."

"Twins," Mom whispered, staring hard at the guppy flapping at her knee.

The mother glared at me again, then got up to retrieve her child. I touched Mom's arm. "I'll watch you dive." She nodded and followed me to the water.

I found a spot on the rough concrete edge while Mom climbed, worryingly, to the high diving board. I'd never seen her dive before. "Springboards are dangerous," Dad had warned, including the one in our backyard that hung three feet above the water. "You might as well leap off a cliff for how safe that thing is. You might as well bash yourself over the head with a two-by-four." He'd had half a mind to get it removed. I'd learned my own awkward back dive from a girl at summer camp, feeling guilty the whole time, as if she was teaching me how to hotwire a car.

It was mostly boys in the diving board lineup. They braved sloppy somersaults and back-breaking cannonballs that sounded a sonic boom. Seconds later, they'd shoot up through the water, grinning like they'd won the gold. When it was Mom's turn, she walked the board slowly, tugging at the loose elastic of her old suit. She put her feet in position, toes at the edge, and stared down at the water.

People in line grumbled. "We're dying of old age here," a kid said. "Next time try the ladies' board."

Mom turned and took a few steps toward the line of waiting boys. They groaned and started shoving each other back down the ladder to let her off. As they made way, Mom pivoted sharply, gripped the railing, and launched herself forward.

The board thundered under her feet as she hurled herself at its edge. She lifted her arms, bounced twice, and sprang up, up into the air. At the highest point, her body seemed to pause,

suspended against the empty blue sky. Then her body jack-
knifed, her arms circling the backs of her knees, before bursting open again and shooting toward the water in a perfectly
straight line.

She surfaced to cheering. The loudmouth on the ladder
was whistling through his fingers. Mom swam toward me,
smiling, as surprised as I was. The sun sparkled all around her.

"I must look a fright," she said when she reached the edge
of the pool. She slicked her hair back from her face.

"That was amazing," I said. "Do it again."

She grinned coyly. "Always leave them wanting more."

We bought celebratory Cokes at the concession stand.
The Girls needed it more than we did. They hadn't moved on
their towels and they were slick with sweat. The young mother
and her twins were gone. Mom sat on her towel, smiling at
everything.

"You're soaking wet," Suzanne said, peeling a magazine
off her thigh. Her makeup had slid half an inch. She looked like
the oil-blurred woman on the cover.

"I was in the pool," Mom said. "You know, that big blue
rectangular thing over there."

"Mom dove off the high board," I said.

"You were diving?" Lorna said, pulling a flask from her bag
and tipping it over their cups.

"Didn't you hear everyone clapping?" I said.

"Was that what that was?"

After their rummy Cokes, the Girls turned onto their stomachs and fell asleep. Mom and I went to the changing room and got in line for the toilets. Mom was in a stall when two women joined the back of the line. They wore V-necked one-pieces and saltwater pearls.

"Dear lord, it's like a Third World country," one said. "How did I let you talk me into this?"

"I know. I know," her friend said. "I thought a change would be fun."

"You want change, go to Palm Springs."

"You're right. You're right."

"That trash on the grass."

"In the bikinis, I know."

"And Elaine Fisher!"

"I almost didn't recognize her."

"On the high dive, showing off like that. Who does she think she's fooling? She's making a fool out of her*self*, that's who. I feel sorry for her, I do, but it's no excuse."

"You're right. You're right."

"If my husband did that, I'd bury my head in the sand. I wouldn't be running around with trash half my age. I wouldn't be flaunting it, you can believe that."

"You know, she still has my punch bowl. The one with the etched daisies? I guess I'll never see that again."

"What a pity."

A girl came out of a stall and I nearly knocked her down trying to get past. I sat on the toilet, staring at the roll of paper and wishing I had my lighter. I thought Mom had looked beautiful up there, but maybe they were right. Maybe she was embarrassing herself. Or maybe I should've busted out of that stall and told those old hags where they could put their punch bowl. Instead, I waited until I was sure they were gone. I could still see Mom's feet under her door when I slipped out. Like mother, like daughter.

When Mom came back to the towels she was smiling so hard it had to hurt. "Everyone ready to go?" she said, already packing up. Lorna and Suzanne complained that it was too soon, their tans wouldn't be even. "We'll come back next week," Mom said, smiling even harder, so I knew we never would.

I found out that Monday that Jamie wasn't really one of us either. He was in a college prep program and they could eat lunch wherever they wanted. For some unfathomable reason he had elected to get locked into the lunch yard with us hooligans every day. But after he punched the door, he didn't come back.

It was barely a dent, but he had done it. He had left his mark. Alone in the front hall once, I placed my own fist gently inside the grooves, marvelling at how neatly it fit, wondering if this was one of Carol's signs.

8

Mom seemed determined to make up for all those years she hadn't swum. She spent whole weekends in the pool. When she wasn't practising her typing, she was perfecting her front crawl, her fingers either smudged with ink or pruned and white. She bought a bathing cap and smeared herself with lanolin whenever she got the chance.

The Girls came over on Saturdays to play gin rummy, but only after they'd spent a few hours baking beside the public pool. They always stayed until somebody asked for their phone numbers. Their tans were so dark their teeth glowed.

They told us about the men they'd met, Tom from Michigan or Minnesota, Dan who did something or other in banking. They didn't seem especially interested in the particulars, but I suspected this was beside the point.

"We aren't getting any younger," Suzanne said.

"Or smarter," Mom said.

"Oh, Elaine, you're a riot."

When it was just Mom and me, I'd do my homework on the patio table, mumbling about how useless math was while I counted her laps. Mr. Grant said it was important to have goals, she told me. "Your most important competitor is yourself!"

She spoke to Mr. Grant on the phone almost nightly now. When Dad's old clients called, she hurried them off the phone with cheap platitudes and mixed metaphors. "You know what they say. When God shuts a door, he opens a new can of worms. Okay, you take care!" Heaven forbid the man got a busy signal.

I don't know what they had to talk about every night after talking to each other all day, but Mom assured me that Mr. Grant was a very inspiring man. After one of his calls, she'd moon around for hours, grinning at the TV, grinning at a book. Sometimes she'd change into her swimsuit and go grin in the pool.

"You wouldn't believe his stories," she said. "He grew up dirt poor, you know. He washed dishes to put himself through law school. He had a lot of doors slammed in his face, but that only made him try harder. The man won't take no for an answer."

"I'll bet."

Mom stopped towelling her hair and looked at me through a screen of wet hair. "Maybe Lorna and Suzanne are spending too much time over here," she said.

———

Summer's empty days stretched out this way for so long it was easy to forget about fall. September was a lifetime away. Then, suddenly, summer school was over and a new school year rushed toward me at meteoric speed. I saw it in every cloud and leaf. There was nothing to do but stand still and wait for it to flatten me.

Labor Day weekend, the grey over Golden was pulled tight as an eyelid. A storm was coming, but our neighbours didn't seem to care. Boys scrubbed their fathers' cars for a dollar and little sisters did cartwheels on front lawns while their parents grilled burgers and mixed mojitos in their yards. As I watched them from the window, Mom talked to Mr. Grant on the phone behind me. She'd spent the whole episode of *Mary Tyler Moore* in the kitchen with her hand cupped around the receiver. By the time she hung up, the lasagna was burnt.

"Oh no!" Mom cried, opening the oven door and waving away the smoke. "Why didn't you turn this off?"

I didn't answer. I'd been too busy eavesdropping to notice. Mom never said anything interesting on those phone calls anyway. She didn't say much at all, except to tell him how wonderful he was. *Oh, Brian, you're hilarious. Oh, Brian, you're too much. Oh, Brian. Oh, Brian.*

She'd started calling him that. *Brian.*

"So what do you want to do on your last weekend of freedom?" Mom said, excavating a crispy square of noodles from the pan, cutting around the black edges with a spatula. "Aren't you excited? You're a sophomore! Oh, don't look at me like that."

She poured me some wine to celebrate. When I didn't drink it, she tipped it into her own glass. She was always in an annoyingly good mood after those calls.

"How about a new outfit for your first day? You could get a pair of those bellbottoms you want."

"That was two years ago," I said.

"Was it?" Mom was wearing a pair of my old cut-offs and a sleeveless top with a stain on the front. Her clothes were riddled with them now, blue dots of fountain pen ink and smudges of black from the typewriter ribbon. Once, a scuff on her shoe would've sent her back to her room to change. A tear in her pantyhose would've ruined her whole day. We had to watch expenditures, she said, a word she'd picked up at work. We couldn't just throw things away because they weren't perfect. But I suspected that really she was proud of these stains the way boys were proud of their scars.

"Okay, fussy pants," she said. "Get whatever you like."

"Great," I said. It was like a warden telling a prisoner he can have anything he wants for his last meal. *How about some mashed potatoes and a nice prime rib!*

The mall was crowded with summer-beat families soaking up the free air conditioning. Little kids ran wild in the food fair while teens loitered in tight jeans, swapping spit and shoplifting. Mothers marched from store to store, checking things off their lists while husbands slouched on hardwood benches, watching the fluorescents flicker. I wandered around, trying on costume jewellery, perfume, wigs. I was realizing too late that summer's solitude had been a gift, and I was glad for these last hours to trickle away slowly.

I was at a record store, leaving my fingerprints all over the new Doors album, trying to imagine my life as a girl who longed for the acid poetry and leather pants of Jim Morrison, when the singing began. Loud and off-key, it drowned out the Led Zeppelin vibrating from the store's speakers. A group of kids in yellow T-shirts were standing in the atrium, belting out "He's Got the Whole World in His Hands" like it was the grooviest tune on earth. I recognized Carol Closter's tone-deaf rendition before I saw her yellow hat.

"Donations for injured Christian soldiers!" she shouted over the singing. "Your dollar could save their life and your soul!" She shook an empty ice cream bucket at people as they passed. Some dropped a few coins, but most ignored her. She pulled her hat down tightly and tried a more aggressive tack.

"You're letting Christians die, you know! You're making Baby Jee-sus cry!" I turned around and headed to Bertram's discount department store, where senior citizens rummaged in bins for huge bags of pantyhose and day-old bread.

Mom's money went far on a discount rack. I picked out a pair of patchwork jeans I actually thought were pretty snazzy, a simple white blouse, a couple of T-shirts, and a pair of knock-off Keds. A security guard trailed me for a while. I guess I looked suspicious loitering in the sleepwear section among the racks of long cotton nightgowns that belonged in a Mennonite museum. I was in no rush. When he got bored of following me and started watching a pack of hippies by the perfume counter, I found the changing rooms.

Since the night of the fire, I'd done impressive acrobatics to avoid seeing myself naked. The image of myself in a mirror was too startling. For months there had been no part of me—not an elbow or a knee—that I could identify as my own. But here, standing in the Bertram's changing room, under the unkind fluorescents, I saw myself. There were my sceptical eyes, my downturned mouth, my sunburnt nose. There my long neck, my narrow shoulders, my small breasts. My cock-sucking lips.

I stripped down to nothing. There I was.

I pulled on the jeans slowly, buttoned the crisp white blouse. I pictured the girl in the mirror walking down a hall, head high, shoulders back. I swung my arms and she did the same. I pulled my mouth into a smile and she smiled back.

I heard someone rustling around on the other side of the curtain. "I'm fine," I said. "I don't need any help."

Fingers slid through the gap between curtain and wall.

"Somebody's in here!"

The hand drew back the curtain, inch by inch. I could already feel it moving over my body, unbuttoning my jeans, folding over my mouth. I tore out of there, arms thrashing, wrapping myself in the curtain and bringing it down in a crashing heap.

Carol Closter stood over me holding a mannequin arm. "You scare easy," she said.

"What on earth?" A saleslady stood behind Carol. She pulled a tissue from her cavernous cleavage and dabbed her flushed face. "What is going on here?"

"My friend wants to buy crotchless panties," Carol said. "Where would she find those?"

The saleslady crossed her arms. We hurried away, pressing our laughter into our hands. Clear of Bertram's, we stopped and let it out. "What are crotchless panties?" I said. Carol laughed so hard she snorted. I bent over, hands on my thighs. My side hurt in a good way.

"I saw you before, by the fountain," Carol said, catching her breath. "I thought you saw me too, but I guess not."

"I guess not," I said.

"Summer school was fun, huh?"

"If you say so."

"I don't have to go back yet," Carol said. "Want to get an Orange Julius? I have two dollars."

Carol did not, I realized, understand the rules of summer. In a few days, Moody Miller would go back to warming the chair outside Mr. Galpin's office, Jamie Finley would rejoin the chlorine brotherhood, I would eat lunch with the square dancers, and Carol Closter would resume her role as resident Jesus Freak. Our tans would last longer than whatever temporary friendships we had cobbled together in the last two months—if you could even call them that. Carol Closter and I were not going to double to prom. We were not going to sleep over at each other's houses and braid each other's hair.

"My mom's picking me up," I lied. "She gets really mad if I'm late."

Carol's smile disappeared. "Okay, Robin. I'll see you at school, I guess." She started walking away, then stopped and turned around. "I like your outfit, by the way."

I looked down. I'd left my clothes in the Bertram's changing room, along with the money my mother had given me and my bus fare home.

———

The sky was sketched in pencil. A storm wasn't far off now. I waited at the bus stop. I didn't know what else to do. I watched haggard shoppers shuffle out of the mall. The hippies from the perfume counter congregated near the doors, bumming for change. The guys had beards. The girls had dreadlocks. One of them dug around in her large fringed purse and pulled out a chocolate bar. She broke off pieces and handed them to her friends. I'd heard about the kids who lived in vans on the edge of town. Draft dodgers and acidheads, guys who sandpapered their fingerprints, girls who read your aura for money. They weren't like the kids at school who wore hemp clothing and stickered their lockers with peace signs.

The rain started, lightly at first. People hurried to their cars, hands searching pockets for keys. A bus pulled up to the stop. I told the driver I'd lost my fare. "Hippies," he said, sneering at my patchwork. The real hippies were dancing on the grass behind me, singing and laughing, the girls catching the rain with their long, twirling skirts. *Come with us*, I imagined them saying. *We don't go to school. We sleep under the stars.*

The rain came down harder, raged. There were buckets of it. If Dad were there, he would have been telling me about China's Huai River for the millionth time. After several years of severe drought, the winter of 1930 brought one of the country's heaviest snowfalls, and the following spring, some of its heaviest rains. The Huai River rose more than fifty feet. As many as four million people perished. Survivors sold their wives, murdered their children, and ate the dead to stay alive. They believed the river would rise forever, that the gods were done with man. Their thirst for punishment would not be slaked. Dad told this story every time it rained, which was almost never. Even he had to admit he couldn't give flood insurance away.

The hippies shouted and swore at the sky. One of them thumbed a ride from a Volkswagen van with snakes painted on the side, and they jumped in, laughing again like it was all part of the game. I didn't like sleeping outside anyway.

My stolen clothes pulled at me, heavy with water. The blouse was nearly translucent, the jeans dark with water. There was rain in my eyes and in my ears. I wondered if it was possible to drown on a sidewalk. I thought of my mom, how she liked to stand outside on stormy nights and wait for the sky to empty itself. I found her in the backyard once, standing in the grass, her nightgown soaked through. I had watched from the safety of the awning, worried and curious, not quite Mommy's or Daddy's little girl.

A car pulled up in front of me and the window rolled down. From where I was standing, all I could see was the driver's mouth.

"Did you win?" the mouth said.

"Win what?"

"The wet T-shirt contest."

I crossed my arms over my chest.

"Yeah, I didn't think so."

I couldn't see the guy in the passenger seat at all, but I could hear him laughing. They high-fived each other inside the car.

"I'm just kidding around," the mouth said. "Hey, I know you, right?" He tilted his head so I could see the rest of him, right up to the buzz cut. He looked like one of the guys who'd terrorized us with garbage. I glared hard and tried to remember the zingers I'd thought up later while I flicked Mom's silver lighter on and off in my room.

"Can we give you a ride? You look really wet. Do you feel wet?"

His friend snickered beside him.

I turned and crossed the meridian quickly, slipping and sliding inside my sneakers. My hair stuck to my face in clumps. I heard a door slam, then shoes slapping the wet road behind me. He grabbed my arm and spun me around. He was a foot taller than me and twice as wide. Behind him, his friend slid into the driver's seat to watch.

"Hey, what's your problem? I'm just offering you a ride home."

"Thanks, but no thanks."

"I'm trying to be a nice guy here and I'm getting fucking soaked." His meaty hand tightened around my bicep. "Why don't you be nice back, huh? My friend Troy says you're a real nice girl."

The name was like a gong ringing in my head. I pulled back but he wouldn't let go of my arm.

Something small flew between us and hit him in the face. He yelped and tipped backwards, a hand to one eye. The other eye blinked at me. "What was that?"

His one good eye darted around. The parking lot was empty except for a few abandoned cars. The rain was coming down like it wouldn't ever stop.

"Fuck, it really hurts," he said. He took his hand away to show me. There was a small mark under his eyebrow, a magenta *V* where the corner had struck. The lid was already swelling. In an hour he'd have one hell of a black eye to explain.

"It doesn't look too good," I said.

"Yeah?"

"Yeah."

He ran back to the car and shoved his friend over. "I was just screwing with you," he said loudly, like he thought someone might be listening. He stuck his head out the window. "I wasn't going to do anything. I swear."

I glared at him until he was good and gone.

The rain stopped as suddenly as it had started, as if someone up there had turned off the tap. The sun broke through the clouds. What my mom liked most about storms was how sweet the air was after. "Makes you wonder how we breathed before," she'd said that night I found her in the rain. "You get so used to the heat you don't even know you're suffocating." What I liked most was how clean everything seemed, as if my whole town had gone through a car wash. Even the colours were brighter. I breathed deeply. Within a few hours, a layer of dust would settle and the heat would sink back in, but for now the air was fresh and cool.

I looked around for whatever had hit him. It lay beside a car, fanned open and swollen with water.

"I told you, you never know when you might need it," a voice said.

Carol stood behind me, soaking wet. White petals stuck to her like confetti. She'd been hiding inside a rhododendron bush.

"It's ruined," I said, handing her the Bible. "Sorry."

"That's okay. I've got more."

A horn beeped. This van was windowless and white, the kind kids called the Chevy Abductor. The side door slid open. Eyes blinked at us from the dark. A dozen kids in yellow

T-shirts sat on the bare metal floor like illegal immigrants. Carol's Ark.

Carol made everyone move over, and I settled in beside her on the floor. She gave me a yellow T-shirt to dry myself with. "You can keep it," she said.

The van started up and we headed toward home, rocking lightly from side to side as we drove. I couldn't keep my eyes open. It felt like I'd been trying to fight a flood with a spoon.

"I was handling things fine on my own," I told her.

"I know," she said. "But you don't have to."

I took a clean, clear breath and rested my head on Carol's shoulder. I didn't want to eat the dead to stay alive. "At least your aim's getting better," I said and closed my eyes.

9

The literary types called us Fire and Brimstone. Those who'd summered in Europe tried out Tart and Vicar. But Joyce preferred the names she had herself once bestowed. "Pyro Slut and Jesus Freak, together at last," she crowed across the hall. "It's a match made in hell."

"Like your nose and my fist?"

That would shut her up for a while. Joyce was very careful about her nose.

"Why do you care what she thinks anyway?" Carol asked. The only answer I could come up with was that I hated to be the one responsible for Joyce's happiness.

Melanie, mortified by any lingering associations, ignored me with renewed vigour, as if I was still capable of ruining her life from a distance. Troy Gainer, newly anointed senior, had perfected the art of looking right through me. After a while, kids mostly left us alone. In its own odd way, our friendship made sense, as did our partnership in Mrs. Maxwell's home ec class. Nobody wanted to bake brownies with the girl who was actually capable of burning down the school, and nobody wanted to bake brownies with Carol Closter because she was Carol Closter.

I was not discouraged. I tried nowhere so hard as I did in Mrs. Maxwell's class, where we were assured daily that our efforts would be rewarded with vital homemaking skills. Half the week we sewed, the other half we cooked. These were the days I looked forward to, the hours when I could, in theory, transform a few raw ingredients into something whole and nourishing. In practice, the glandular smell of oil brought bile bubbling up the back of my throat. Butter and mayonnaise were out of the question—the Girls had taken care of that. Eggs were the worst, those swollen globules bobbing in albumen, those yellow accusing eyes. They triggered a gag reflex that started in my knees.

"You have to get your hands in there," Mrs. Maxwell would say, pushing mine into a bowl up to the wrists. "You can't be squeamish about it. You are making something beautiful that will feed your family. The most important ingredient in every recipe is love."

It was no use. As much bile as I swallowed, everything I touched came out flat, gritty, lopsided, and burnt. I julienned my fingertips, grated my knuckles into the batter, but no offering was good enough. My sauces were both lumpy and runny. I could've used the mashed potatoes to spackle a wall. Cakes simply gave up the will to live. My love, it turned out, was inedible.

"It comes naturally to some," Mrs. Maxwell said, wiping her hands on a dishtowel so the egg never really came off, just got moved around. "Others have to try a bit harder." I imagined the yolk drying under her nails until her next shower, and then I thought of teachers showering and it was all I could do not to run out the door. "There's no shame in a nice TV dinner," she said, shaking her head, because there was shame in it and we both knew it.

Carol Closter said I shouldn't listen to Mrs. Maxwell. She was a dried-up old egg who couldn't get anyone to marry her so she was stuck here teaching us for all eternity. Carol was happy to let me fail brilliantly day after day while she thumbed through floured recipe pages and talked about her saints. Applying ointment from Mrs. Maxwell's first aid kit to my tender skin for the millionth time, she'd ask Saint Lawrence to watch over me. The patron saint of cooks, he'd famously told his tormenters as they roasted him over coals that they should turn him over—he was done on that side.

At the end of every class, stuffing my handiwork into her dainty mouth like it was the most delicious thing she'd ever tasted, Carol would invite me once again to her teen Bible study group. "Everyone keeps asking about you," she'd say. "We get free chocolate bars."

I pictured them sitting in the back of the van, eating Kit Kats and praying for me. "Maybe next time."

Carol would just tilt her head and smile. She said God had a plan for all of us. It wasn't our place to question what that plan was. The world and everything in it was preordained, our stories already written in permanent black marker on that big locker in the sky. "You'll come when you're ready," she'd say, glowing with the certainty of it.

Deep down I suspected she was right. I already had the T-shirt.

Saturday mornings, Mom and I drove to a Lucky's where nobody she knew shopped. We sang along with the radio while we made a list of new and exotic foods she'd read about somewhere, added the ingredients for one of Mrs. Maxwell's practice recipes I wanted to try. At the store, we abandoned the list and filled our cart with Kraft slices and Wonder Bread and bottles of discounted red wine. Back at the house, Mom would pull on her old swimsuit and do laps while I'd lie in the pale autumn sun, flipping through magazines and keeping count. Now and then, I'd look over at the pool house. Those afternoons were so perfectly uneventful, so wonderfully ordinary, I half expected to see cigar smoke escaping from the door.

When the Girls came in the afternoon now, they no longer exiled Mom in the kitchen with talk of contraceptives and coat hangers. Now it was their suburban fantasies that drove her from the room. What had Dad paid for the house? Were the schools in the area any good? Did Maytags really never break down? June versus September weddings? Niagara Falls versus Acapulco? Veil versus tiara? Their left hands were bare, but they were confident. They had hot dates later with men named Cliff, Carl, Ray, or Ron, salesmen from out of town who took them to Chinese restaurants near the airport. They counted down the days until they could quit their jobs.

"I enjoy my work," Mom said.

Lorna laughed. "And we all know why, don't you think?"

"Actually, I've been thinking of taking a correspondence course," Mom said. In fact, she'd already driven to the university on the other side of town on her lunch hour and brought home a slim correspondence brochure that she'd pored over for days, underlining and circling things until it looked like one of my graded essays.

"What the heck for?" Suzanne said.

"Don't you want to understand what you're typing all day?"

The Girls scrunched their noses. They did not.

At five o'clock, they got ready for their dates. I'd bring them cocktails in Mom's bedroom, and they'd give me old lipsticks they'd grown tired of. They liked me more when they needed me, which didn't seem unreasonable. Between refills, I'd sprawl on Mom's bed, thumbing through one of Suzanne's magazines while they got dressed. Suzanne and Lorna were the most exciting thing that happened to me all week.

"Don't you go on dates?" Lorna asked one evening, words garbled around the bobby pins in her mouth. I shrugged, pretending to read.

"A girl as pretty as you?" Suzanne said. "When I was your age, I was out every Friday and Saturday night." She was setting her hair with Mom's rollers, leaning toward the mirror in her bra and panties, both red but not a matching set. "What about your mom? Does Elaine go on dates?"

"She's married," I said.

"But not buried." She grinned at Lorna in the mirror.

"She talks on the phone a lot, I guess. Mr. Grant calls here all the time."

That look again, whizzing over my head.

"Is that so?" Lorna said.

"He says she has a lot of potential," I said, rolling my eyes, trying to mimic the way they talked. I was enjoying the attention. We were in cahoots. "He *admires* her *initiative*."

"I'll bet he does."

Lorna reached for the dress she'd hung on the closet door, slipped her legs inside the smooth red fabric, and shimmied into the bodice. Suzanne took Lorna's place in the mirror. When her towel slipped she didn't bother to cinch it back up, just sat there brushing her hair like that, smiling at herself in the mirror when I would have cringed. I felt the scratch of envy in my chest, sharp as the business end of a rat-tooth comb.

"She'll probably get a raise soon," I said.

Suzanne pursed her mouth sourly. "Oh, someone's getting a raise, all right."

After the Girls left, Mom spoke to *Brian* for twenty-six minutes. Every giggle was chalk on a blackboard.

"Are you fooling around with your boss?" I said after she hung up.

"Don't be silly. We're just friends."

"Lorna says men and women can't be just friends."

"Your father and I managed it for fourteen years."

But when Mom talked to Brian on the phone, she didn't sound the way she had when she talked to my dad. She sounded sunny and eager, like a game show contestant being interviewed before a live studio audience. "Oh, yes, Brian," she'd say. "Yes, of course. Yes, yes." After, she'd smile like she'd won something, though to me it sounded like she'd given something away.

"You're still married, you know," I said. Her smile flattened. Cakes weren't the only thing I knew how to ruin.

"How could I possibly forget with you always here to remind me," she said.

That Friday morning, Mom gave me ten dollars to order a pizza when I got home. "I'm having dinner with Brian," she said. "We're going to discuss my future."

"Is that what you kids are calling it these days?"

"Har har," she said and made that awful kissing sound near my ear.

I was thinking about this during home ec while Carol talked about her saints. "First of all, you have to be a servant of God, obviously, and then you have to be venerable. That means you lived a life of heroic virtue. After that comes the hard part—the miracles. You need two miracles. That's the way the Catholics do it, and if you're going to be a saint, you definitely want to be a Catholic one. It's the one thing they got right."

"Sure," I said.

"If you're a martyr, you only need one miracle. And you don't have to part the Red Sea here. You could cure a blind person or something like that."

"Turn Joyce Peyton into a human being."

"Exactly."

As I wondered how many martyrs it would take to make my dad come home, Carol lifted her nose delicately to the ceiling and sniffed. It took me a little longer to notice the smoke. I was that used to it.

"Perhaps another elective," Mrs. Maxwell said, holding my smoking dishtowel under the tap. I didn't even remember leaving it in the oven. Kids fanned the air with their aprons. "You mean well, dear, I know. But you don't respect your oven. You don't respect the heat."

The bell rang, and we filed out of the smoky room, down the hall to our lockers.

"If that old cow likes ovens so much," Carol mumbled, "she should go put her head in one."

I shoved my hands in my pockets. One held Mom's silver lighter. The other, her ten bucks. I didn't see how the evening could end well. When I asked Carol if I could come over to her house after school, she didn't seem the least surprised. I guess it takes a lot to shock somebody who believes in miracles.

When you are young, other people's homes are foreign countries where strange languages are spoken and private rituals are best left private. I assumed this would be doubly true of the Closters. Not knowing what to expect, I prepared myself for crucifixes and rosaries, altars and shrouds. I pictured her mother in habit and wimple, her father with a white square at his neck. But the Closters were like everybody else. I tried not to feel disappointed.

They lived in one of Golden's newer developments. Their house, like those beside it, had aluminum siding the colour of iceberg lettuce and a short porch shaded by a white canvas awning that you cranked in and out by hand. There was a basketball hoop over the garage and a flag over the front door. Two clay pots of bright pink flowers flanked the front step. String beans threaded a picket fence. I was met inside by fuzzy wallpaper, brown wall-to-wall, fake wood panelling, gold velvet furniture attired in plastic. The kitchen cupboards were dark orange, the avocado backsplash tiles hand-painted with the requisite fruits and vegetables. There weren't even any crucifixes hanging around, though they did have an oil painting of Jesus in the hall where a mirror should have been. I guess the Closters trusted that God wouldn't let them leave the house with spinach in their teeth.

"We've heard so much about you, Robin," Mrs. Closter said. She stood at the stove where pots bubbled musically and filled the air with the heady scent of gravy. She looked nothing like Carol. A ruddy brunette, Teutonic and imposingly tall, she had to bend deeply at the knees to kiss her frowning daughter hello. "Robin this and Robin that. I guess I should ask you about yourself, but I feel as if I know you already."

"Mother, you're embarrassing me."

"Oh, now. I'm sure Robin's mother would say the same thing about you."

"Sure," I said. In truth, I'd never mentioned Carol to my mom. Carol rolled her eyes, and I smiled. She was horrible to her mother. We finally had something in common.

Mrs. Closter took Carol's coat, asked about her day, her allergies, if she'd had enough to eat for lunch. Carol gave curt responses, pushed her mother's fussing hands away. Mrs. Closter gave up and stood holding our coats, smiling as though she expected a tip. "Can I make you girls a nice snack?"

"We want to be alooooone," Carol said.

"I'll surprise you!" her mother said and disappeared into the kitchen.

I followed Carol to her bedroom. It was small but pretty, festooned with stuffed things and ruffled things and porcelain things, all of it purple and white. Lilac floral wallpaper peeked out between posters of Bible verses and biblical scenes. Jesus with a lamb. Jesus with Mary. Mary with baby Jesus. Baby Jesus with a baby lamb. A two-foot figure of the saviour in a glitter-trimmed robe watched from atop a shelf. It was like hanging out in a Christian gift shop.

Carol asked what I wanted to do. She had a bunch of Christian board games and a 500-piece puzzle of *The Last Supper*. "Judas's head is missing," she said, "but I think it's actually better that way."

"Why don't we just watch TV," I said.

"We don't have one. My parents say it gets me too worked up."

I sat on her bed and flipped through a magazine. It was full of stories about photogenic teenagers who were making the world a better place. Some of the pages had been torn out and stuck to the corkboard above Carol's desk. Her inspiration board, she called it. "This boy teaches retarded kids to play the ukulele," she said and sighed dreamily.

Mrs. Closter knocked on the door. Carol sighed again, undreamily. "Yes, Mother?"

"I was wondering if Robin would like to stay for dinner."

"Why would she want to do that?" Carol said, rolling her eyes to the ceiling, or God maybe.

"Actually," I said.

When Mr. Closter came home at five-thirty, everyone ran outside to greet him.

"This is Robin," Mrs. Closter said, beaming at him.

"Well, well," he said, beaming back at her, then me. He was an engineer, Carol had told me, and when he shook my hand I could smell the pencil lead. "Well, well," he said again.

Mrs. Closter poured her husband a glass of orange juice while he described the new McDonald's restaurant he'd seen driving home from the office. "It's got these two big arches," he said. "Sort of, um . . ."

"Golden?" I said.

"Why, that's right."

"Isn't that something," Mrs. Closter said, settling back into her work.

Carol's kid brother popped a pinch of grated cheese into his mouth and said the neighbour bought a new car.

"You don't say." Mr. Closter reached over to ruffle his son's hair, and the little guy smiled up at his dad. I tried to remember why it had bothered me when my dad did the same thing.

When dinner was ready, I set the table. Mrs. Maxwell said I was good at things that didn't involve actual cooking.

"It looks lovely," Mrs. Closter said, touching my arm.

She'd made a roast and mashed potatoes. There were glazed carrots and green beans with almonds and cheddar biscuits shaped into hearts with a cookie cutter and love. I'd seen these huge wedding cakes in a bakery once, dizzying towers of whipped white perfection. I thought they were beautiful until the lady behind the counter told me they were made from Styrofoam. You can't tell the fake layers from the real ones, she said, because everything is covered in frosting. That had been my family, Styrofoam drowning in Betty Crocker's Vanilla Cream. Carol's family probably milled their own flour. While Carol said grace, I opened my eyes just enough to confirm what I already suspected. Everyone was smiling with their eyes closed.

After dinner, Carol walked me to the end of her block. All the houses were lit up with televisions and refrigerators and families. I thought of Mom, out with her Brian. We were missing the *Mary Tyler Moore Show*.

"I guess my family's pretty weird, huh?" Carol said.

"Your parents are nice."

"They aren't my real parents," she said. "I'm adopted."

"Sorry," I said, which seemed like the only appropriate response.

"Don't be sorry. It means they really wanted me."

I looked at the ground so I wouldn't have to look at Carol. The details of a drug-addled birth mother would eventually come out. In fact, many women, drug-addled and otherwise, would lay claim to Carol Closter within the year. But it wouldn't make what she said that day any less true. Mr. and Mrs. Closter had chosen her. They had pointed to the fluff of orange hair through the nursery window and said, *That one. That's our girl.*

There it was, that rat-tooth comb again, scratching its tip across my heart. But this time it was worse. This time I was jealous of Carol Closter.

When I told Carol I had to go, she threw her arms around me and squeezed. Her hair was in my mouth. It was really soft. I'd always imagined it wiry.

"What's that for?" I said, spitting it out.

"Jesus wants you," she said. "Remember that Jesus wants you tons and tons."

When I got to the end of Carol's block, I turned to make sure she'd gone inside, then took Mom's silver lighter out of my pocket and flicked it on. The little flame leapt into the darkness, its warm bubble lighting my way. I was feeling better until the flame began to shrink. Smaller, smaller, smaller, then nothing. No amount of flicking could coax it back to life. There was no ceremony to a lighter dying, no audible fizz, no lingering trail of smoke. The dark slammed back, cold and unwelcome, and that was that.

There was a gas station a couple of blocks away where kids bought beer without getting carded. I pocketed the empty lighter and felt for the ten bucks.

I picked out a Coke and a Bic. The guy behind the counter gave me a look.

"For my dad," I said.

He shrugged and turned a page in the car magazine he was reading. "Like I give a crap."

Back home, I lay in bed, playing my favourite Carpenters album while I flicked my new Bic on and off. It wasn't like Mom's silver lighter. There was nothing elegant about it, nothing substantial. Disposable by design, its weight hardly registered in my palm. Nobody would ever engrave their initials in its blue plastic shell. But I liked it all the same. I liked the red switch, a little tongue egging me on. I liked how when I flicked it, the squat flame woke slowly, unfurling itself begrudgingly. I liked that I had to hold the tongue to keep the lighter going. If I let go, the flame disappeared. Each bright second was a choice I had made.

Mostly, I liked that it was mine and nobody else's.

I didn't hear Mom come in until she knocked on my door. I slid the lighter between the box spring and mattress just as the door opened. She stood in the doorway, cigarette between her fingers. One of her nails was broken. She used to wear fake ones that broke off all the time, but this one was real.

"Are you sleeping?"

"Would it make a difference if I said yes?"

She smiled a little and sat on the bed, right above where I'd hid the lighter. Close up, I saw that her mascara had run and she hadn't fixed it. She either didn't care if I knew she'd been crying, or she didn't know it herself. Neither option seemed good.

"How's *Brian*?"

"Not the man I thought he was."

"Who was he?"

Mom tugged at her skirt. Her pantyhose had a long run that climbed her knee and disappeared under the fabric. "He said I shouldn't get worked up about all this feminism mumbo-jumbo. He said women should stick to what they're good for."

"What are they good for?" Really, I wanted to know.

"He had a key to a motel room," she said, then laughed and waved her words away like smoke. "Blah, blah, blah." It was always this way with us. She told me too little or too much. I wanted to know more. I didn't want to know anything.

"Saint Catherine is the patron saint of secretaries," I said. Spinsters too, but I left that part out.

"Is that right?" Mom said. "This must have been her night off, then."

She reached out and fingered the fraying edge of my comforter. She could never abide loose ends. "We don't really talk about boys, do we," she said, singling out a broken thread and giving it a gentle tug. "Do you want to? Talk about boys?" She had attempted to explain the birds and the bees to me the week after my first period. Her mention of a special kind of love between mothers and fathers had only confirmed that I knew more about sex than she did. She tugged again.

"You'll rip it," I said.

She patted the thread back down, folded her hands for a moment. "I don't know what I was expecting. Everyone makes it looks so easy."

"Nothing looks easy to me," I said.

She regarded the loose thread as if it might have an opinion on the matter, then plucked it between two fingers. She went for it this time, really put her elbow into it. The old satin split as smoothly as a seam.

"Oh," she said, frowning at the rip. "Oh," as if she didn't have a clue how it had gotten there.

10

Mom made me call her office and tell them she was really, really sick and couldn't come in for a few days, maybe a week, maybe longer. While I spoke, she coughed like a consumptive in the background. "Uh-huh," the switchboard lady said and hung up. That woman never did like her, Mom said. "I guess now I know why." Anyway, it didn't matter. She wasn't going back.

When Lorna finally dropped by the house with a box of Mom's things, she wouldn't come to the door. Lorna had on oversized sunglasses and a scarf around her hair. At first I'd thought she was one of the neighbourhood women coming to collect some imaginary piece of Tupperware along with a peek inside our house. They did this now and then, kept tabs. But Lorna seemed content to stand on the step with the box crooked in one arm. The other skewered the air before me, left hand proffered limply so I could get a better look—a slice of gold around one finger, a diamond so small you had to squint.

"I'm engaged! Can you believe it?"

"I guess miracles do happen," I said.

"Excuse me?"

"Congratulations."

"You should see it when it catches the light!" Lorna bent her hand back at the wrist, wiggled her fingers, frowned. "Suzanne is dying of envy, of course. All the girls are. I keep telling them, their time will come. Oh, but poor Lainey! Everyone feels just awful for her. We tried to warn her, you know, but really she should know better. That man can have his pick—and trust me, he does."

I took the box. A dog-eared paperback, an ink-stained cardigan, a half-dead African violet. Free of it, Lorna stretched her arms and wiggled her fingers again. "There!" she said. "See that?"

"What?"

Lorna frowned again and folded her empty arms. "You just remember to keep your knees together," she said. "You wait till there's a ring on that finger. Nobody buys the farm when the milk is free."

"Cow," I said.

"Excuse me?"

"Nobody buys the cow."

———

Mom pored over the want ads, circling postings for secretaries, receptionists, shop girls. She went to interviews every day in her smart blue suit, her hair a stiff French twist. Every evening, I found her rumpled and defeated in front of the TV, feet tucked under her housecoat, smoking her way through every-one else's bad news.

"Everybody wants a twenty-year-old in a sweater," she said. "I might as well try to get blood from a stone."

I circled an ad for blood donors.

"Very funny," she said.

"Ten dollars is ten dollars."

The brochure for the correspondence class sat undisturbed on the phone table in the living room where Mom kept the bills. The bills too, I noticed, sat undisturbed.

"My shrine to wishful thinking," she called it.

"The desk of dead dreams," I said. We laughed so hard our cheeks hurt. We were becoming a family of quitters.

More interviews, more cigarettes in front of the news. She went on like that until one morning the television wouldn't turn on. Or the toaster or the coffee maker. Mom didn't seem too concerned about it. She sat in front of the dark TV, staring at her reflection in the curved grey glass.

That Sunday, I got up early. I was going to church. With Melanie, I said.

"What on earth do you want to do that for?" Mom said.

"I'm going to pray for electricity."

Carol, for her part, didn't seem the least surprised.

I had envisioned the stern sermon, hard polished oak under my knees, cramped confessional, pitiless priest, but Carol Closter's church was more like the show homes of the future Mom used to drag me to. There were white stucco walls and cream-coloured carpeting and blue-veined marble floors. Pastor Bob, with his wavy hair and brown turtleneck, could have been selling dishwashers from that marble pulpit. He talked about how you needed to love your enemies even more than you loved yourself, and reminded everyone about the swap meet on Saturday. He had it on good authority— here he pointed up and winked—that there'd be some real bargains.

While Mr. and Mrs. Closter chatted over coffee cake in a room beside the chapel and Carol's brother chased girls in frilled dresses around the lawn, Carol and I joined the teen Bible study group. A dozen kids sat on beanbag chairs, eating free chocolate bars while a college student with lopsided bangs tried to get them to open up about their hopes and dreams. "It's my hope to be a better person all the time," Carol said. "It's my dream to make the world a better place through the teachings of the Lord."

"Thank you, Carol," the college student said. "But maybe today we can hear from somebody else."

At the end of the hour we prayed. We prayed for poor President Nixon and for the godless youth of America who were making things so difficult for him. For the American soldiers, because they were on the side of God, and the Vietnamese on both sides who weren't. For the poor Mexicans who would be better off in their own country and the poor blacks who would probably never be any better off. For boys who threw their lives away for marijuana and girls who threw their sacred gift away for boys.

"And why do we pray for people who won't pray themselves?" the college student asked. Carol's hand shot up. The college student sighed, nodded.

"Praying for the helpless is our job," Carol said. "Just like judging sinners is God's."

I thought praying seemed a lot like judging. But it was nice in that room, with the chocolate bars and beanbag chairs and free-flowing electrical power, so I kept that particular judgment to myself.

When I got home, Mom was floating on her back in the pool.

"So?" she said. "Did you find Jesus?"

"Yeah," I said. "He was under the sofa cushions."

"Isn't it funny how he's always in the last place you look."

The electricity came back on two days later. For all I knew, Mom had sold a pint of her O positive. "It's a miracle," she said, walking around the house, flicking everything on—lamps, stove elements, the blender we never used. "Praise the lord!" she shouted over the noise. "Hallelujah! Let there be light!"

Mom always said Thanksgiving was overrated in America, not to mention six weeks late. Dad, who paid out too many Christmas tree fires, would have been happy to let all winter holidays pass quietly and without threatening strings of electric lights. Most years we'd gone to the country club's turkey buffet, attended largely by widowed men who tucked their napkins into their golf shirts, awkward evenings that left us unavoidably grateful for whatever it was we did in fact have. But Christmas, Mom loved. Christmas could not be stopped. It blew through our house like a jolly Arctic storm. She'd recreate the Canadian winters of her youth with plastic holly and snow-dusted windowpanes that came out of a can, persistent sunshine be damned. All month she'd answer the phone with "Hello-ho-ho." It was the one time each year when she insisted on entertaining. She would invite everyone, and everyone would come. "We wouldn't dream of missing it," they told her. "We look forward to this all year." Some of the women actually wore bells, tiny ones dangling from their ears. Even Mrs. Houston could be coaxed away from her widow's solitude and into her green Chanel suit. Dad would spend the evening holed up amiably in a corner with whoever brought the good Scotch.

Not that year. No invitations went out. The mantel remained clear of holly. The windows were dusted only with actual dust. All week long Mom hammered out copies of her half-page resumé on Mr. Grant's typewriter, which she'd never returned— her "booby prize," she called it. She must have sent one to every company in Golden, or at least that was the idea. She kept the phonebook beside the typewriter. When she'd written another address on another envelope, she'd tear out a corner of the yellow page, crumple it up, and toss it across the room. "If they hire me, we'll know how to find them," she said. "If they don't, well that's it for Wilma and her bargain wigs." Slowly, an Everest of crinkled yellow balls rose in the corner of our living room where an eight-foot noble fir had usually stood.

Mom would not lose hope, not even when she got to Zeb's Fish Palace, not even when she realized Zeb sold actual palaces for fish. She checked the mail that month like she used to check the phone. Every day brought the usual flyers, catalogues, and bills. When a few Christmas cards arrived, somebody's best wishes for a joyous holiday in embossed gold script or—horror!—a photo of some smiling family in matching reindeer sweaters, Mom dropped them into the trash. "They can shove their best wishes up their you-know-whats," she said. "I need their season's greetings like I need a hole in my head." A job at Hallmark was definitely out of the question.

As usual my grandparents sent me twenty Canadian dollar bills along with instructions not to spend them. We didn't hear from Dad at all, not so much as a dumb card. Not that I'd expected anything. He'd managed to forget our phone number, so it stood to reason he'd also forgotten our address. When Carol gave me a Bible the week before the break, I tried to feel thankful since I was pretty sure it was the only present I'd be getting that year. At the same time, I tried not to imagine the mountain of gifts under the Closter tree. I failed miserably at both. I couldn't look at Carol without picturing her house festooned in holiday splendour. I saw a magically snow-capped roof, chimney puffing happily, windows sparkling with tinsel and joy. Carol would be in her room cheerfully praying for the Mexicans and fornicators while Mrs. Closter roasted a perfectly moist Butterball and Mr. Closter helped elves build a bicycle on the front lawn. "My mom wants to know when you're coming over again," Carol kept saying, and I kept making excuses. My imagination was bad enough. Faced with the real thing, there was a fairly good chance I'd hang myself from the Closter mantel with somebody's homemade stocking.

School itself gave unexpected respite. Public education can always be counted on for depressing bits of coloured cardboard and sagging crepe paper bunting. The plastic tree was duly propped up in the hall outside the school office and trimmed with last year's tinsel. The old fringed foil runners were tossed over air ducts, and paper snowflakes were stapled to anything that stood still long enough. There were Mrs. Maxwell's home ec stars knitting socks for soldiers, and John Lennon and Yoko Ono's "Happy Xmas" tinkling morosely from car radios and guitars. There were poorly conceived green and red mashed potatoes in the cafeteria that nobody ate, and a pancake break-fast with Mr. Galpin in droopy red flannel pyjamas, trying his best to smile under his cotton-batting beard.

The shining glory was the Christmas assembly, when they unveiled blown-up yearbook photos of the boys from Reagan High who'd died in Vietnam that year. They smiled out at us from their art class easels at the front of the auditorium stage as the senior class president read their names along with the captions that had run under their graduation photos in their final yearbooks. Too-short lives reduced even further to a hundred words or less, nicknames and inside jokes and remember-whens that none of us remembered. After the ceremony, the photos would be hung outside the office along with the others, where they could smile at us for all eternity. Saint Steven. Saint Eddie. Saint Bobby. Saint Mike.

I sat at the back of the auditorium with the dazed and musky stoners, none of whom seemed to understand what was happening on stage. Melanie sat three rows up, beside Joyce Peyton, engraving letters into her inner arm with a ballpoint pen. It was where she tattooed all her crushes so her mother wouldn't see. I imagined the tall, bending *J*, the long, slender *F*. Jamie Finley was sitting near the front with the freshmen. He'd become a rare sight at Reagan that fall. When Troy and his gang of crewcuts held court in the parking lot at lunch, Jamie wasn't with them anymore. I'd heard that he'd quit the swim team, but nobody knew why. Surrounded now by weeping girls, he stared up at the dead boys on their easels, his head and shoulders as still as theirs.

I didn't know where Troy was, and for the first time since the fire I didn't care.

Once the senior class president was finished, Carol took the stage. She hadn't mentioned anything about the assembly, but this didn't surprise me. Carol was always popping up in places she didn't belong. When the school band held a bake sale to raise money for new sweaters, Carol had her own bake sale for Russian orphans. "New sweaters?" she called out to kids stuffing themselves at the other tables. "These orphans don't even have *old* sweaters. They don't have anything. Some are so hungry they eat their poop!" It probably goes without saying that she couldn't give those cupcakes away.

Carol stood neatly at the podium, her little white Bible clutched in both hands, while Mr. Galpin lowered the microphone for her. Anticipatory snickering rippled softly through the audience. The microphone was still too low by a few inches, but Carol was used to these small indignities. She placed a sheet of paper on the lectern and slowly, delicately, lifted her chin. "The Lord is my shepherd," she began. "I shall not want." Dear God, I thought. Anything but that. Somebody cracked a joke about lying down in green pastures. Joyce Peyton said something to Melanie about virgin births. Carol lifted her chin even higher and kept reading. She was used to these indignities too.

Someone booed. Then another. They were timid at first, seeing what they could get away with. As more kids joined in, they grew bolder. Carol's voice struggled to rise over them, hitting a pitch that made my eardrums itch. It was Moody Miller's job to run the spotlight at assemblies—nobody else had the patience to sit still for an entire hour—and as he trained it on Carol I could see her hands trembling, struggling to hold on to that piece of paper and keep it from flying away.

I couldn't hear her anymore, but her lips were moving. One way or another, she was finishing that prayer.

Mr. Galpin hurried up the stage steps, yelling so hard his face was as red as those pyjamas. The way he held up his hands, you couldn't tell whether he was pissed off, giving himself up, or trying to conduct the chorus to its crescendo. As if in answer, the voices swelled. The sound became a wave, a tsunami. Down in the front, Jamie Finley was unmoved. He sat as motionless as the boys on their easels, smiling out at us beneath their hair-creamed cowlicks, in their Sunday suits and their fathers' ties. I shrunk lower in my seat. I dug a foxhole inside that back row. It was only a matter of time, I was sure, before they remembered there were two parts to this freak show now. In seconds, that swarm of hissing vipers would turn their tongues on me. The dead boys kept smiling. Those smiles ripped my heart out. It's not like I'm really her friend, I explained to them. It's not like this is even my life.

And then the worst thing that could happen happened. I glanced up and saw Carol looking right at me, mouth open but mute, chin quivering dangerously. Her cheeks were shiny. Was she crying? It had to be Moody's spotlight. She was sweating under it maybe. Carol Closter ranted. She raged. She walked into a hailstorm of garbage, singing the national anthem. What she didn't do was cry. So I did the only thing I could do. I jumped up from my foxhole, stepped on a dozen dirty Converse sneakers, and slunk out of there like the traitor I was.

It was official. I wasn't just the world's worst friend, I was possibly the world's worst person. As punishment, I stayed inside for the whole holiday break and helped Mom ruin Christmas. Christmas Eve, she always made me watch *It's a Wonderful Life* with her, but not that year. Instead, she watched soldiers gum it up for the TV cameras while backup singers in sequined dresses swayed their hips to "Jingle Bell Rock." "It would be funny if it didn't make me want to tear my hair out," she said.

I went to my room and tried not to think about my lighter. I'd only had this one a week and it was almost empty. To make myself feel worse, I flipped through the small, white Bible Carol had given me. "It can't be easy for you this time of year," she'd said at my locker. "Just remember, you're never alone if you have Jesus." I had bristled at Carol Closter thinking of me as lonely, made worse for being true. The Bible was just like hers, except for my name written in purple on the first page. It weighed almost nothing in my hand. It didn't seem right that something men went to war over could weigh so little. A Bible should be a thousand pounds, I thought. It should be written on stone tablets. The pages were so thin and flimsy I could almost see through them. When I started imagining those pages floating through the air on a current of heat, I threw the Bible in my closet and slammed the door.

A minute later Mom stood in my doorway, dropping ash on my carpet. "Everything okay in here?"

"Oh yeah," I said. "It's a regular winter wonderland."

"I guess I haven't made this the nicest holiday for you, huh?"

"You were the one who liked all that stuff," I said.

"Tell you what. I'll be right back. Don't go anywhere." As if I had an option.

She came home an hour later with bags of groceries. "I found a Jewish deli!" she said, jiggling her keys like bells. "What do you think of your old mom now?"

I unpacked a bag of day-old dinner rolls, a box of mashed potato flakes, a can of Cool Whip, and the tiniest turkey I'd ever seen.

"There's something wrong with this turkey," I said.

"It's a chicken."

"We can't eat chicken for Christmas dinner."

"Sure we can. We can have whatever we want. We can have ham. We can have goose. I felt like chicken. What do we need with some big bird?" She flapped her arms and bobbed her head. I didn't laugh. A thunderbolt was probably going to crash through our roof any minute now and kill me, and this was my last meal—this chicken?

"Can't we just order Chinese food?" I said.

"You'll change your mind when you smell it!" she sang.

It's a Wonderful Life was on television again. Channel 3 was playing it non-stop. I sat on the couch and watched for a while. It was at the part where Jimmy Stewart realizes he's dead when I realized I hadn't heard so much as a lid rattle in the kitchen. My stomach grumbled. I got up to see how dinner was coming. Chicken wouldn't really be so bad.

The bird lay headless and naked in a roasting pan in the middle of the table. Mom sat in a chair, staring at it. This went on for a while, the two of them gawking at each other.

"Do you ever get the feeling," she said, "that your life is happening, but you're not in it?"

"Okay, fine. I'll eat the stupid thing."

"It doesn't matter."

"Should I turn the oven on?"

"Sure, terrific, I'll stick my head in it."

Mom lit a cigarette and poured herself a glass of wine. I pulled on a sweater and got my bike out of the garage. In Golden the gas stations never closed and there was Christmas money burning a hole in my pocket.

The guy behind the counter grumbled when he saw my Canadian dollar. He pushed it back across the counter along with a chocolate Santa wrapped in foil. "Happy Hanukkah," he said, waving me away.

I stepped back outside, bouncing the full lighter in my palm. I'd chosen a red one this time. Mom could ogle poultry until New Year's Eve if she wanted, but I was getting into the spirit of things. Under the electric hum of the gas station sign I heard a radio-cracked version of "Silver Bells." The pumps were draped with coloured lights. They blinked in the settling dusk. I flicked the Bic on and off, keeping time.

"What are you, crazy?" the attendant shouted at me through his little window. "You can't do that here."

There was a newly vacant lot across the street where a patio furniture store used to be. As I pushed my bike out of the gas station lights and toward the dark, a flame sparked up ahead. Jamie Finley came into focus, ghostly behind the fizzing end of a match. He had salvaged two folding chairs from the pile of rubble and pointed them at the gas station like it was a fireplace. He sat in one.

"Haven't you heard that smoking causes cancer?" he said. I let go of the Bic's tongue and stuffed it in my pocket. Jamie lit another match. He was wearing a red sweater with a snowman on it. His hair fell into his eyes.

"And what are *you* doing out here?" I said. "Working on your tan?"

The second match sputtered and died.

"I needed some air," he said.

"Me too," I said, because I couldn't think of anything else to say.

Neither of us spoke for a while. I could hear the squeak of the folding chair, the jiggle of Jamie's long, skinny leg. The gas station attendant came outside, lit a cigarette with his own Bic, and smoked it leaning against one of the gas pumps.

"This is the worst movie I've ever seen," I said.

Jamie chuckled, and I heard the scrape of metal in dirt as he pushed the other chair toward me. He lit a match so I'd know where to sit. It was the most romantic thing anyone had ever done for me.

As I hooked my foot under my kickstand, a car pulled into the gas station. Doors swung open and kids tumbled out, waving their hands at the dust they'd made. Reagan kids. Melanie and Joyce. Troy Gainer's red Mustang rolled up to a pump beside them.

Troy got out and somebody put a beer in his hand. Melanie and Joyce arranged themselves on the top of the convertible's back seat. Melanie said something that made Troy laugh. He walked over and handed her the brown bottle, nodded approvingly as she chugged it back. She wiped her mouth to hide her huge smile. A breeze pricked my face and neck like ground glass. My whole body shivered. It wasn't a *J* she'd been carving into her arm at the assembly. I clutched my handlebars so I wouldn't fall over.

I could feel Jamie looking at me in the dark. "Shouldn't you be in one of those cars?" I said sharply.

"Shouldn't you?"

Tanks finally filled, car engines started. Troy held his passenger door open, waited while Melanie reapplied her lip gloss in his side mirror. As the Mustang peeled out, its horn roared in my ears like a stuck game show buzzer. Wrooonnnggg. And then they were gone, swallowed by the night, nothing left but gas fumes and dust.

Jamie lit another match. This time he let it march toward his fingers. He lit another and did it again. The air was sour with sulphur. He had half a pack left.

"You know that movie with Jimmy Stewart?" he said.

"*It's a Wonderful Life*?"

"Yeah, that one. I hate that movie. Fucking bullshit." Another match flared. This time he held it up to his face. The flame carved his cheeks with shadows and hooded his eyes. I wasn't sure what he was trying to say, but suddenly I wanted to go home and make sure the oven wasn't on.

Before I did, I dug in my pocket for the chocolate Santa. Saint Nicholas, patron of sailors, pawnbrokers, thieves, and children. I gave him to Jamie. "Merry Christmas," I said.

"Yeah, sure." Jamie lit another match and flung it into the air. We watched the orange tip arc, fall, and die in the dirt. I heard foil unwrapping. "Merry whatever," he said.

It was after eight when I got back, but Mom was still sitting at the kitchen table. So was the chicken.

"I've decided to go back to school," she said.

"Cooking school?" I said. My stomach was gnawing a hole in itself.

"Har har. College. I'm going to finish my degree. I can take classes part-time. If I buckle down, I could graduate at the same time as you."

"Great," I said. We were never getting to Minneapolis at this rate.

"I have to do something with my life, honey."

"You're doing something. You're my mom."

"And then you'll grow up and what will I have?"

That chicken, for one thing.

The phone rang. I answered it in the living room. Anything to get away from that bird. "Hello-ho-ho," I said dryly.

"Hey," Jamie said. He didn't say his name and he didn't need to.

"Hey," I said back.

"So I was thinking about those kids who died," he said. "That's what I was doing out there. I've been thinking about them a lot. I can't stop, actually."

"It's really sad," I said.

"No, that's not it. I mean, it is sad, really fucking sad, but also, I don't know, I keep thinking about how lucky they are."

"Lucky?"

"Everybody loves them now, right? They can't ever screw up or let anyone down, you know? Nobody cares if they quit the swim team or failed trig or whatever."

"Why did you quit the swim team?"

"See, that's exactly what I mean. Nobody remembers the stupid stuff those kids did or didn't do. They just remember that they went to war and fought for our country. So they're heroes forever. Well, anyway, that's what I was doing out there."

"Jamie?"

"Yeah?"

I fumbled for the right words. I needed to explain that, despite all evidence to the contrary, I wasn't really the world's worst person. I needed him to know that I was Carol Closter's friend, that I liked her, actually. I also needed him to know that there were times when I hated her a little too. Not for being a freak, not even for having a perfect family, but for going from someone I once pitied to someone I almost envied. I hated her sometimes because nothing and nobody was the way they were supposed to be. Most of all, I needed him to understand that I hated myself for feeling this way. I didn't know why Jamie Finley was the one I had to say all this to, except that he was on the other end of the line and I wanted these things out of me. But I couldn't tell him. My lungs were filling up with all the things that needed saying—I was drowning in them, and it's hard to talk when you're drowning.

"So, okay," Jamie said after a while. "I just wanted to tell you that. That and Merry Christmas."

I put the phone down and stared at it for a minute, hand resting lightly on the receiver. I could dial the operator and ask for the number of every Finley in the phone book. If I didn't do it soon, I'd lose my nerve. While I debated, the phone rang under my hand, and for a second I believed in Christmas miracles, if no other kind.

"I'm sorry!" I said.

"I forgive you," she said.

My chest emptied, but I didn't feel any better. "Carol?" I said. "You what?"

"I forgive you. I've been thinking all week about how you probably felt really bad about it, but you shouldn't, Robin. Do you know why? Because being my best friend is the best present you could ever give me. Plus, my pastor says I need to be more forgiving. So there—I forgive you."

Carol waited, but I didn't know how to respond. I didn't even understand what conversation we were having. After what felt like an hour, she tried again. "I said I forgive you, Robin. For not getting me a present?"

"Oh," I said. "Right. Sorry."

"You already said that."

"Right. Okay. Well, thanks then, I guess."

"You're welcome! Anywho, see you next week. 1972—can you believe it? Okay, bye!"

Mom was smoking at the sink. A dishtowel covered the bird. "How about Chinese food?" she said. "*It's a Wonderful Life* is on. We can eat in front of the TV, if you want."

"It's a great idea, Mom. Really, I mean it. College—wow."

She was quiet for a moment, as if waiting for the punch-line. When one didn't come, she smiled widely, grabbed me by the shoulders, and kissed my cheek with a smack. She flipped through the Yellow Pages, looking for Chinese restaurants. "What do you have without chicken?" Mom barked into the phone. "Beef and broccoli! Wonderful! Let's do the biggest order of beef and broccoli you've got! Let's do a double order! We want beef and broccoli coming out the ying-yang!"

On television, Jimmy Stewart was running around town, accosting people. He couldn't get it through his thick skull that nobody knew him anymore because he didn't exist. I changed the channel. I was starting to hate that movie too.

11

On New Year's Day, a lady in a pink suit and pink hat stood at our curb, holding a small pink suitcase and staring a hole through our front door. "Now what?" Mom said, standing at the kitchen window, tapping her ashes into the sink. We'd passed a pleasant-enough week playing cards and eating leftover Chinese, but she'd have to start looking for a job again in the morning and she was already on edge. She made me go outside to get rid of whoever it was. All that pink was making her uncomfortable.

"May I help you?" I said, like a counter girl at Macy's.

The lady smoothed her pink skirt and lifted her head, adjusting her frown into something resembling a smile. She held the suitcase in front of her with white-gloved hands. A sprig of plastic holly was pinned to her lapel. I almost didn't recognize her without a martini.

Vera Miller took me in through heavily shadowed eyes. "Hello, doll. Is your mother home?" She didn't wait for an answer.

As she reached the front door, it swung open.

"Elaine?" Vera said. The white glove tipped back the pink hat to get a better view. Mom's hair was in its usual weekend shambles. She was wearing old jeans and a pair of my flip-flops, her toes dangling over the too-small soles. "Is that really you?"

"What do you want this time?" Mom said. "I don't see a casserole." She kept one hand on the door, the other on her hip.

"Casserole? No, darling. I'm here to introduce you to the beautiful world of Katy May."

"You sell Mary Kay?" I said.

"Katy May," Vera corrected, tapping her pink case. *Katy May Kosmetics* was emblazoned on the front in frilly dark pink letters. "I have in here the secrets to every woman's eternal happiness. And it's no casserole, I promise you that."

"Don't Mary Kay women wear pink?" I said.

"This is blush," Vera said. "A far more sophisticated colour. But I can teach you all that. That's why I'm here. In the nick of time too, by the looks of it. New year, new you—what do you say?"

"I suppose you'll want to come in," Mom said.

"I can't work magic on your doorstep, Elaine."

Mom sighed and stepped aside.

Vera stood in the foyer, taking in the piles of newspapers, the plates of toast crusts, dishes turned ashtrays, tiny funeral pyres on every dirty plate and mug. "I love what you've done with the place."

Mom moved the want ads, and Vera set up on the dining room table. She laid her little case delicately on the water-stained oak top and unlocked the brass latch. Layer upon pink layer was lifted and peeled back, as if her white gloves belonged to a surgeon and the suitcase was the belly of some poor beast. Its bowels revealed dozens of pots, sticks, and tubes. I'd asked my mom once why she reapplied her lipstick so often. "It's my job," she'd said and slicked on another coat. Now she peered into the satin-lined case and frowned. Vera did the same as she studied her blank canvas.

"Why, you're naked, Elaine. I don't do the laundry without a bit of rouge."

"I get around that problem by rarely doing the laundry."

Vera shook her head. "Beauty should never be a chore."

Vera worked slowly, applying something to Mom's eye or cheek, then rubbing it off with a damp sponge. Mom sat quietly, submitting to a barrage of powder, liner, and well-intentioned insults. Now and then, Vera would pause to frown at the results. "Funny, this colour usually works wonders for sallow skin."

While she toiled away, I asked Vera about her job. It didn't seem as glamorous as being a roller-skating waitress, but it had to beat giving blood.

"Well, first of all you don't do this for the money," she said. "Though many of the girls—Katy May beauty ambassadors, I mean—many of them do very well. But it's really about the satisfaction you get helping other women discover their most beautiful selves. You can't put a price tag on that."

"Apparently you can," Mom said, thumbing through the Katy May catalogue.

"A girl can always use pocket change," Vera said. "My mother called it mad money. 'Put something aside for yourself, Vera. Don't be a fool like I was.' But that's what I thought she was—a fool. Who listens to their mother?" Vera winked at me.

"Your husband doesn't mind you working?" Mom said.

"Cal doesn't care what I do, now that he's got a girl in the city."

"I'm sorry," Mom said.

"I was always good at catching lipstick on a collar, but these new girls don't even have the decency to wear any." Vera's laugh caught in her throat. "It was the wheatgrass juice that gave him away. How do you like that for modern? He reeks of it now. Have you tried it, Elaine? Lawn clippings in a glass."

Vera's hand fanned away something invisible. "I don't know why I'm telling you this. You must find this all very tasty."

"I've lost my appetite for gossip," Mom said.

They stared at each other for a moment, like they were waiting for the other one to blink first. Finally, Vera reached into the case for another pot of shadow. "This will really bring out the gold in your eyes."

Mom lit a fresh cigarette. Vera worked on in silence, pulling a mascara wand through Mom's lashes, then curling them with a horrifying instrument she claimed was a woman's best friend. The eyelashes succumbed, curling up and back until they kissed the lid. *Who are you?* I imagined one saying. *Who am I? Who are you!*

At last Vera stepped back and handed Mom a mirror. "What do you think?"

Mom's eyes bulged at her reflection.

"Gorgeous, isn't it?"

"I hardly recognize myself."

"That's our motto!" Vera said. "With Katy May, you're a whole new you. Now don't feel obliged to purchase everything I used. I wanted to show you what we could do, but Katy May is so good you can make do with just eight or nine products."

While Vera arranged products carefully on a square of pink satin, Mom made a face at herself in the mirror. I got up to peruse the little pots of colour.

"How about you, doll? It's never too early to establish a regimen. Remember, beauty is a privilege, not a right."

I shook my head. Vera sighed. "Youth truly is wasted on the young."

"I can hardly get her to brush her hair," Mom said, forgetting her own ratted ponytail.

"At least she talks to you." Vera said, packing up her case.

"How are your boys, Vera?"

"Blaming me for screwing up their lives, as usual."

"Did you give them makeovers too?"

Vera arched one perfectly groomed eyebrow at her, then laughed. "Oh, Elaine, you look like a hooker who got ready in the dark."

"It really is awful, Vera."

They doubled over with laughter, gripping each other's arms for balance. Then suddenly Vera wasn't laughing anymore, only crying, diluted black liner dripping onto the pink satin square. Mom shooed me out of the room to fetch a glass of water.

"How do you do it?" I heard Vera say. "How do you not fall apart?"

"When I figure that out, I'll let you know."

An hour later Mom stood on the front step, a pink box full of cosmetics she couldn't afford cradled in one arm. Vera honked as she drove away. She didn't even drive a pink Cadillac, just the same boring brown station wagon like everyone else in the world.

———

The next morning, I woke to the sounds of things breaking. I followed them through the house. Earthquake? Burglar? Mom. She was rummaging around in the pool house, butt poking out the door. At last she emerged. "Ta-da!" She held Dad's Rolodex above her head like a trophy. She was bright-eyed and pink-cheeked. She'd put on her Katy May.

Mom arranged everything on the dining room table. The Rolodex sat in the middle, orbited by her coffee cup, cigarettes, notepad, and pen. The cards held the names and numbers of Dad's insurance clients, country club cronies and sundry wives, people whose calls she'd avoided for months, wearers of reindeer sweaters. After two cups of coffee and three cigarettes, she was ready. She pressed her palms against the sides of the Rolodex and closed her eyes, Carson's Carnac the Magnificent without the feathered turban.

"You can do this," she told herself. "You are a whole new you." She pulled out a card. "Ken James. Shit, shit, shit."

And so it went.

"I'm not asking for handout," she told Ken James and Ed Stephens and John Bartlett and Barbara Green. "I need a chance, not charity." Then she'd nod, light another cigarette, and thank them, exhaling, for their generous time. After each call, she tore up the card and added it to the tree of crinkled yellow balls. This went on all afternoon. The conversations were short—it was the cigarette breaks between calls that were long, the ten or fifteen minutes it took for her to hurl the Rolodex over my head through the open sliding doors and then scramble on all fours in the grass, gathering up the cards again.

She was in tears by the time she got to Mildred Howard, a woman who had worked in Dad's office when I was little. My parents had gone to Mildred's daughter's wedding, but I hadn't heard her name in years. Now here was Mom crying into the phone, to this stranger, "Oh Mildred, Mildred, what am I going to do?"

After a few minutes, the last tear was snuffled back, black raccoon eyes dabbed with the back of a sleeve. Mom walked the phone into the kitchen and stayed there through a whole episode of *The Monkees*.

"So?" I said as the credits rolled.

"So I guess I have a job," Mom said. Mildred Howard ran the billing department at Golden General Hospital. Under her were half-a-dozen housewives who translated doctor scribble into neat rows of billing code. They were middle-aged women with empty nests and no interest in learning bridge. It was perfect. "It's not as prestigious as blood donation," she said, "but it'll keep the lights on."

With that, Mom took out her new pink compact, peered into the small mirror, let out a long whoosh of breath, and snapped it shut again. She put down the compact and picked up the stack of bills. Every few minutes I heard the tear of an envelope, followed by the resigned scratch of pen on her chequebook.

Anencephaly. Giardiasis. Herpangina. Quadrantanopia. Ulcerative colitis. Xerostomia. Mildred Howard gave Mom a medical dictionary so she could look up the correct spellings. It was a stern, sober tome with tiny type and a black cover, the kind of book you'd expect to find on a doctor's shelf. "It's awful all the things that can go wrong with the human body," Mom said as she leafed through its pages, an exclamation mark between her brows. She went to the hospital on Mondays and Wednesdays. The rest of the week she worked from home. Some nights she fell asleep at the table, dictionary open beside her, cradling someone's alarmingly thick medical record like a pillow. I found her there at midnight once, collapsed and sobbing over a file. "This world breaks my heart," she said, lifting her head, DECEASED stamped in reverse across her wet cheek.

Mom had another dictionary for her college courses, which were far more mysterious than the records she transcribed. She'd signed up for Introduction to Economics and something called Gender Politics, which she said she clearly knew even less about. This dictionary, bought with her first paycheque from the hospital, had a faux-leather cover and gold lettering, like the one in my junior high in which certain entries—*fellatio, cunnilingus*—had been fingered to near transparency. "Well, there's another word I'll never use," Mom would say. I'd felt the same way in junior high.

Mom pressed on, made regular trips to the library, spent whole weekends reading, going through highlighter pens the way she used to go through hair spray. I rarely saw her without a book in her hand that January, and none were by Julia Child. There was Germaine Greer and her *Female Eunuch*, a word I was sorry I looked up. Betty Friedan and her *Feminine Mystique*, which was indeed a mystery, though not the kind I had expected. Kate Millett's book came wrapped in brown paper the way we were made to wrap our textbooks at the beginning of each school year. Then came the women from Mom's study group, the flesh-and-blood versions of her books, and no less mystifying. They had mythical names like Willow, Aurora, and Celeste. The Sisters.

The Sisters were as strange as sea anemones, fluid and bright and infinitely beautiful in their thrift-store jeans and sandals bought at Mexican markets. They brought jugs of blackberry wine and drank, laughed, and ranted through purple-stained lips dangling clove cigarettes. They propped their elbows on the coffee table, slung their long, tanned legs over the sofa arms, or sat lotus on throw pillows on the floor. They spouted poetry and fifty-cent words and had opinions about everything. They over-powered with their funky tea bags and their enthusiastic anger. No matter how much bleach I used, the house always smelled of patchouli.

Mom tidied around them, hovered with the coffee pot, put out plates of cookies. "They're store-bought," she said, apologizing for the white flour, the refined sugar. The Sisters told her domesticity was just another word for oppression. Whole generations of female power had been destroyed by the invention of floor wax. Mom would gaze down at the Pepperidge Farm and frown, as if discovering some long-silent enemy, one more insidious betrayal beneath her own roof.

While Mom bused their empty mugs and glasses, the Sisters talked about their own mothers, how empty their lives were, how they just didn't get it. They admired Mom for working, they said. They told her she gave them hope.

"I'm not saving the world," Mom said. "It's nice to feel useful, I guess."

Don't do that, they said. Don't put yourself down. Don't minimize your contribution. She was an extraordinary woman. Look at their mothers—not a paycheque in the bunch.

You *are* saving the world, they said.

"It must be wonderful to have your life ahead of you," Mom said later, as we watched them pull out of the driveway, someone's bare feet jutting out the back window of a dusty white Beetle.

"Everyone has their life ahead of them," I reminded her.

"You wouldn't understand," she said, which was true.

Mom found a natural food store on the other side of town and brought home hard, dry things made of spelt. She stopped shaving her legs. She missed a salon appointment, then another, until her hair brushed the tops of her breasts. The part was an ever-expanding strip of brown. Her Canadian roots, we dubbed them. One day she came home with a box of brown hair dye and a pair of rubber gloves. "It'll be easier," she said. "Less fuss." For the first time I could remember, our hair was the same middling brown, but she'd never looked less like my mother. Staring at herself in the mirror, she said, "I remember you."

It was a Pandora's box of hair dye. Suddenly, Mom despised all her clothes. She took away a garbage bag full of skirts and dresses and brought it back filled with plain cotton blouses and wide-legged pants that smelled of mothballs and garages. She abandoned Chanel No. 5 for a small, oily bottle of sweet almond and cherry blossom. She bought a silk caftan at a campus market and wore it instead of her housecoat, floating from room to room in swirls of indigo and green. "It's so freeing," she said. "I feel light as air." As if she'd been suffering in corsets and petticoats all those years.

On weekends, the Sisters left their books behind and brought their own garbage bags full of clothes. The houses they shared near campus had Japanese futons on hardwood floors and French philosophy on second-hand bookshelves, but no washing machines. While our Maytag did its magic, they'd strip down to their panties and plunge into the pool. Their tans were deep and seamless. Their long hair gathered around them in amber swirls. Mom would fish it out of the drain for days.

She didn't swim herself when the Sisters were there. Embarrassed by their bobbing naked breasts, she buried her face behind a book. I barricaded myself in my room. But the Sisters were determined. They would stop me outside the bathroom, ask where I was in my cycle, if I was eating wheat. I shouldn't use bleach, they said. I shouldn't bathe so often. I shouldn't watch network television or listen to AM radio or eat processed foods or anything with a face.

They pulled me into living room one afternoon. *What's your take?* they asked. *How do you feel? We want to know what young people are feeling.*

"About what?"

Everything.

"I guess I think—"

Don't think. Feel. What are your feelings? Do you feel power-less? Let down? Abandoned? Pissed off? Dig down into your solar plexus. How do you feeeeel?

Mom sat mutely on the sofa during this exchange, crumbling the brownie in her hands back into cocoa powder. There were more in tin foil on the coffee table. How the Sisters managed to bake without stepping foot in a kitchen was a mystery to me. I reached for one.

"No!" Mom shouted, knocking it out of my hand. "These are special brownies. They're only for the grown-ups."

The Sisters' giggles stalked me to my room, as if "special brownies" was some genius code a fifteen-year-old couldn't crack. How do they expect you to feel, I wondered, when everyone's convinced you're a moron?

My teachers found kinder synonyms. *Unfocused. Distracted. Lacklustre* was my favourite—it made me think of old pearls forgotten at the bottom of a jewellery box. Miss Blumberg said I was a bright girl and there was no reason I shouldn't be getting at least a B, but it's hard to trust someone who's wearing a feathered headdress. Mrs. Maxwell continued to dole out generous C's. "You've earned it," she said. "Lord knows." Mr. Galpin told me that his office door was always open, which is probably the most worrisome thing anyone in a sweater vest can tell a person.

My counsellor, Mr. Boyd, told me I needed to get serious about my future, that life was more than boys and sock hops. "You're on the verge of failing Math and English. Your other grades aren't much better. I know you girls think getting married will solve everything, but nobody's going to marry a high school dropout."

"I'm not getting married," I told him. "I'm going to be a broadcast journalist."

"Can you *spell* broadcast journalist?" he said.

Carol said Mr. Boyd wasn't qualified to guide turds into a toilet. In general, she trusted teachers about as much as she trusted textbooks. They all got an earful of Bible quotes supporting her position against cellular biology or quadratic equations or square dancing. Most placated her with high B's or independent study. In gym, she carried the clipboard, exempt from participating in any sport for health reasons, though everyone knew it was the showers she was avoiding. Carol wouldn't even go inside the locker room, but stood outside the door in her turtleneck and cords, checking our names as we passed. She'd always give me a sympathetic smile. Being a suspected arsonist got you out of nothing. I had to suffer through dodge ball like everybody else.

When Carol wasn't arguing in class, she was usually in the library drafting letters to evangelical ministers or Republican politicians to ask them for advice. It was one of the many tasks on the ongoing list of good works she kept at the front of her purple binder. She checked it daily and found no greater joy than when she carefully crossed off an item with a purple pen and ruler. Carol wrote to President Nixon to apologize for America's youth and wish him luck in the next election—she'd be voting for him in her prayers. She wrote to Governor Reagan to tell him how bad she felt about the trouble he was having with capital punishment and to assure him that she'd see all his movies as soon as she was allowed to watch TV. She asked Oral Roberts how one went about applying to his university and commiserated with Herbert W. Armstrong that, once again, the end of days had not come to pass. Next to her saints, Carol Closter's favourite conversation topic was the Rapture, when the righteous would be called to heaven and the sinners condemned to their slow, painful deaths. She kept a gallon of water and a flashlight in her bedroom closet for the event. My dad had kept similar items in the trunk of his car, along with a first aid kit, a flare gun, and an old *Playboy*. He was nothing if not a practical man.

While she waited for the Rapture, Carol started another list in her binder, one of all the kids in our school who she needed to pray for. These were mostly potheads and burnouts, the girls who were doing it, and a sexy foreign exchange student from Paris. "It's not Guillaume's fault," Carol explained. "French people are just born that way." She had a book at home that proved it. She'd taken it from a book burning she'd gone to in Montana with her old church group. She relayed this casually, like *bonfire* was another word for *yard sale*. Not that I was one to talk.

Carol prayed for the kids on that list every night, she told me. She cried for their endangered souls. She wrote encouraging notes with cheerful drawings and slipped them into lockers and desks. *Jesus loves you*, she wrote, *even if you don't*. It was all part of her plan.

"You have to show heroic virtue," Carol told me. "They need to know that you tried your whole life to be a holier person. You can't even get venerated without that, forget beatified."

"Beautified?" I said.

She rolled her eyes, pausing at the top as if to say, See what I'm working with here?

"Be*at*ified. The fourth step? I told you they do this by the books. They don't mess around."

"Who's they?"

"*They*, Robin. *Them*. You know, sometimes I think you don't even listen to me."

Joyce Peyton and Melanie D'Angelo were also on Carol's list, but she didn't talk about them and I didn't ask. I figured she'd seen Melanie making out against Troy Gainer's red Mustang at lunch, their tongues down each other's throats, his hands groping inside her back pockets as if he was looking for change.

The Closters were spending spring break in Montana, where they'd enjoy wholesome activities like visiting relatives and burning books. Before she left, Carol made me a copy of her list on the school's mimeograph machine.

"Promise me you'll pray every night," she said. "Promise! Promise!"

"Okay," I said and mostly meant it. There had to be a hundred people on that list, but I was determined to support anything that would keep Carol off the auditorium stage.

Aside from prayer duty, I had fully intended to study all week, to get it together, buckle down. Every afternoon I lay on a blanket in the backyard, surrounded by textbooks, but Mussolini and mitochondria couldn't compete with the sound of the war in the living room. Mom left it on in the background while she transcribed, glancing up between cardiac arrests and brain tumours.

The Saturday before school started, the Sisters came with jugs of wine and no laundry. They'd been to a rally in the city. People had been arrested. Tear gas was used. They fluttered around Mom, telling the story in bits and pieces, shouting over each other, lit up with anger and possibility.

"It sounds very exciting," Mom said, perching on a dining room chair, her spine straight beneath her caftan, the line between her eyebrows wriggling this way and that. My dad was always waiting for the other shoe to drop, but my mom preferred cautious optimism. She said things like "The grass is always greener" and "Well, you never know."

Exciting doesn't begin to describe it, the Sisters said. *This is it. Things are really happening now.*

"What's happening?" I asked. "What things?" I really wanted to know. I wanted to feel what they did. I wanted to be optimistic, not cautiously, but wholly, utterly.

Everything, they said. *Can't you feel it? Can't you feeeeel it?*

I got on my bike and rode to my old junior high. I'd started going there again. The playground was usually overrun with little kids during the day. At night, high school kids gathered with their stolen bottles under the seductive glow of street lamps, but for a few quiet hours between dusk and dark, I would swing. I would try to remember the names on Carol's list and wish them all straight A's and eternally clear skin. I'd made a promise. Plus, it kept me away from gas stations.

One good thing about a school was that you knew it would always be there. Nobody was going to tear it down and put up a mini-mall. Still, whenever I arrived at the edge of the playground, it was always with some relief to find it where I'd left it. Except this time. This time there was someone on my swings. The interloper dug a Ked into the sand, twirling her body round and round. The chains twisted above her, clicking like old bones. When they wouldn't twist any more, she lifted her feet. There was a heartbeat's pause before arms, legs, hair flew out—everything spinning for a few brilliant seconds before the chains jerked and whipped her back the other way. Settling, she spiked her Ked again and started twirling the other way. As I began to turn my bike around, Melanie looked up.

"I forgot how much I liked it here," she said, squinting against the setting sun.

"Best swings in town."

"Yeah," she said and smiled.

I dropped my bike in the grass and lowered myself into the swing beside hers. We rocked ourselves forward and back, feet never fully leaving the ground. Melanie poked her sneaker in the sand and dug a hole. We hadn't spoken to each other in months. We'd become experts at avoiding each other at school. But here, on these swings, those rules didn't apply.

"Remember the day we met?" she said.

"You had braces."

"You had a bowl cut."

"What a couple of dorks."

"What happened?" she said, like she really didn't know.

"I stopped letting my mom cut my hair."

"You know you were supposed to be my maid of honour," she said. She sounded mad. I guess I'd be mad too if I had Joyce Peyton for a best friend now. I pushed off a little, just enough to get air between me and the ground. Melanie gripped the chains loosely and dug her feet deeper in the sand.

"Do you want to know if me and Troy are doing it?" she said. I lifted my feet, angled my legs so they wouldn't drag. Melanie kicked at the sand. "We're going to. Probably next weekend."

"Why?"

"His parents are going out of town."

"I mean why are you doing it? I thought you wanted to wait until you got married."

"God, you sound like Cloister. You really do. You know she told Joyce that Jesus watches people do it? I'm not kidding. Like He's some kind of pervert or something."

"You don't even know her," I said.

"Weren't you at the Christmas assembly? Or, like, any-where? You know, I felt really bad about what happened last year, but it's almost like—I don't know—like she asks for it."

I didn't say anything. Melanie stuck a clump of hair in her mouth and chewed. I leaned my body back, pulled hard on the chain, and kicked forward. Her head followed me. Tick-tock, tick-tock. Neither of us wanted to talk about Carol Closter anymore.

"Joyce said you'd be jealous," Melanie said finally. "You know, Troy never even liked you. He was telling everyone what a mental case you were for burning that house down and Joyce said yeah, well you liked her, and he said no, he never did. He didn't even know your name till after everything happened."

I arched my back and pumped my legs as hard as I could. I pumped like that swing would actually take me somewhere else. I pumped like God was watching. My thighs and hands burned. The wind whistled in my ears. But high as I went, I always had to come down again. The chain thumped at the top as gravity yanked me back to earth. I hated that rush of air from behind, the world flying away from me.

"If I do, he'll love me! Don't you get it? He'll love me!"

I let go of the chain and launched myself into the sky. Away, away. I could see the whole town. I could see the curve of the earth. One second I was arcing up, up, up. The next I was flat out on the ground.

I flipped onto my back, panting. There was sand in my mouth, and blood. Melanie bent over me, blue eyes blinking, blond hair tickling my arm. I remembered him heavy on top of me, grunting and groaning, pushing his way inside. He hadn't even known my name.

"Jeez, are you okay? Robin? Say something. You're freaking me out."

Little stars sparked around her. Her eyes were filling with tears. I turned my head and spit red dirt.

"How high did I get?" I said.

"I don't know. Fifteen, twenty feet? Who cares how high you were?"

I sat up carefully, palms and knees burning, everything on fire. "Don't do it," I said. "You don't have to do it."

Melanie wiped at her eyes roughly. She'd written *TROY* on her forearm, gouged it. The skin was red and angry around the sharp blue lines.

"Give me one good reason not to," she said.

I could see that she really meant it. She wanted one good reason.

"He should love you first."

"You're one to talk," she said and left me in the dirt.

My street was jammed with crappy hatchbacks and beat-up Volkswagen vans when I got home, our house lit up and swaying like a lava lamp. There were about thirty people clustered

into little groups here and there, everyone in animated conversations, beer bottles swooping this way and that with their
gestures. I pushed my way through the wheat fields of long
hair and hemp clothing. Mom was running around putting
coasters under everything. I followed her into the kitchen.
There was beer on ice in the sink, a baggy of grass on the
wedding china.

"I leave you alone for a few hours and you throw a party?"
I said. "This isn't how I raised you."

"I don't know what happened," she said. "They made some
phone calls and then all these people started showing up. I
didn't know there would be this many. I thought a few friends
meant a few friends."

A shirtless guy came up to us, holding a record. Mom
wrinkled her nose as if he was about to ask her for money.

"You got the *White Album*?" he said.

"Sorry," I said. "We've only got that colour."

He nodded like he was thinking about it, then walked away.

"I guess I'm not very good at this college thing either,"
Mom said.

"You could tell them to leave. Or I could."

"But they're having such a nice time," she said.

Someone turned up the hi-fi. The Sisters made a dance floor
in front of it. Their thin bodies swayed side to side, bare feet

never quite leaving the ground. Mom was right. They did look like they were having a good time. It was probably the best time anybody had ever had in our house.

"What happened to you?" Mom said, noticing the hole in my jeans.

"I fell off the swings."

"I wish I could still play on swings," she said.

She lit a cigarette. I handed her one of the beers from the sink and got myself a Sprite from the fridge. The cold felt good on my torn palms. We took our drinks outside, where a group sat lotus style on the overgrown lawn, comparing their parents to Nixon.

"Oh, I almost forgot." Mom pulled a postcard from the endless folds of her caftan. "This came for you today." On the front was a picture of a mountain in Montana. On the back were two words: YOU PROMISED.

"It isn't signed," she said.

"It's from my pen pal," I said. "I promised to write her this week, but I forgot."

"I didn't know you had a pen pal. I think that's just terrific. It's good to be open to new things."

"What if you still like the old things?" I said.

She put her arm around me. "Maybe you can have both," she said unconvincingly.

Two of the people on the lawn started shouting at each other.

"You want to be drafted?" he said.

"I want the *right* to be drafted," she said.

"Only because you know it'll never happen."

"That's the stupidest thing I've ever heard you say."

He kissed her so hard he knocked her over. "I love you so fucking much," he said.

"Now *that's* the stupidest thing I've ever heard you say."

They rolled around in the grass, laughing and kissing and shouting about how stupid they were.

"I'll give them fifteen more minutes," Mom said. "Then I'm calling the police."

I nodded and drank, washing away the last of the sand and blood. My palms were raw with gravel. My knees throbbed. But for a few seconds I'd been flying. For one perfect moment I'd had wings.

12

You could tell it was spring in Golden by how many convertibles had their tops down. All else stayed the same. The war limped along on our television sets. Vietnam didn't seem to have seasons either. Afternoons, through Mrs. Maxwell's window, I watched Melanie slide into Troy Gainer's red Mustang. She skipped class almost as often as Jamie Finley, who'd spent the last half of his senior year under the football bleachers, getting drunk or stoned with the resident potheads and deadbeats, kids who'd been bound for that particular patch of withered grass since grade school. At night, with nobody to watch over but myself, I went through a rainbow of lighters, flicking them on and off just to hear the hungry snap of red tongue, the soft sucking birth of flame. When I emptied one, I added it to the shoebox under my bed, along with Mom's silver lighter and the other Bics. I was beginning to understand how Carol felt waiting for the Rapture.

Then suddenly June arrived. That, at least, was a kind of salvation I could count on.

The school year's end was hailed, as always, with visionary violations of the dress code and the constant clamour of untethering youth. Drama stars practised breathless soliloquies in the halls while jocks scrambled to memorize the periodic table. Hippies lolled on the grass, decorating each other with henna and swapping spit. Honour roll students skipped class to sit behind the portables with smoke-pit kids, sipping peach schnapps and crème de menthe pilfered from parental liquor cabinets. Classroom maps were regularly taken off and rehung upside-down. Garbage cans were up-ended, toilets asphyxiated with cherry bombs. Toilet paper bunting perpetually decorated the trees. We could often hear Mr. Galpin in the halls, pleading with people to go to class or just go home.

"I hope they're enjoying themselves," Carol said, glaring out the window of Mrs. Maxwell's sewing room. It wasn't even two o'clock, but upperclassmen were already spilling into the parking lot, fiddling with radio knobs, shouting to each other over impatient engines, giving directions, making plans. Carol paced back and forth in front of the glass. "I hope they're making magical memories that they can look back on fondly when they're burning in the fiery pits of hell."

Carol had been in a bad mood all week. She never did hear back from the president or poor Mr. Armstrong, though she did get an autographed headshot from Governor Reagan and a long letter from Mr. Roberts in which he encouraged her to forward a sizable donation. Now, to add insult to injury, her parents were making her go to camp. Mostly she was grumpy that she hadn't gotten further with her good works. A whole year had passed and she didn't have anything to show for it. It's called high school, I told her.

"Saint Vitalis converted the prostitutes of Alexandria," she said. "I can't even save a cheerleader."

A pack of them jumped up and down on the field, white teeth and panties flashing. Troy Gainer watched them, nodding to an eight-track's beat. He'd won a partial athletic scholarship to Arizona State. He'd been wearing a Sun Devils jacket for weeks. Melanie had it on now. It was so big on her you couldn't see her hands.

"Camp can't be any worse than this place," I said.

"At least school ends at three o'clock."

Carol slumped into a chair and groaned. I was no good at cheering people up. Outside, Troy got in his red Mustang and Melanie jumped in beside him. He blasted the horn and the cars behind him answered. Fists punched out open back windows while girls squealed their approval.

I looked down at my sewing machine. They *were* making magical memories. And I was making culottes.

The Sisters were already gone, fleeing Golden for communes in Big Sur and family beach houses in Montauk. The house seemed quieter than ever. We heard the sounds of our neighbours again—weed whackers, barking dogs, TVs at all hours echoing our own.

Mom had passed her courses, but barely. "What a bunch of nonsense," she said, burying her grades in the coupon drawer. "I'm glad, actually. It's a relief. Saves me from wasting any more time." But she didn't sound relieved. She sounded like she wanted to go to bed and stay there for a really long time.

She took on more transcribing work. She spent three days a week at the hospital. The other two, she worked under the backyard awning, patio table for a desk, medical records stacked neatly beside her in wicker baskets she'd bought for the task. We reacquainted ourselves with the Lucky's across town where everything was made with sugar and wheat and wrapped in cellophane. We picked up things for Mrs. Houston, who didn't like to drive.

"You're sure it's no trouble?" she said that Saturday as she did every Saturday, standing on the other side of the fence.

"It's our pleasure," Mom said.

"I suppose I wouldn't mind some nice peaches. Or black plums. Do you think they'd have some nice plums?"

"I'm sure we can manage that."

"Only if it's no trouble."

"Poor thing," Mom said when we were in the car. "Where are her children? That's what I'd like to know. Promise me you won't abandon me when I'm old."

"What do you mean *when*?" I said.

At the store, Mom spent a long time with the produce, cradling, squeezing, sniffing, weighing. I wandered off in search of new ways to consume sugar. I was in the cereal aisle when I heard her shouting my name. She never did that. She said Canadians only raised their voices when it was absolutely necessary, like at rodeos and weddings.

I found her beside a magazine rack, various pieces of fruit congregating on the floor around her feet.

"Juggling?" I said.

Mom's face was flushed and wet. Tears darkened the newspaper trembling in her hands. She lifted it to show me. A naked girl ran screaming down its grainy grey cover. Carol, I thought. Then: No, not Carol. Another girl.

"It was the napalm," she said, crumpling against the *Life* magazines. "*Our* napalm. It burned the clothes right off her body. Burned them right off."

I scanned for an exit, but it was too late. The cashiers were already circling. They liked Mom, who was always upbeat and complimented their frosted hair. They closed the express lane and sat her down on the stool behind the register. Shoppers with ten items or less were ushered, tongues clucking, to other lines.

"She needs water," one cashier said, fanning Mom with a coupon sheet.

"She needs sugar," another offered, scanning the wall of chocolate bars behind her.

Someone got the manager from the back, a sweaty little man with a pricing gun slung into his waistband. He escorted Mom to our car, hand cupping her elbow. Men often did this. Her lean frame gave the impression of fragility. Only Dad knew better, would give her jam jars to open, passing them silently over the breakfast table. The manager patted her arm and told her she was doing fine, just fine.

Mom speared him with a look and pulled her arm away. "Thank you so much for your assistance," she said coolly.

"Well," he said and scurried away.

Mom made me drive. I'd never done more than steer for her while she lit a cigarette. While I concentrated on not killing us, she stared out the window.

"How do they do it?" she said.

"Do what?" I was irritated by the store manager, the stares of the other women, the fact that this was my first time behind the wheel. I should have been excited. Dad should have been sitting where Mom was, filling the car with cigar smoke and telling me, *Take it easy, Tiger.* Would all my firsts be ruined?

"How do you see something like that and go home and make dinner?" Mom said. "How do you go on as if something horrific isn't happening?"

"You don't even vote," I said.

"I can't vote," she said and started crying again.

"Now what?"

"We left the groceries. Silvia's beautiful plums."

On the bright side, we'd gotten a free newspaper. Mom had walked out of Lucky's with it crumpled in her hands and nobody, not even that sweaty little manager, had said a word.

At Harvard University in the early 1940s, a chemist combined naphthenic and palmitic acids into a sticky gel that could be mixed with petroleum and then ignited. Because it clung to everything, including skin, the gel was a particularly efficient weapon against human targets. More than sixteen thousand tons were dropped on Japan during World War II. Almost twenty-five times that was used in the Vietnam War. This wasn't one of Dad's stories. There was no personal policy that protected against napalm. Acts of government are like acts of God: unfathomable and uninsurable.

We had seen the bombings on TV, though we didn't know what we were seeing. The planes dove low to the ground, then shot back up to the clouds as the earth exploded with fire beneath them. Now the photo of that little girl bombed us. It ran on every front page until it reached even *The Golden Gazette*.

Missy Carter went from class to class handing out copies and telling us why we should care. Kids listened, riveted, unable to peel their eyes off that picture. They couldn't put their finger on why exactly. There was just something about that photo.

When they finally figured it out, they papered the school with the picture, augmented it with doodled bucket hats. *You'll all burn in hell!* floated above her in speech bubbles. *He maketh me lie down in green pastures.* It was superfluous. You couldn't look at that picture and not think of Carol Closter screaming down the hall, hand clutching her wet towel.

Teachers appealed to Mr. Galpin. It was obscene, they said. The girl was naked, forgodsake. But Missy Carter argued civil liberties and freedom of speech and alienation of our basic rights, by which she meant that her father was a corporate lawyer with a large discretionary fund. From homeroom to last bell, that naked girl chased us, limp-armed and open-mouthed. Whenever Carol passed one of those photos, her whole body tilted away. For days she seemed to walk at an angle. "What's wrong, Cloister?" Joyce barked. "Remind you of somebody?" Carol only lifted her head a little higher, walked a little faster. I didn't know how she did it. Sometimes I could swear I heard that little girl screaming. Screaming! At least she'd screamed. At least she'd run. I wanted to shout every time I saw Troy Gainer punch the air to his Eagles eight-track, every time I saw Melanie sink into the dark of the Mustang's back seat. Instead I locked myself in a bathroom stall—there I was again—and flicked my lighter on and off, counting down the hours, minutes, seconds. Those last days of school had the metal clench of a steel trap.

When my Bic was empty, I flung open the stall door. Enough was enough.

Jamie Finley lay flat out under the bleachers with a six-pack tucked into his armpit. A few feet away, a guy snored under a swarm of stringy black hair. Jamie's right hand choked the neck of a Pabst Blue Ribbon. An opener stuck out of his front pocket. That and a lighter.

"Can I borrow that?" I said.

Jamie opened his green eyes behind a flop of bang and grinned. "Hey, hey! You're just in time to help us celebrate." Jamie took a swig of beer and wagged the bottle at me. I shook my head. "What? You're not celebrating? Didn't you hear? Troy got a scholarship to Arizona State. How about that?"

"Partial scholarship," I said.

Jamie held up his beer. "To Troy and his partial scholarship."

"So what? You're going to college, right?" Jamie was smarter than Troy Gainer. Jamie was smarter than most of us. I pictured him on a campus out east, hugging his Kafka against his wool coat, surrounded by stone buildings and snow-dusted trees.

"College is for suckers," he said. He tipped the bottle back. Beer went everywhere—his chin, his shirt. He wiped his mouth, pointlessly.

"Aren't you worried about the war?" I said.

"Are *you* worried about the war, Robin Fisher?"

"They say it'll end soon," I said. I heard this on the news a lot, but I didn't really believe it. It felt like the war had been going on my whole life.

"Why does Troy get everything?" Jamie said. "He gets the scholarship. He gets the girl. What do I get?"

It was like swallowing a ball bearing, realizing what he meant. Jamie liked Melanie. I'd messed it up for both of them. I was like napalm, destroying everything, burning it all to nothing with one touch.

Bottle empty, Jamie tossed it over his shoulder and took another from the six-pack. "Troy gets everything and I get warm fucking beer."

"Some people don't even have warm beer," I said.

"I know that. Don't you think I know that? It's just that—fuck, you know, everyone keeps saying these are the best years of our lives. What if they're right? What if it doesn't get better than this?"

"That's not even funny," I said.

"Do you see anyone laughing?"

Jamie drained the bottle in one go. This one hit the bleachers, ringing out like a gong. The sleeping guy mumbled under his hair.

"Hey," Jamie said, "wake up. Today is the first day of the end of our lives."

The guy rolled away from us, hands over his head as if he expected more shelling.

Jamie's eyes closed. He let his arms flop to his sides. I marvelled at anyone who could sleep on his back with his arms open, like a dog or a baby, beings that don't know the world is a dangerous place. I always slept bent at the waist, my whole body a fist.

His breath grew ragged edges, then he was snoring. When I was sure he was asleep, I knelt beside him. I reached out, fingers hovering at the top of his thigh, and slid the lighter carefully from his pocket. I was close enough to feel the heat of his body. His beer breath was not unpleasant.

"What are you doing?" he said.

"I need this for a while. I'll bring it right back."

"Take it," he said. "You deserve it. You deserve everything, Robin Fisher. I hope you get the partial scholarship of your choosing. I hope you get a beautiful fucking life."

Jamie rolled over and spooned what was left of his six-pack. I pushed the lighter back inside his pocket. Something told me he needed it more than I did.

When the fire alarm was pulled that afternoon, nobody threw so much as a snide glance at me as they rose from their desks and filed out the door. It was the last day of school—a false alarm could be counted on as surely as the dry heat. While men with axes stormed the halls, kids dispersed quietly into the shadows of emaciated trees and the hot recesses of parked cars. A half-hour later, they shuffled their boneless bodies back to class, disappointed their school was not a smouldering pile but uncomplaining. It would be another hour before anyone noticed the missing pictures. Every one of them had been torn down, every screaming naked girl gone.

Mr. Galpin called me to his office during last period. Moody Miller was leaving as I got there.

"We have to stop meeting like this," I said.

Mr. Galpin sat in one of his own visitors' chairs, looking uncomfortable. Mr. Boyd stood over me, breathing loudly. I could smell the peanut butter he'd eaten for lunch.

"Where were you during the fire alarm?"

"On the field?"

"Were you? *Were* you?"

"Now, hold on," Mr. Galpin said. "Let's back up a bit here. Miss Fisher, you've probably noticed that somebody took those pictures down. It appears to have happened while everyone was outside." My dad had the same tie he was wearing, little white diamonds on a navy sky. I'd picked it out for Father's Day from a mail-order catalogue. *For the disappointed man in your life*. "Nobody is accusing anybody of anything, you understand. We're trying to get some information, that's all."

"The janitor found the pictures in the boiler room," Mr. Boyd said. "What was left of them. Someone put them in the furnace. It doesn't take a genius to figure out that whoever put them there was the same person who pulled the alarm."

"Apparently not," I said.

"Are you being smart?"

"With my grade point average?"

Mr. Galpin stood up and waved his hands. "This isn't getting us anywhere. Like I said, Miss Fisher, we're just hoping to clarify a few things."

"So if we were to look inside your locker," Mr. Boyd interrupted, "we wouldn't find matches or anything else of that nature?"

"Probably," I said.

"Probably?" Mr. Galpin's eyes crinkled at the corners. Kind, my mom would have called them. Sad, I would've said.

The counsellor tried, unsuccessfully, to hold back a grin.

"People put stuff like that in my locker sometimes," I said. "Matches and lighters."

"I see," Mr. Galpin said. He shook his head. "I see."

A fire truck cruised by outside, probably en route to another high school. It wasn't in any rush.

"Anyway, you wouldn't need matches if you had a furnace," I said. "Or vice versa, I guess."

"No, you wouldn't," Mr. Galpin said. "No, you sure as hell would not. Thank you, Miss Fisher. Thank you very much for your help. Have yourself a good summer."

"That's it?" Mr. Boyd said. "I guess we'll just let them burn the school down, then."

"Yes, Mr. Boyd. I'd say that's more than enough."

I stepped out of Mr. Galpin's office and into a giant snow globe. The halls had exploded with a million pieces of paper, tests and essays with fat red letters on them that didn't mean anything now. At the other end of the hall, the janitor swept up flurries of foolscap. It was after three, I realized. Somehow I hadn't heard the bell. I ran to the front doors and threw them open. Not a single car or soul remained in the parking lot. Toilet paper fluttered silently in the trees.

My throat tightened, then my chest. The ending I'd been praying for had came and gone without my knowing it. I'd been holding my breath for over a year and now—was that really it?

Whoosh. My chest sprung open. My throat released. I gasped and sputtered, something halfway between a laugh and a cry. And then I did cry.

I pushed my fingers against my eyes. I didn't know what was wrong with me. I headed to my locker to get my things. There was nothing in there that I wanted, but that's what you do on the last day of school—you clear out your locker. As I rounded the corner, I saw Carol. I'd never been so glad to see anyone in my whole life.

When she saw me, she tugged her hat down low on her forehead and crossed her arms.

"Why did you do that?" she said. "I never asked you to do that."

"Do what?" I started to shove my hands in my pockets, but Carol grabbed my wrists and held them tight between us. For a small person, she was surprisingly strong. She turned them in her own small hands, over and over like a palm reader who's forgotten how to do her job.

"I hope you're happy," Carol said. "You're ruining my life."

As she stormed off down the hall, I examined my hands. For the record, they were as clean as a newborn's. That myth about fire alarms staining your hands with ink was just one more thing I'd heard in school that turned out to be bullshit.

13

When the great Krakatoa erupted in the summer of 1883, the sky over the surrounding Indonesian islands was already choked with ash. There had been a series of smaller eruptions that spring, an ellipsis en route to the exclamation point. This was the part of the story that really got my dad—not that thirty-five thousand people had sunk to their ocean graves, but that the Krakatoans had seen it coming and done nothing. "For months they woke up, ate their papayas, and went to work as if everything was hunky-dory. Can you believe that? Months."

"What should they have done?" Mom said. "They lived on an island. What choice did they have?"

"That's not the point, Lainey. That's not it at all."

"No, Jim. I suppose it's not."

The summer of 1972, it felt like we were the ones living beside a volcano. The air was oven-hot at all hours, so hot you wanted to run away from your own skin. Families fled west for the ocean breeze or east for cold clear lakes. Those who stayed put made the most of their air conditioners, their pools, their ice-makers. The town council asked the good citizens of Golden to cut back on water usage, to use the AC only when absolutely necessary. Resources were scarce. Americans everywhere were pitching in. But conservation was not a popular idea in Golden, where lawns were green twelve months a year and nobody minded too much if in the evenings, when all the fathers came home and turned on their televisions, the living room lights sometimes flickered and dimmed.

In our house the television was almost always on. I had gotten used to the voices, the soothing electric hum, that eternal blue glow. It was a third presence in the house, one that I could count on. Now, suddenly, Mom wanted it off. Hadn't I heard about peak oil? Energy shortages? Didn't I watch the news?

"How can I watch the news if the TV's off?" I said.

Mom couldn't stand television anymore, that was the real problem. She got mad at everything now, even the game shows. She threw a slipper at Richard Dawson's head because he called a contestant "sweetheart." But I liked knowing that somewhere out there people were winning washing machines and snow blowers just for knowing the price of canned gravy. Mom still read the newspaper, cover to cover, every day, though it made her just as miserable. "They're all a bunch of con men," she'd grumble, holding the morning paper with one hand and raking a brush through her hair with the other. "Who put these maniacs in charge?" Later, I'd find the paper in the kitchen garbage, shreds of newsprint wilting under wet coffee grounds and clumps of hair.

She'd started working at the hospital full-time by then, covering other people's vacations and enjoying the industrial air conditioning. "Why anyone would want to travel in this heat is beyond me," she said. Meanwhile, she couldn't sit still. She had struggled with her college classes but was restless without them. Restlessness coursed through my own teenaged limbs, but mothers were supposed to stay put, like furniture.

Weekends, there was nothing to anchor her down. It was too hot to be outside or inside, too hot to stay awake, too hot to sleep. I moved as little as possible, fanning myself ferociously with magazines and trying not to think of the crisp, blue pool close enough to dive into. But Mom was always on the move. She'd go from room to room, picking things up and putting them down again, as if she'd lost something. At night, I heard her haunting the fridge, the liquor cabinet, a ghost with no social life. At least when she did laps in the pool she had some-where to go—shallow end, deep end, shallow end, deep end. "Why don't you come in?" she'd say. "I just washed my hair,"

I'd lie. And Mom would shake her head, grinning, like it was some old joke she'd half forgotten. She used to wear a swimming cap. Now she let her hair get green and stiff with chlorine. Once in a while, she'd bend over the kitchen sink and let me rinse it with lemon juice and soak it with olive oil. Her salad days, she called them.

One Saturday, while Mom wandered the house in her towel turban, I sat at the dining table, thumbing through one of the grade eleven textbooks Mr. Galpin had given me to take home for the break. I had managed to avoid summer school this time, but just barely. "Let's see if we can't keep that momentum going," Mr. Galpin had said, like it was a group effort, like we were a team. "If we get a bit ahead of things, I don't see why we can't try for a few B's next year." I had thought of a few good reasons, all of which I kept to myself. Now here I was trying to care about the early American settlers, for Mr. Galpin's sake, if not my own. An hour in and I hadn't cracked the first chapter, while Mom had made excellent progress touching nearly every object in the house with the tips of her fingers, as if tallying our possessions. There were one or two clear ovals on every surface. It was the most dusting I'd seen her do in weeks. Eventually, she came to a stop beside me and bent down to see what I was reading—or not reading, such as it was.

"What's so fascinating?" she said.

"Nothing, unfortunately."

She flipped slowly through the pages, pausing here and there to squint and frown at something. "What's that they say—those who forget history are doomed to repeat it?"

"So my history teacher keeps telling me."

"I was never very good at history. You probably get that from me. I wasn't very good at any of it." She squeezed my shoulder and wandered away again.

An hour later, I found her outside, cigarette in hand, staring hard at the back of the yard. There was no mistaking what she was staring at. Then she turned suddenly, went back inside, and picked up the textbook I'd finally abandoned. She turned the page, then another. Finally, she sat down on the sofa with it. When I went to bed she was still there, feet tucked in the crack between the cushions against the evening chill.

Sunday, she was there again, this time with a hefty hardcover novel she'd once said was the reason people invented movies. I thought she'd thrown all her college books away, but one by one they reappeared. She read every evening, long legs folded inside her caftan. She was all angles again, sharp corners and switchbacks, hollows where once hills might have been. My own body had become unwieldy. I had dreams where my legs grew so long they snapped at the knees when I tried to walk. I made do with cut-offs and bare feet. I could've walked around naked, for all Mom would've noticed. She could sit that way for hours, lingering over pages like they were fabric swatches and she just couldn't decide. When the college books ran out, she went to the library downtown. The only thing piled higher than dirty dishes in our house were books. She was soaking it all up like a sponge, which was more than I could say for the actual sponge. Mom's housekeeping had become increasingly sporadic since Dad left, but lately her neglect had vigour, a sense of purpose. "Appliances are the backbone of the domestic industrial complex," she said when I lifted my eyebrows at the state of the kitchen, the island of dirty dishes, the fields of toast moulding on countertops. The mound of coffee filters in the garbage was a tiny Krakatoa waiting to happen.

"Housewife," she told me, "is just another word for indentured servant."

"What's another word for dysentery?" I said.

Our neighbours' prim lawns, conspicuously clean cars, mailboxes decorated with painted wood flowers—Mom glowered at these things as if observing the rituals of some barbaric tribe. "Those garbage cans probably cost more than I make in a week," she said. "They're for holding garbage, for Christ's sake."

Our house was next. Mom hated the wallpaper, the carpeting, the artwork, the tablecloths. Oh, the tablecloths! The abomination! Objectionable items were put out with the weekly trash. A small footstool, a box of fringed hand towels, the guest soaps we hadn't been allowed to use, the iced-tea spoons. "What do we need with iced-tea spoons? Is the Queen going to drop by for Hamburger Helper?" The nautical watercolour that had hung in her bedroom for years, the hand-knotted rug we weren't supposed to walk on, the sheers, the phone table. "A phone needs its own table? Well, la-de-da."

The kitchen was left alone only because she so rarely went in there anymore. Same for my room. The rest of the house Mom scrutinized with the diligence of a minesweeper. "Such clutter," she said, admiring the growing pile at the curb. "Such waste." She thought this was a great success, this stripping away of the things she once loved.

It made her no happier. Every morning, she got into the Buick in her practical black slacks, hair pulled back in a tidy French twist, looking like someone on her way to a tax audit. There she goes, I'd think, turning the world on with her smile. I was glad for the reprieve, but not for long. Within minutes the relief would give way to disquiet. The house was too empty. There was too much space, shadowy indents where lamps and chairs used to be. She'd agonized for months over the fabric of those chairs.

I would invent reasons to call her at the hospital. I couldn't find the can opener. I'd lost my keys. "Now what?" she'd say instead of hello. Evenings were okay. I could watch her, camped out on the sofa, nose in some book. But at night it hovered over me in the dark, this sense that something was missing or misplaced. It sat on my chest and whispered in my ears. It wasn't the house she was stripping away. Waking every few hours, I'd creep down the hall and press my ear to Mom's door until I was sure she was still there on the other side.

One night, ear pressed against pine, all I heard was the blood pumping through me. I opened the door one inch, then another, until I saw the empty bed. The rumpled sheets did not reassure me—she'd stopped making her bed long ago. I hurried through the house, throwing open doors and finding only more emptiness. In the living room, I saw the half-drunk bottle of red wine left just inside the open sliding door. I scanned the yard. It took a minute for my eyes to catch hold of her standing in the doorway of the pool house. Her caftan fluttered around her. An empty wine glass dangled from one slack hand, the swooping tip of her cigarette in the other, a lightning bug in the dark. The cigarette disappeared inside the pool house. Mom followed.

I could hear her moving things around. I didn't know what she was doing in there, but I knew it couldn't end well. Did she notice what was gone, the many small flammable objects that could be easily ferried to vacant lots at dusk and not be missed?

After a minute, Mom stepped back out onto the grass. Her placid face was lit up bright as the moon overhead.

I couldn't see what she'd lit, but I could see the flames lapping eagerly at the air. Whatever it was burned furiously. A few more hot seconds and there would be no stopping it. Everything in that pool house was as dry as moth wings. I suppose I should have warned her or called out in alarm, but I didn't feel alarmed. Memories of the fire I'd set—when I let myself remember it—always brought with them the purest disbelief and wonder for simply, remarkably, being something that I had done. One moment I was a nice kid, a normal kid, someone you might like well enough but hardly think about, the next I was someone you would not say those things about at all. So I stood at the sliding door, watching quietly. If I felt anything it was curiosity. If I was a pyro freak, maybe it was in my genes.

At last Mom reached into the pool house and pulled out a box. For a few seconds it blazed gloriously above her head like an Olympic torch. She stood tall, hoisted it a few inches higher, and pitched it into the deep end, where it bobbed a few times, sizzling loudly, before sinking, unceremoniously, to the bottom of the pool. Seconds later, one of Dad's oxford shirts swelled to the surface like a giant jellyfish. Mom lit a fresh cigarette, reached for the pool skimmer, and wrestled the shirt back under water. I went back to bed and slept through the sunrise for the first time in days. What can I say except that it's reassuring to realize you aren't the only mental person in your family.

The next morning, I found Mom standing at the sliding door, drinking coffee and staring at the pool. As I joined her, I saw the box still crouched at the bottom of the deep end. Dad's shirt had gotten tangled in the gutter. It waved its arms in the water like a drowning man. She turned her back to it.

"Let's do something," she said. "Let's go somewhere. Wouldn't that be fun?" She made herself smile.

"Where do you want to go?" I said.

"Anywhere but here."

Finally, something we could agree on.

The Buick expelled suffocating gusts of volcanic air when we opened its doors. We rolled down all the windows, laid beach towels on the seats, and tried not to think about the heat. We drove to the new McDonald's and ordered ice cream cones through the drive-thru window. That was as far as our planning went. After that, we let the green lights guide us, dripping chocolate everywhere, glad for simple things like napkins and a breeze. At first the radio did the talking for us. Soon we were singing along. We tipped our melting cones together like glasses of champagne, grinning our chocolate grins.

These drives became our thing. When we'd had enough of summer's heat, of the television's war, we jumped in the Buick and drove. Mom would toss her pumps in the back seat and drive in bare feet. I'd stick mine out the window and let the wind tickle my toes. We cruised by the new golf course being built into the hills. We zipped past the old mall coming down, the new mall going up. We zigzagged, circled, doubled back. Hamburger wrappers rustled in the footwells. Wads of used napkins flowered from the door pockets. You'd think somebody lived in that car. Getting low on gas was a sign of accomplishment. Mom called it clearing out the cobwebs, which made us smile because the actual cobwebs in our house remained perfectly intact.

Mom decided it was time I learned to drive. I must have ground that gearbox nearly smooth in those first few days, but she only put her hand over mine as I steered and said, "Transmissions cost money. Try not to drive us into the poorhouse." Her teaching method consisted of watching for stray dogs and police cars while I skulked around back roads, hands strangling the wheel. Sometimes I'd glance over and she'd have her eyes closed. Cigarettes found their way to her mouth by habit.

"You're not watching," I said. "I could drive us off a cliff."

"Don't do that," she said.

Her faith in me made me nervous, as undeserved faith always does, but soon enough I was zinging down the asphalt, the radio powering my right foot.

"If we kept north we'd reach the redwoods," she said one afternoon. "They're so tall, you get vertigo just looking up at them. If you cut down a redwood, it would have a thousand rings."

"We could go there," I said.

"Sure we could. We can do whatever we want."

"We could go somewhere cold. Alaska or Canada."

"Not Canada," she said.

"You don't miss it?"

"Now and then, I suppose." She took a long, thinking drag. "Everything seems better from far away."

I tried to imagine snow-capped mountain peaks reflected in ice-blue lakes, but the world on the other side of the windshield was red and orange, a landscape of fires and earthquakes that made you hot just looking at it. Mom leaned her head against her door and shut her eyes again. Across the country, kids were turning on, tuning in, and dropping out. Middle-aged women were swapping their tennis pros for tantric gurus. Californian ashrams were full of them. But we weren't going anywhere. No matter how long we drove, we always ended up back where we'd started.

Near the canal, traffic barely crawled. Heads poked out of windows, necks stretched, trying for a glimpse of something. Kids in back seats pulled faces at the people behind them. The guy behind us leaned on his horn. We were sweating through our towels by the time we reached the bridge. A crowd had gathered along the railing, everyone peering down. A policeman stood in the road up ahead, gesturing with white-gloved hands, a whistle in his mouth.

"Don't stop," Mom said, sitting up straight. "You don't have a licence."

"We're Bonnie and Clyde now?"

But the policeman hardly glanced at me as he waved me to the shoulder. I parked behind the row of cars, and we put on our shoes and walked over to see what was going on.

"It's awful," a woman was saying. "I want to cry. I do."

"It's unsanitary, is what it is," the man beside her said.

"Do you have to be like that?"

"Now, don't go getting all emotional. It happens every summer. That's what the grates are for."

"Is it a deer?" Mom said.

The man turned and took in how pretty she was right then with her hair back in a messy braid, her caftan waving around her like some exotic flag. "You ladies don't want to see this," he said.

"Oh, now you're concerned for the fairer sex," the woman said. He sighed, tipped his hat, and followed her back to their car.

We took their places along the bridge rail. Men in green overalls were piled on the grate below, reaching and grabbing for something, trying to get hold. A few stood back, wiping their brows and shaking their heads. A construction truck idled at the edge of the canal, its yellow claw hovering over the water, waiting. "This isn't going to work," one of the men shouted.

"Got any better ideas?" another shouted back.

"It's the thirst," the old man beside me said. "They wander off from the herd, looking for water. They go crazy, I guess. I saw it happen once. I was about your age. That was a real heat wave. We fried eggs on the sidewalk. That deer just climbed up and walked in, like it was getting into a bath."

Below us, the men untangled themselves and scuttled back. "Oh hell," the old man said.

Her long brown legs were bent at impossible angles. A bulging black eye stared up at us. I covered my face with my hands.

"She's so beautiful," Mom said quietly.

"Don't look," I said.

"Someone has to."

"What are they doing now?"

"You don't want to know."

Seconds later, I heard the unmistakable whine of a chainsaw. Mom grabbed my elbow and we hurried back to the car. We nearly ran. I was glad when she got behind the wheel. I kept seeing that black eye, like the sun's bright orb burned onto the insides of your lids. "You'd better believe we're leaving," she told the policeman and he stepped aside to let us by. She drove fast, paying no mind to speed limits or stop signs. For the air, she said. "Sometimes I just can't breathe in this place."

That was the last time we went driving. Gas was too expensive, Mom said. It was too damned hot. The Buick would bust a gasket, or she would.

"How am I supposed to get my licence if I don't practise?"

"You have somewhere important to go?"

Afternoons, I sat on the front lawn, memorizing the booklet I'd gotten from the DMV and waiting for her and the Buick to get home. She'd usually let me take a few turns around the block by myself while she sat on the step and smoked. When I got tired of studying, I'd watch ants carrying bits of leaves through the grass. I'd lay my hand in their path, but it wouldn't stop them. They'd marched up and onward, unfazed by this mountain that had magically appeared.

This is what I was doing when a brown station wagon slammed to a stop in the middle of the street and Carol's face popped up in the driver's window. I ran over, surprised by how happy I was to see her. It was refreshing to miss someone who actually came back.

"How was camp?" I said.

"Hell on earth. Come on. I need to show you something." She unlocked the passenger door and I got in.

"Since when do you drive?" I said.

Carol let go of the brake and we lurched forward. "I'm sixteen, aren't I?"

Sixteen or not, Carol could barely see over the steering wheel even with a Bible and a pillow under her. We inched down the street slower than those ants. She took a right turn, then two more. "I'm not so good with lefts," she said.

Carol followed the canal all the way to the other side of town. At our speed it took twice as long as it should have, but that was fine by me. Finally, she pulled into the parking lot of a small shopping plaza. She parked in front of a doctor's office and turned off the engine. There was a pet shop on one side and a beauty parlour on the other, the kind that catered to old ladies who still called it that.

"This is what you needed to show me? I've seen mini-malls before."

"It's not a mall," Carol said. "It's my destiny." She gripped the wheel with both hands and leaned forward, peering through the windshield at the doctor's office. "Robin, do you know what Roe versus Wade is?"

"Sure," I said, though what I knew wasn't much. Whenever they mentioned it on TV, Mom threw a shoe at the dial.

"We prayed about it at camp a lot," Carol said. "One night, we were sitting around the fire, praying, and everyone was crying—they cried about everything there, I was going out of my mind. But this one night, one of the older girls stood up and told us she'd done it."

"Done it?"

"Had an abortion. She killed her unborn baby, Robin. Now do you see?" Carol lifted a hand from the wheel and touched her fingertips to the windshield. Her voice was a whisper. "And that's where they did it. Right. In. There."

I followed her gaze, trying to see what I'd missed before. It was the middle of the week, but the doctor's office looked closed, the curtains pulled tight. The window announced DR. H. WINKELMANN, OB-GYN, in classy gold letters. Winkelmann didn't sound like the name of somebody who killed unborn babies. It sounded like the name of someone who made balloon animals for a living.

"I was thinking we'd call ourselves the Crusaders," Carol said. "Do you think it's too much?" Carol loved the Crusades. She knew everything there was to know about them the way I used to know everything about the Cassidy brothers. "Or maybe the Guardians. That's not bad."

"What are you guarding?"

She turned her head. Her eyes were wet but she was smiling. "The babies, Robin. All those babies. We're going to save the unborn."

"How are you going to do that?"

"Not me. Us."

"Us?"

"You're my best friend. You want me to reach my destiny, don't you?"

"I don't know, Carol."

"What don't you know?"

I thought of the bloody skirt on my mom's bedroom floor, the blood on my hands. How many times had I washed them in the days that followed? How many times had I scrubbed under scalding water until they sung with pain? I tucked them under my thighs now.

"What about the women? The girls?"

"What about them?"

"Maybe they don't have any other options," I said, sensing a truth under the words that I didn't yet have the vocabulary to describe. I was worse at English than I was at history.

Carol blinked at me slowly, like one of those dolls with working eyelids that opened and closed. "Do you know where aborted babies go?" she said.

I shrugged. "Purgatory?"

"In the garbage, Robin. They throw them in the garbage, like trash."

"They don't really do that."

"How do you know?"

I shifted in my seat. My thighs made a sickly sucking sound as they peeled off the vinyl. It was hot in that car. It was getting so I could hardly breathe. I'd never seen that skirt again and I was glad for it. I didn't know what had happened to it and I didn't want to.

"Maybe you're right," Carol said. "We shouldn't stop them from killing their babies, we should help them. Hey, I know, we can have an abortion drive at the mall. We can all hold hands and sing 'Kumbaya.'"

"I didn't mean that." I pulled the neck of my T-shirt away from my chest. I wasn't sure what I'd meant.

"Forget it," Carol said, putting the car in gear. "So what if it's my destiny? Just forget the whole stupid thing."

We drove home in silence. After what felt like hours, the car slammed to a stop. Carol still wouldn't look at me. I didn't much want to look at her either. Fat tears rolled down her pink doll cheek, and I thought of her running down that hallway in a towel, her wet feet slapping the floor, soap in her screaming mouth. I put my hand on the door, turning my face away like I had that day.

"I know you all think I'm a big joke," she said. "But this really is my destiny. I'm sure of it."

"I don't think you're a joke, Carol."

Carol nodded, but she didn't say anything else. I got out of the car and shut the door. The Closters' station wagon was halfway down the block before I realized she hadn't dropped me anywhere near my house.

I passed the gas station on the way home. I didn't need a new lighter. I just felt like one.

"Bad habit," the attendant said as I handed him a dollar for a Bic and a pop.

"Nobody likes a quitter," I said.

When I stepped outside again, a yellow Pinto was parked near the air pump. Jamie Finley squatted beside one of the front tires, air hose in one hand. His clothes were coated in a layer of dirt, as if he'd rolled around in a sandbox. When he lifted his arm to shield his eyes from the sun, I could see the sharp line where his tan ended and his T-shirt began.

"Robin Fisher," he said and smiled slowly. His cheeks were shadowed with stubble, but the dimple was still there. "What do you think of my new wheels? Pretty sweet, huh?"

"It's great," I said. It was the ugliest car I'd ever seen.

"It's butt-ugly, but it was cheap. People keep flagging me down for cab rides. On the upside, I already made twelve bucks."

"So it's paid for itself," I said, and Jamie laughed.

I stood in the shade of the pump, drinking my pop while he finished checking his tires. He told me about his job working construction at the new mini-mall across the street where the patio furniture store used to be. "Well, not so much construction as shovelling rocks," he said. "I move rocks from one pile and put them in another. I figured it was better than working in some mailroom, wearing a tie."

"Ants can carry a hundred times their own body weight," I said.

"I guess I should be glad I'm not an ant then," he said. "It's not so bad, actually. I do a lot of thinking."

"About what?"

Jamie squatted back on his heels and rubbed his chin. "I guess I'm trying to figure out when exactly everything in my life went to shit. You ever think about stuff like that?"

"Maybe," I said. What I meant was *all the time*.

"Buddhists say you should live in the present, but my brain has a mind of its own."

"Those who forget history are doomed to repeat it," I said.

Jamie smiled like it hurt to be right about some things. He stood up and went inside the store. I thought about going home but didn't. He came back out with a bottle of beer, held it to his forehead before he took a drink.

"So did you?" I said.

"Did I what?"

"Figure out when everything went to shit?"

Jamie turned his beer in his hand, picked at a corner of the label. His fingernails were tipped black with dirt. Mine were bitten. I couldn't remember when I'd started doing that.

"Yeah," he said. "I think I've got a pretty good handle on it."

I studied the ground. The concrete was cracked everywhere. My toes were grey with dust. I remembered the time Dad had sprayed for ants. He'd rented the equipment so he could do it himself, sweeping every nook and crevice with cloudy white liquid. I'd told him he looked like an astronaut with that pack on his back, and he'd grinned behind the mask like he'd found a hundred bucks. This was before the moon landing, before I hated Neil and Buzz.

When I lifted my eyes again, Jamie was staring at me. "What about you?" he said.

I thought for a minute, but I couldn't decide. There were too many things I regretted, too many things I wished I'd done or not done. "I'm pretty sure it all started when we landed on the moon," I said. Jamie nodded, as if he knew just what I meant.

"So now what?" I said.

"Now nothing. It's an exercise in futility, just like the rocks."

I drank my pop. Jamie drank his beer. He peeled a strip of label off his beer, then looked at it like he wished he hadn't.

"What if you could go back in time?" I said. "What if you could go back to that moment and change what happened?"

Jamie peeled another strip, then another, bits of label snowing down. "What, like a time machine?"

"Yeah, exactly. What if you had a time machine?"

"Then I'd change it, I guess. Fuck yeah, I would. But I don't have a time machine. Do you have a time machine, Robin Fisher?"

"No, Jamie. I don't."

"So there you go," he said. "Rocks."

Jamie looked down at the mess he'd made and nodded like it was inevitable too. Maybe it was. Maybe everything was. But I also knew then that I would help Carol, because she was my friend and she needed me. This time I wouldn't let her down. Time machine or no time machine, that was one thing I could change.

14

Carol didn't have a driver's licence after all. While Mrs. Closter was visiting family in Colorado and Mr. Closter was at work, Carol "borrowed" the station wagon. She was supposed to be babysitting her little brother. What she did with him instead, she didn't say. But she did say she might let me drive around the parking lot when we got there. She didn't think God would mind me practising my parallel parking as long as it didn't get in the way of saving the unborn.

This time Carol parked far away from Dr. Winkelmann's office, near the exit to the street. In case there was trouble, she said.

"Trouble?" I said. "Are we robbing a bank?"

Carol frowned. I was trying to lighten the mood, but Carol preferred things heavy.

I helped her get the signs out of the back. She'd spent the weekend making them. Hers was a montage of grisly images jazzed up with red glitter. Mine had Bible scripture all over it in letters cut out from her Christian magazines. You'd think I wanted to kidnap babies, not save them. I asked her to trade, but Carol said I was being ridiculous, it wasn't a beauty pageant.

We stood around getting the feel of them in our hands. We weren't sure what the procedure was after that. I suggested we walk in a circle the way the war protesters did, but Carol objected to doing anything like the hippies. "They're worse than communists," she said. "Or maybe the same." Anyway, our signs were poster board staple-gunned to broom handles. They flopped around in the slightest breeze. Walking in circles was out of the question.

"We can't just stand here like morons," Carol said. "We should say something. We could sing a hymn, or do a chant?" But the only songs I knew all the words to were by the Carpenters, and I didn't think "Do You Know the Way to San Jose" was going to fly. Carol suggested we sit in the car and play I spy until a better idea struck us, so that's what we did. She said the car would give us the element of surprise, but really, I spy was one of her favourite games.

The curtains in the windows were closed though the hours on the glass said the doctor's office was open. A lot of people went through the door, mostly middle-aged women in pastel pantsuits and tired young mothers towing small children.

Every hour or so a hairdresser from next door came outside to smoke. She had shoulder-length hair the colour of new pennies. Once in a while, someone with a dog would walk up to the pet shop and stare in the window. One golden retriever had a plastic cone around its head, though I couldn't see anything else wrong with it. His owner stared at the closed door like he could will it open.

"I spy a dog."

"You're not even trying," Carol said.

We took a lunch break. All that sitting around really tuckered us out. Carol had made Mrs. Maxwell's egg salad sandwiches. Just the smell of them made me burp. I told her I was too hot to eat, which was partly true. While Carol ate her sandwich, I curled up in the back seat and tried to nap.

Carol nudged my leg.

"I spy a cat," I mumbled, eyes firmly closed.

She nudged me again and tapped the window above me. I sat up and peered out. A woman was struggling to get out of her car. She swung one leg out, then the other. Aiming her enormous stomach at the doctor's office, she gripped the doorframe with both hands and catapulted herself up and out.

We'd put the signs in the back of the car, so Carol had to crawl over me to get to hers. By the time she had it, the woman was halfway across the parking lot.

"Lady!" Carol shouted, charging forward, sign hoisted like a lance. "Hey, lady! Laaay-dyyyy!"

The woman turned around just as Carol caught up to her, bouncing off her bulging stomach and stumbling backwards, dropping her sign.

"Oh my goodness," the woman said. "Are you all right?"

Carol took several gulps of air. "Please. Don't."

"Don't what, dear?"

"Your. Baby."

The woman bent down and put her hands on her knees. "Are you out here all by yourself, sweetheart? Should I get someone?" People were always bending down to talk to Carol, calling her sweetheart. I half expected them to pinch her cheeks.

Carol was used to it. "No, ma'am. Thank you."

"Well, all right then," the woman said and carried on to the hair salon.

I got out of the car and walked over to Carol. "She's just fat," I said.

"I know."

I picked up Carol's sign for her. Some of the glitter had come off. Otherwise it was okay. I held it for her while she took a hit from her inhaler. She didn't always need it, but it made her feel better.

"I really thought this was my destiny," she said.

While I tried to think of something comforting to say, a woman in a nursing uniform and pink cardigan came out the doctor's door. She stood on the sidewalk and shouted across the parking lot. This was private property, she said. We had no right. If we didn't leave, she'd call the police. She held up a finger and shook it at us. For once even Carol was speechless.

A small man opened the office door and stood beside the nurse. He had a cap of silver hair and wore baggy brown corduroys under his white coat. He looked like a nice person. He looked like somebody's kindly grandfather. He touched the sleeve of the nurse's cardigan and said something to her. She shook her finger at us one more time before following him back inside. I felt bad for both of them. Nobody said they liked what they did for a living. Maybe their high school guidance counsellors had chosen their careers for them. Maybe they'd had really bossy friends.

"Do you realize what this means?" Carol said.

"That we should go home?"

She stared at me for a minute. "Hardy har har," she said. "You almost had me there."

When Vera Miller knocked on our door this time, she wasn't wearing pink but a pale grey shift and white sling-back pumps.

Instead of a small suitcase, she carried a clipboard and a pen. It looked like she was there to grade us for something.

"Darling," she said, taking in Mom's caftan. "It's your lucky day. We're about to make history." She handed us each a button. She had the same one pinned to her dress. George McGovern's three smiling faces beamed at one another.

Mom handed the button back. "I'm Canadian, Vera. I can't vote."

Vera dropped the stewardess smile and fanned herself with the clipboard. The armholes of her dress were rimmed with sweat. It was August. We all had pit stains the size of sand dollars. "Are Canadians allowed to make iced tea?"

While Mom was in the kitchen, Vera stood in the middle of the living room, smirking at the mess. It was a wonder, I'll admit, how we managed so much of it with so little furniture.

"Still going for the post-apocalyptic look, I see," Vera said.

"When in Rome," Mom said.

"That explains the toga."

They went out to the backyard. We still had chairs there. I settled back on my blanket on the grass, while Mom pushed the medical records to the centre of the table to make space for their glasses. Half the hospital was on vacation, so on top of working full-time, she brought work home on the weekends to catch up. The transcripts didn't make her cry anymore. Now she'd shake her head at them and say things like, "How on earth did they miss that tumour? They can see a putting green from three hundred yards, but this they miss."

Mom lit Vera's cigarette, then her own. "So what happened to transforming the women of America one lipstick at a time?"

"A spectacular failure," Vera said. "You and my maid were the only sales I ever made. They make you buy those kits, you know. There's sixty-two bucks I'll never see again. If you ever want any blue eyeshadow . . . Anyway, who needs women's lib when you've got alimony."

"Has it come to that?"

"My first husband was a big proponent of women's lib. He always said, 'Find something you're good at, Vera, and then find a way to make money at it.' Turns out the only thing I'm good at is divorce."

"I'm sorry things didn't work out for you."

"So am I. There's no stingier ex-husband than a divorce lawyer. Though he did give me this perfume for my birthday." Vera held out her wrist, and Mom sniffed obligingly. "It says Possession on the box, but I call it nine-tenths of the law."

"Oh, Vera. Is it that bad?"

Vera waved Mom's pity away. "On the bright side, the little hippie left him. She said he was giving off bad vibrations. I told him it's the wheatgrass emanating from his pores. He's getting daily colonics now to clear it out. I was thinking I should send her a thank-you card for that."

"You're the Emily Post of post-nuptials."

Vera took a sip from her glass, winced and swallowed. "Now I know who to call when I need a cup of Drano."

"I ran out of tea," Mom said. "If I'd known you were coming, I'd have baked a casserole."

"That's why I didn't call," Vera said, and they smiled at each other.

They drank their iced coffee and smoked their cigarettes. The sun dug in its heels. I leafed through my magazine lazily.

"So you and McGovern are going to change the world," Mom said after a while.

"I've wasted twenty years trying to change men. This seemed easier."

"I'm not sure you can do one without the other."

"You've got me there. Husband number three was president of the Young Republicans in college." Vera tapped the button on her dress with a French-tipped nail. "He almost had a heart attack when he saw this. It was wonderful."

"So a vote for McGovern is a vote for revenge?"

"The volunteer meetings are full of divorced women. There'd be no campaign without us."

"Now there's a slogan."

"You should help out. Join our divorced women's club."

"I'm not divorced, Vera."

"Technicalities."

"That's my life. One giant technicality."

Vera turned to me. "Is this one old enough to vote yet? You're American, aren't you, honey?"

"She's sixteen," Mom said wistfully, I thought, like the heroines in the novels I never managed to finish.

"Too young to worry about the promises of old men," Vera said.

"Or the complaints of old ladies."

"Who are you calling a lady?" Vera said.

She stood up and came over to where I lay, aerating the grass with her kitten heels. She bent down and put her hand under my chin, lifted my face to hers. Her eye makeup was running and powder had settled thickly in the lines around her mouth, but not even Mom's coffee could budge her sly red smile. "Sixteen," she said. "Not a woman but not a child either. It's the limbo of life."

"More like purgatory," I said.

"Talk to me when you're my age," Mom said. But I could no more imagine being her age than I could imagine being a parakeet.

"Dominic Savio was fourteen when he died," I said.

"Who's that?" Vera said.

"The patron saint of juvenile delinquents."

Vera let go of my face and picked up my magazine, fanned herself with it. It was open to the quiz "How Good a Daughter Are You?" I'd passed with flying colours, because I'd lied on nearly every answer. "I'll have to remember to tell Moody he's got his own saint," she said.

Vera settled back into her chair. Nobody said anything for a while. I laid my head down on the blanket and closed my eyes. Maybe I could learn how to feather my hair by osmosis.

"Did you hear about those kids camped out in front of that doctor's office?" she said. I opened my eyes. I was wide awake now. "You know—*that* doctor."

Mom jumped up. "Well, I could sure use another coffee. More coffee, Vera?" She didn't wait for an answer. Vera kept talking, only louder.

"They're just a couple of kids," she called out. "Waving signs around or some nonsense. What do you make of that, Elaine?" When Mom didn't answer, Vera turned to me. "They're about your age. Can you believe that?"

"No," I said, which was true.

I'd met Carol at the end of my block every morning for the past two weeks. Every morning for two weeks, I'd thought about staying in bed, but that would have meant saying no to Carol and, worse, trying to explain why. I didn't need a magazine quiz to tell me I was a crappy daughter, but I was trying, at least, to be a good friend. I wasn't sure I believed in destiny, but it was important to Carol to be in that parking lot and for me to be with her, so there I was. Mrs. Closter would be back from Colorado any day now anyway, and Carol didn't take buses because they were teeming with germs. Soon this would just be another summer memory, something to throw away with the clothes I'd outgrown. In the suffocating heat of Mrs. Closter's station wagon, it was easy to convince myself that it didn't mean anything, that maybe it wasn't even happening. Maybe we were just two normal kids on summer vacation playing I spy. Except that we weren't.

"You don't know anything about it, of course," Vera said, squinting at me. It might have been the sun in her eyes, but maybe not.

An answer scratched at the back of my throat. I wanted to tell Vera everything. Melanie had hated going to confession, but I could see the value, to purge yourself of sin, to say your Hail Marys and be neatly and efficiently absolved. But absolved of what? What had Carol and I done wrong? Most days, sitting outside Dr. Winkelmann's, it didn't seem like we'd done anything at all.

"Vera?" I started. If anyone would understand, it would be Vera Miller, who seemed to me to be the kind of woman who'd done things she regretted but still managed to coordinate her shoes and handbag. She was the closest I was going to get to a priest.

Vera's left eyebrow twitched. "Yes, sweetheart?"

Then again, I wasn't Catholic.

"Were you really a roller-skating waitress?"

"Who was a roller-skating waitress?" Mom said, stepping through the sliding door with a carafe of brown sludge.

Vera leaned back in her chair, something like a smile twitching at the corner of her red mouth. "Nobody you know," she said, holding out her glass for a refill.

15

One Saturday, Mom drove downtown with Vera Miller and came home with a box of McGovern pamphlets. "I guess I've joined Vera's divorced women's club," she said and laughed like it was some big joke. It was hot, even by Golden standards, the air so dry it tasted of dust. But Mom didn't let that stop her. She knocked on doors every evening, sometimes with Vera and sometimes alone. When she got home she gulped water like she'd been wandering a desert and grumbled about where our neighbours could stick Nixon's promises.

"You don't think McGovern will actually win," I said.

"Stranger things have happened," she said, which was true.

Like me walking to the gas station every couple of days, whether I needed a new lighter or not. If I got there around four-thirty, Jamie Finley was usually there after work. I'd stop and talk to him while he checked the air in his tires or rubbed the hood of the Pinto with a chamois. He was a teenaged boy and all teenaged boys love their cars, butt-ugly or not. If Jamie was putting in overtime, I'd sometimes stand in the shade of the gas pumps and watch him work from across the street. Moving rocks from one pile to another was probably the world's worst job, but at least he had something useful to do. I'd spent almost a month sitting in a station wagon outside Dr. Winkelmann's office, and I was still really bad at parallel parking, though I had gotten better at I spy.

"Everyone needs to feel they have a purpose," Mom told me. She was still working full-time at the hospital, but instead of bringing home medical records, now she brought home McGovern paraphernalia to hand out on her evening walks. When she ran out, she would bring home more. It reminded me of Jamie's rocks. Maybe that was all life was, moving things from one place to another.

Around the time the heels of Mom's shoes wore down to the metal nubs, the campaign office promoted her to the call list. She'd sit on the stool under the kitchen phone for hours, reciting the same platitudes she'd once used with Dad's clients. *Every cloud has a silver lining. It's always darkest before the dawn. You can't make omelettes without breaking a few eggs.* When one of Dad's clients did call to worry over a policy, she'd give them her McGovern spiel. "You can't insure against everything," she'd tell them. "Who's going to cover the damage we're doing in Vietnam?"

They gave her more pamphlets, more numbers to call, her very own clipboard with a pen attached by a chain of rubber bands. They told her she was a real asset, they wished they had ten more like her. The senator appreciated everything she was doing. Keep up the good work. Your country needs you more than ever. *Your country needs you.* Oh, how Mom loved that line. She said it to the people on her call list, to the cashiers at Lucky's, to the man who came to fix the pool pump. "America is in pain. America is broken. Your country needs you. Your country *neeeeds* you." The more she told people how miserable things were, the more hopeful she seemed.

Between calls, she stuffed envelopes and made buttons with a nifty machine the campaign office had lent her. Nobody could turn out buttons like Elaine Fisher. They found their way into cupboards and drawers. What furniture we had was covered with them. We had purpose up the wazoo.

Vera came over some evenings to help. She'd spike their coffee with Irish whiskey and rant about husband number three. I sat at the table with them or on the floor, stuffing one envelope for Mom's five or six. She had developed her own system, threading the pamphlets between her fingers and firing them into a cascade of open envelopes. "That could be the vote that wins the election," she'd say, squeezing one last fattened envelope into another full box. "You never know!"

Mom said if I liked volunteering, there were girls who came to the hospital once or twice a week to help out. They handed out flowers or fed the elderly patients. I said I'd think about it, and she smiled at me as if I'd been shortlisted for the Nobel Prize. But really what I liked about those hours stuffing envelopes was hearing Vera's stories, the sound of her and Mom's laughter in the warm air like our own laugh track.

Vera would usually stay until dinner. She was never very eager to leave. Furniture or not, she liked our house better than her own. "There are all kinds of empty," Mom said one night after Vera finally went home. When it was just the two of us again, Mom would put away the envelopes and study for her citizenship exam, eating whatever I put in front of her, never complaining about burnt edges or cold centres as she turned the pages of the little booklet with paper-cut fingers. Later, I'd quiz her on dead presidents and she'd quiz me on speed limits, the two of us firing questions back and forth between her evening laps.

Some McGovern campaigners came to the plaza one day, knocking on doors and stopping to talk to people in the parking lot outside Dr. Winkelmann's office. "Take a good look at the enemy," Carol said, but all I saw were people shaking hands and handing out pamphlets. What they were doing seemed a lot like what we were doing, only they were happy about it. It was the seventies and everybody was having a great time telling everybody else how to live.

I was disappointed when they left. It was the second most exciting thing that had happened in that parking lot all month. The most exciting thing was when the town put up a No Loitering sign. The nurse had come outside to watch two men in reflective vests jackhammer a hole in the sidewalk and stick a signpost in it. When they were done, she'd yelled across the parking lot, "You've got thirty minutes and then I'm calling the police." She was either just trying to scare us, or the police didn't care about a couple of dumb kids with glittered signs, because we didn't see so much as a cruiser drive by. I kept waiting for somebody to make me and Carol go home, but nobody ever did.

I usually drove Mrs. Closter's station wagon around the parking lot when we got tired of I spy, but it was too hot to be in the car that day and the air conditioning triggered Carol's asthma. While she walked to the mini-mart to use the bathroom and buy another cold pop, I sat bored and sweaty under the pet shop awning with my DMV booklet on my lap and quizzed myself. When the road signs started to blur together, I leaned my head back against the stucco and closed my eyes.

Traffic hummed sweetly in the distance. I could almost see the steering wheel and that long, cool road north.

The hairdresser with copper hair came outside and taped a hand-lettered sign to the salon window. It took her a really long time to get it straight. Taping up banners was apparently the kind of skill you perfected in school, then promptly lost, like algebra.

When she was done, she stood back and scrutinized her work. SPECIAL!!! 2-for-1 PERMANENTS!!!

"For people with two heads?" I said.

"You kids are bad for business," she said.

"Sorry."

"Are you Mormons or something?"

"I don't think so. What's a Mormon?"

She pulled out a cigarette from behind her ear and stuck it between her lips. She patted her smock and, finding nothing but a comb, sighed loudly. I took out my lighter. As the hairdresser leaned in, her copper hair fell forward, glinting in the sun like a wall of fire. I cupped my hand around the flame so her hair wouldn't catch fire for real.

"I'm from Utah," she said. "Everybody in Utah is always sticking their nose into everybody else's business, and not a single one of them with good hair. Says something, don't you think? How I'd love to get my hands on some of those heads now. I couldn't help your friend with the hat though. Hair like that won't even take to straighteners they use on black girl hair. You've got good hair. You just need a little volume at the crown. Ever try sleeping with Coke cans?"

"In my bed?"

"In your hair." She gave me a look. "What are you doing here, kid?"

I opened my mouth to answer her, but I wasn't sure how. What I wanted to say was that I thought I once knew the difference between right and wrong, but lately all the choices on offer seemed as dubious as the sea monkey families advertised in the backs of magazines. What I said instead was, "Is it hard to be a hairdresser?"

"It's not brain science, but you have to pass a test." She took a drag from her cigarette. "What I really wanted was to be a nightclub singer. My mother was the one who signed me up for hairdressing school."

"Maybe you could sing to your customers."

She shook her head. "I never said I was any good."

"I'm going to volunteer at the hospital," I said. "They give you your own old person to feed."

"That's nice," she said and smiled like she meant it.

The guy with the golden retriever came back. The plastic cone was gone now, but the pet store was still closed. Someone had put a new sign on the door. It would reopen next month as a shoe store. He studied the sign for a while, as if he was trying to understand why someone thought dogs needed shoes.

"You'd think they'd have worked it out by now," the hairdresser said.

"You'd think," I said. I thought she meant the guy and his dog.

"I mean, you take trash out the back, don't you?" She exhaled out the side of her mouth. "Oh hell, what do I know? I came to California to get away from all that. Right. Wrong. Who's to say? I mean, Dr. Mengele over there isn't so hot for business either."

The hairdresser stubbed out her cigarette and went back to work. Carol came back from the store. She'd brought me a root beer.

"I think I'm starting to burn," she said while I drank. Her entire face was the colour of cooked ham.

"This isn't working," I said.

"I know."

"Let's go home."

"Okay."

"Really?"

"Yeah, but you don't have to look so happy about it."

There wasn't really anything to pack up. We didn't bother to take the signs out of the back anymore.

"They were really good signs," I said.

"You can't go wrong with glitter." Carol popped the latch. "No point keeping them, I guess."

She gathered the signs in her skinny arms and went around back to look for a garbage bin. Carol was a lot of things, but she was no litterbug. I opened my booklet, and tried to remember what a squiggly black line meant. It was a minute before I heard the shouting.

I ran toward the sound of Carol's voice. The back of the plaza was a lot like the front, except there were no windows, only a series of grey doors every thirty feet or so. Carol had somebody pinned against one.

"What are you doing?" I said.

"I'm saving them," Carol said.

"Well, stop."

Carol stepped back from the door. The girl crumpled to the ground and sobbed into her hands. She was wearing a sweatshirt with a D'Angelo Dry Cleaning logo on the front. *Where cleanliness is next to godliness.*

"Melanie?" I said.

"I told you!" Carol said, hopping up and down. "I told you this was my destiny! Now do you believe me?"

A row of black garbage bins squatted against the wall beside us. I wrapped my arms around my stomach, imagining a dead baby in one of those bins, mixed in with the hair clippings and cans of expired cat food. I thought of my mom, how she had cried alone behind her bedroom door for days.

"I'm sorry," Melanie whimpered. "I'm sorry."

"It's okay, Mel. It'll be okay."

"What do you mean?" Carol said. "It's not okay! Why are you even talking to her?"

"I can talk to anyone I want to," I said, but then I couldn't think of anything else to say.

Carol stared hard at me, her hands curling into tight little fists. "I knew it," she said and launched herself at me.

She was heavy enough to send me flailing a few feet before I slammed down on the concrete. Then she was on top of me, knees digging into my ribs, hands scratching everywhere—at my hair, my clothes, my face. Melanie was shouting at her to stop. I covered my face, but I didn't fight back. I deserved it, if not for this then for other things. Carol would wear herself out soon enough anyway. I could already hear her asthma rattle. I was more worried about her than me.

Somebody laid on a car horn. Carol's fists froze in the air above me. We turned our heads and saw a red Mustang idling on the side street. The driver honked again. Melanie rose and bolted for the car, mashing her hands into her eyes. She'd barely shut the passenger door when Troy hit the gas.

"That does it!" The nurse stood in the doorway behind us. She tugged on her lumpy cardigan. "That's assault. This time I'm really calling the police." The hairdresser was at her back door too. She shook her copper head as though she'd expected this from me all along, good hair or not.

Carol climbed off me. Her face was shiny with snot and tears. She'd lost her hat in the shuffle, and her hair sprung out in every direction, like a dandelion gone to seed. She stuck her inhaler in her mouth and took a sharp breath, then another. "Your nose is bleeding," she said, giving me her handkerchief. "Pinch it and tip your head back."

We walked back to the station wagon. She took another puff from her inhaler, but her breath still scraped inside her lungs. I thumbed my lighter, but it didn't make me feel any better either. Carol got in behind the wheel and started the engine. I stood beside the passenger door.

"Are you coming?" she said.

I shook my head. I didn't know how I was going to get home, but I knew I wasn't getting in that car.

Carol nodded at the steering wheel. "I knew it," she said again. She took a right out of the parking lot, even though we lived to the left. What was it she knew? I wondered as I watched her drive away. Why didn't I know it too?

While I looked around for a bus stop, two old ladies came

out of the hair salon. They locked their bony arms at the elbows and shuffled down the sidewalk, chatting happily and touching their freshly curled hair. For friends, I realized. 2-for-1 permanents for people with friends.

16

In September of 1900, a hurricane made its way toward the Gulf of Mexico. It was a beautiful day and the dawn of a bright new century. The economy was booming and life was good. If you are pleased with the world and your place in it, nature's most powerful displays can be a spectacular confirmation of all you believe to be right and true. "A Category 4," Dad said, "now that would be something to see." The people of Galveston, Texas, must've agreed with him. Locals and tourists alike had ignored the warnings and gathered near the water to watch the waves. A fifteen-foot storm surge hit the island city in the evening. By morning, more than six thousand people were dead. The beaches were closed for months while the bodies washed ashore.

This was what I was thinking about as I ate my toast and stared out the kitchen window at George McGovern's smiling face on a piece of cardboard stuck in the front lawn. The sky was a clear cerulean. The only cloud was the one that had been following me around for the past week. I had failed my driver's test, among other things. Now this awaited: the first day of my junior year.

Mom had planted the sign the night before, pounding the stake into the lawn with a dusty can of tomatoes while Vera Miller stood by in the grass, supervising their tumblers of sangria. It was rumoured that our town, by miracle or mistake, was being considered as a stop on the candidate's tour. If he came, everyone working on the campaign would get to see his smiling face in person, along with the rest of him.

"We could meet the next president of the United States of America," Mom had said, pressing the can of tomatoes to her chest like an Academy Award. "Isn't that something? Doesn't that beat all?" I hadn't seen her this happy since she stopped wearing dress shields.

A newspaper rustled behind me, followed by the cheerful snip of scissors. Mom had started a scrapbook. Every morning she cut out articles about the election or McGovern and carefully pasted them onto a fresh white page.

"You've been staring out that window for ten minutes," she said. "Are you nervous?"

"Only that our neighbours will egg our house."

"Don't be nervous. Junior year won't be all that different."

"That's what I'm afraid of."

Mom gave me a sympathetic smile. She was wearing lipstick again, a serious shade I still think of as Democrat Beige. The night before, sign firmly rooted, she'd knelt in the grass and made me take a photo of her with cardboard George. She'd squished her face in close to his and matched his cardboard smile tooth for tooth. Between the two of them, it was hard to say who was more delusional about the future.

Reagan High was the same slab of oatmeal-coloured stucco, same bleached-pink doors, same asbestos-ridden walls, same unblinking windows. Newly anointed seniors loafed on the stairs, nodding along to someone's car stereo and sucking on their minty-fresh coolness. Inside, underclassmen waltzed from locker to locker, showing off straight teeth and new noses. The PA system asked Moody Miller to please report to the vice-principal's office. And so another year began to unfurl, ten months of polyester gym shorts, creepy health class filmstrips, and powdered potatoes coming out our ears. At lunch I heard someone counting the weeks until Christmas break. In these ways, Mom was right—junior year wasn't all that different. In other ways, it was.

I hadn't seen Carol since that last day in Dr. Winkelmann's parking lot, and that was fine by me. When I opened my new locker, I found a postcard of da Vinci's *The Last Supper* with

Judas circled in purple pen. I put it in the first garbage can I passed and went to home ec, where Mrs. Maxwell told me Carol had developed a peanut allergy over the summer. "What a shame," our teacher lamented. "She would have made an excellent homemaker. Such lovely buttonholes, such conscientious darting." I was paired with Moody Miller, who'd been permanently banished from shop class at the end of sophomore year for playing Russian roulette with a band saw.

"Who's Carol Closter?" he said.

"Just a girl," I said.

Melanie came to class, but now she slumped in the back rows, eyes on her desk, hair in her mouth, checking the clock over the door every five minutes. Hearing her name spoken by a teacher made her jump. "Where'd you go?" Miss Blumberg would tease. "Earth to Melanie." At the bell, she'd dash for the washroom, where she seemed to live between classes. I heard her in there once. I didn't need to see her white espadrilles pigeon-toed under the stall door to know who it was. Her voice was unmistakable, muffled though it was with a mouthful of hair. "Leab us nod indo dempation but deliber us from ebil . . ." She wore a D'Angelo Dry Cleaning sweatshirt every day. She had dozens.

At lunch, squeezed between Joyce Peyton and other girls, Melanie rolled her sandwich bread into little white balls between her fingers. Outside of class, nobody seemed to notice that she didn't talk much. I took my lunch to the bleachers, where the breeze brought the smell of cut grass and the sound of birds chatting in the trees. Even the cheerleaders' chants were kind of nice until I realized they were just another kind of prayer.

Hallelujah for home ec, for Mrs. Maxwell's ordered classroom, for the scrubbed linoleum and bleached aprons and shelves of gleaming Pyrex. It wasn't so bad being paired with Moody Miller. To everyone's surprise, he not only came to class but demonstrated actual ability. Who would have suspected him capable of such velvety hollandaise, such impossibly fluffy meringues? Mrs. Maxwell couldn't deny it, not even from Moody, whose eyes were usually bloodshot, if not half-closed, and who'd once asked where she kept the foods in aerosol cans. She made everyone gather around to watch him whisk things.

"How is it you know how to do this?" Mrs. Maxwell asked cautiously, the foundation of all she knew to be good and right resting on this pothead's answer.

"My mom doesn't cook much," was all Moody said.

To me, Moody admitted that he liked watching cooking shows. His favourite was *The Waltons*. "There are all these people," he said, "like kids and dogs, and everyone's always going in and out of the kitchen while the lady makes the food."

I told Moody that wasn't a cooking show. It was a drama about a family in rural Virginia during the Great Depression. I felt bad being the one to tell him, but I thought he had a right to know. Moody took it in stride. "That explains the long johns," he said.

I told Moody about *Mary Tyler Moore*. He said his mom watched it sometimes, but it gave him the willies. "You ever notice how that chick's hair never moves?" Moody flicked his own greasy bangs out of his face. He didn't mind wearing an apron, but he could not be coaxed into a hairnet. "I mean never. That's some freaky shit."

"You're right," I said, thinking about it. "That is freaky shit."

This was as deep as our conversations ever got. Most days I sat on my stool and watched Moody work. It restored some small faith in me to see a person enjoy himself so much with a set of measuring spoons. It was a lot like sitting at Mrs. Closter's kitchen island, without Carol there to point out how Jesus had fed the multitude with just two fish and five loaves of bread.

It may be true, as some have said, that things might have solidified here. Better still, courses might have corrected and life returned to its equilibrium. Carol might have come back to school, joined the yearbook committee, and discovered a real talent for writing snappy photo captions. I might have finally learned to feather my hair and gone on to cure cancer. But the textbook version of that year was already being written by men who had never set foot in a home ec classroom. We marched unwittingly toward events that had been put in motion long before the day Missy Carter stood in front of Rona Blumberg's class, shaking *The New York Times* at us.

"We can't sit here and pretend it's not happening," Missy said. "They'll send boys to die in Vietnam, but here in America life is precious? How does that work? Who's running this country? I mean, hello, is anybody home? We're too young to vote, but we have to live by their laws. When do *we* get to decide?"

Our teacher, dressed in a teal and silver sari, applauded enthusiastically. "What a fantastic opportunity to put our learning in action," she said. "Why don't we make posters? Posters are a wonderful way to communicate. Different posters could represent different points of view." We were studying colonial India. Somehow I couldn't see Gandhi sitting lotus on the cafeteria floor, filling in bubble letters with tempera paint.

"They'll just take them down," Missy said. "We've got to think bigger than posters. We've got to do something they can't destroy." She barked a list. Sit in, walk out, shut down, picket, boycott, rally, march. She'd gone to a special summer camp in Oregon where instead of archery and nature walks, she'd learned the fundamentals of civil disobedience and human rights law. "We should call ourselves something," she said.

"Students for Civil Rights?" someone suggested.

"Students Against Tyranny?"

"SAT?"

"Students Against Governmental Oppression and Tyranny?"

"Goodness," Miss Blumberg said. "I'd better write this down."

"What's the difference between oppression and tyranny?"

"Excellent question!" She wrote the words on the blackboard. "Can anyone explain the difference?"

Everyone joined in now, shouting ideas while Miss Blumberg scribbled furiously on the board.

Melanie hadn't come to class that day, and I was glad. I'd chosen my own seat by the window that year, away from the swimming pool vent, where I could enjoy if not actual freedom then at least the illusion of it. I stared out the window now, watching for the water planes. The front page of the newspaper that morning was devoted to the wildfires that had started in the forests south of town. They happened most years, blooming in late summer like fields of scarlet salvia. Carol would have said it was one more sign of the coming apocalypse, but really it was just some moron forgetting to put out a campfire. Below the fold was a small story about Troy Gainer. "Golden Boy Makes a Splash in Arizona." There were two pictures, a grey, pixelated blob in a pool and Troy's senior yearbook photo. Melanie had probably seen it too, over her bowl of cereal and under Mr. D'Angelo's bald spot. My mom, cutting out a McGovern article on the next page, had snipped Troy's grinning head clean off.

I didn't see any water planes yet, but there was someone on the school roof. The only person who ever went up there was Moody, but he was snoring in the seat in front me. Whoever it was dropped their head back and cupped both hands around their eyes. I pressed my face against the glass and tried to see what they were looking at, but all I saw was the same blue sky.

"Let's vote on it," Miss Blumberg said. "All those in favour of Students Against Governmental Oppression and Tyranny raise your hand."

I scanned the roof again, but the person was gone. A bird flew overhead, and I followed it as long as I could, tracing a flight path around trees and telephone wires, headed somewhere that wasn't here.

The school mailed out a memo the following week: "A number of students have expressed the desire to organize a special event here at the school. We believe that this is an excellent opportunity to create a dialogue around important issues of our time and demonstrate democracy in action. All points of view will be represented, and everyone is invited to participate." There was no mention of *Roe v. Wade*. Missy Carter's Students Against Governmental Oppression and Tyranny had become Rona Blumberg's Pageant of Ideas!

Mom thought it was a terrific idea. "I wish I'd done something like this when I was your age," she said. "I wish I'd been more involved." If we wanted to make buttons, she would lend the machine to us. *We. Us.* Me and all my civil liberties friends.

"I'm not really involved," I said. "It's just a thing some kids are doing."

"Why not? It sounds like a great idea. You know, after your father—" She paused and swallowed. We never talked about him, only around him, like a hole in the ground nobody had bothered to throw a board over. "Well, anyway, look at me now. I'm part of something. I'm contributing. I want to get out of bed every morning. George is the best thing that ever happened to your old mom." She'd started calling him that. *George.* "Why don't you give it a try? What's the worst that could happen? You might even enjoy yourself. How about that? That wouldn't be so awful."

"I was actually thinking I'd volunteer at the hospital," I said. "You know, feed some old people?"

"Really? Well, that's great, sweetie. I'll talk to Linda about it today." She put an arm around me and gave me a sideways squeeze. "Show up and join in—isn't that what they say?"

"No, Mom," I said. "Nobody says that."

The next day, Mom left a button for me on the kitchen table. It was the kind she slipped through the neighbours' mail slots, except instead of "Come home, America," this one said "World's Greatest Kid." I put it in my pocket with my lighter. Maybe one would cancel out the other.

I really had intended to volunteer at the hospital. While I rode the bus to Golden General after school that Friday, I pictured myself in a striped uniform with that button pinned to my blouse, pushing grateful old people around in wheelchairs. I saw myself feeding them with plastic spoons, fluffing their pillows, gently brushing their fine, silver hair. They would be happy to see me. They would tell me I was a nice girl, that I reminded them of their granddaughters. They would give me things—quarters, trinkets—which I'd leave on their nightstands after they'd fallen asleep. But when I got to the hospital, I couldn't go in. I couldn't get past the front doors. I stood on the black rubber mat while the automatic doors clunked open and shut. There were dead people in a hospital. Dead old people, dead parents, dead children, dead babies. I might see blood. Or worse. All I could think about was how many garbage

305

bins you'd need for a whole hospital. No button was worth that.

The water planes came as I rode the bus home. They flew in pairs, carrying water from the ocean to the fires south of town. You could hear them coming like thunder. I got off the bus and stood on the sidewalk to wait for them to pass overhead. As the planes roared by, I lifted a hand to the sky. They flew so low, you'd think you could almost touch them.

I was half a mile from home, but only a few blocks from the gas station. I hadn't gone for weeks. When I got there I saw a sign in the parking lot that hadn't been there before. In a couple of months it would be a Dunkin' Donuts, but that day it was still a gas station.

Jamie was stretched out on the hood of his yellow Pinto. "Did you see them?" he said, taking a toke from a joint. "Man, I love those planes."

"So what—you're a stoner now?" I said.

"Is that your way of saying you'd like to partake?"

"No, thanks."

Jamie lay back against the windshield and stared up at the sky. He jeans were less filthy than usual.

"Are you still moving rocks around?" I said.

"Nah, they promoted me. I move bricks now." Jamie took another toke and held it so long I thought he'd forgotten to breathe. "Troy's picture was in the paper today," he said.

"So was Nixon's," I said, and Jamie nodded.

The gas station guy came outside with two cans of Coke and gave them to us. He didn't mention the joint. He shrugged when we thanked him. "I'm a sucker for young love." We didn't correct him. Free pop was free pop.

Two more planes flew overhead. "I'm moving to Texas," the guy said, going back inside. "If I have to sweat my balls off all year, I want to do it while eating barbecue." I wondered if he knew how many hurricanes they got there.

"They're pretty brave, huh?" Jamie said.

"Gas station attendants?"

"Pilots."

I looked up at the empty sky. The planes were great steel beasts. It hadn't occurred to me that people were involved. Suddenly, I was worried about them.

"My cousin did it for a summer," Jamie said. "He wasn't a pilot, just ground crew. I was thinking I could do that. You don't need any special skills or anything."

"The Peshtigo wildfire killed twelve hundred people and destroyed a million acres of land," I said.

"Shit," Jamie said and lifted the joint to his mouth again.

In truth, the forest fires around Golden weren't that bad. A thousand acres of sugar pine and sycamore would probably go up in flames, but damage to home property was uncommon, casualties even more so. At the first whiff of smoke, our phone would start ringing, everyone clamouring to update their policies to include wildfires, but Dad had rarely paid out on one. Still, within a few days he'd be out there hosing down the house just like all the other crackpots. Mom was more philosophical about it. If the town burned down, she said it served us right. "Who lives in a desert, anyway? Who sees a hundred square miles of dirt and says, 'Now this is more like it'?"

"Some people think they're good for the forests," Jamie said. "They say they burn away what the forest doesn't need so new trees can grow. Nature finds its balance, right? Good and bad. Life and death. You believe that?"

"You're stoned," I said.

"I'm cool."

"Let me see your eyes." I moved closer. His eyes were more deeply set now, as if they were trying to see less of the world. I focused on his pupils—officially huge. He'd let his hair grow past his shoulders, but it still smelled like apples. "You're okay," I said.

"You're not too bad yourself."

We smiled at the ground and drank our pop.

Another plane rumbled over us. Jamie reached up to graze it with his fingertips. "Maybe I can learn to fly planes in the army," he said.

"Yeah, right," I said.

"I'll be eighteen next month."

"You're joking, right? Nobody signs up." It wasn't true, but it should've been.

"Maybe I want to protect my country."

"Protect it from what? We shouldn't even be over there."

"What am I doing here that's so great? Moving rocks and stacking bricks? Those pilots save people. They risk their lives. Maybe I'll get a medal or something."

"Maybe you'll get killed."

Jamie shrugged and took another toke.

The gas station guy was making a lot of noise inside. It sounded like he was tearing down the walls in there. It sounded like bombs going off. I stuck my hands in my pockets and found the button Mom had made me. *World's Greatest Kid.* I gave it to Jamie.

"What's this for?" he said.

"Just don't go to Vietnam," I said and went home. I probably didn't deserve my own old person anyway.

17

In January 1965, on a highway outside a town in British Columbia, a small avalanche forced four drivers to stop their cars. They idled a few minutes, deciding whether they should turn around. It could be they'd never heard of fault lines and shear zones, that the rubble on the asphalt was just something between them and home. While they thought about the time they were losing sitting there doing nothing, a second avalanche triggered a landslide. A hundred million tons of earth crashed down, enough to displace all the water in the lake below and strip the surrounding forest bare. Those four people died, of course. Two of them were never found. Their bodies are still there, buried under the rubble because they couldn't decide which way to go.

This was the only disaster story my mom ever told me. She said that my grandmother had called from Alberta to tell her about it. It was the only time she could remember hearing her mother cry. It was the largest landslide recorded in Canada. It's known as the Hope Slide. I always thought that meant something, that it was some kind of commentary on the nature of life, but it wasn't. Hope is just the name of the town.

I was discovering several benefits to not being friends with Carol Closter. One of them was sleeping in on Sundays and not worrying if I was damning my soul to hell for all eternity. I had done bad things that nobody cared much about and well-meaning things that hurt people. It seemed to me that we'd all be a lot safer if I just stayed in bed. I was contemplating the feasibility of doing so for the rest of the day when Mom knocked on my door. "You won't believe this," she said. "You've got to come outside."

We stood on the front step with our hands over our mouths and noses, trying not to breathe too deeply. The wildfire had spread north to the valley on the other side of the hills. From there, the gentlest wind carried the ash to Golden. Everything was soft and muted, coated in a fine grey snow. We stood on the step watching it fall. It would have been beautiful if you didn't know what it was.

Surfaces were dusted, swept, mopped, and covered. Rugs and crocheted wall hangings were beaten and put away. All schools and most businesses were closed for two days. But you couldn't escape the ash any more than you could your own senses. On the news they were telling everyone to stay inside, warnings that carried about as much weight in Golden as water restrictions. Our neighbours were outside at all hours, hosing down their cars and driveways. Sprinklers were spitting on every lawn but ours.

"Where is their sense of civic duty?" Mom said. "We're in a drought."

"It's always a drought," I said. "We live in a desert."

Mom shook her head. "This is exactly what's wrong with this country. Nobody wants to deal with reality. Nobody wants to see what's really going on. It's always easier to close your eyes."

"It keeps the ash out," I said, wiping mine with my sleeve.

"George says apathy is the death of democracy. George says doing nothing is the most dangerous thing we can do." Mom was helping organize the reception for the senator's visit to Golden. She'd spoken to one of his personal assistants on the phone, so now it was *George says this* and *George thinks that*. It reminded me of the way she used to speak for my dad, the other deaf-mute in our lives.

"George says people would care more if they participated in the political process." She looked at the Cardboard George on our front lawn as if he might have something to add. It was a new Cardboard George. There were a dozen more like it in the foyer. Every night, somebody stole the sign from the lawn. Every morning, Mom got the dented can of tomatoes out of the pantry and pounded another George into the grass. It seemed to me that everyone on our block was participating in the political process just fine.

Ash swirled prettily in the runoff around Mrs. Houston's slippered feet as she hosed off the lime tree in front of her house. Behind her, the lime leaves dripped, impossibly green and glossy against all that grey sky. Grey water streamed down the sidewalk and into our driveway. We followed it with our eyes. "We can't hose our problems away," Mom said. The Buick's windshield was thick with ash. We couldn't drive away from them either. When Mrs. Houston was done with her tree, she dragged her hose across our lawn. "You're welcome to it, Elaine. I have another one out back." Mrs. Houston got started on her azaleas. Mom looked down at the hose coiled sinisterly in her arms.

"I give up," she said.

"Promises, promises," I said.

When school reopened, hand-painted banners announcing Miss Blumberg's *Pageant of Ideas!* hung on every wall. A day later, someone tore them all down. The day after that, more went up. "They won't silence us this time," Missy Carter said, storming the hall with a roll of newsprint under one arm, thrusting a handful of paintbrushes in the air.

Mr. Galpin, suddenly beside me, asked me to step into his office for a moment.

"I didn't do it," I said, hovering in his doorway. It might have been my imagination, but I thought I smelled booze.

"What didn't you do?"

I tipped my head back toward the hall. "Participate in the dialogue."

"Oh that." He scratched at his neck under his collar. His unattended stubble had become a patchy beard. "I'll leave that to the poster police."

Mr. Galpin settled behind his desk and motioned for me to sit. "I wanted to speak to you about Miss Closter, actually. She's missed a bit of school."

"It's probably the ash," I said. "Her asthma's pretty bad. She's allergic to the world, basically." Mr. Galpin nodded slowly. I didn't actually know why Carol wasn't at school. The truth was, I hadn't even noticed. I hadn't torn down Missy's posters, so I assumed she had.

"Well, let's hope that's all it is," he said. "I wouldn't want her to fall too far behind. Junior year can be a tough nut. It's normal to feel overwhelmed, isn't it?"

"I guess so." I didn't know how much further Carol would fall behind seeing as she rarely went to class to begin with, but Mr. Galpin seemed pretty worried.

"If you think of anything she might be having trouble with, if there's anything I could do—well, I'd like her to know that she has a friend."

"Okay," I said and stood up to go. But Mr. Galpin leaned back in his chair and kept talking. I figured he didn't have anywhere better to be either.

"I suppose this business with the posters is to be expected," he said. "Some people aren't happy with the idea. I can't say it's the sort of thing I generally lean toward—better to let sleeping dogs lie, I've found. But some parents have voiced their support. And parents, let me assure you, do not voice their support. What do you think about it?"

"I think you have a really hard job," I said.

He smiled a little. "Harder than some, not as hard as most. But I think you're right. There might not be any clear answers here, which is more often the case than not, I'm afraid."

He scratched his neck. There was that smell again. My dad had smelled the same way on Sunday mornings sometimes. I hated that smell. Even more, I hated to think of Mr. Galpin drinking alone in his empty house.

"Why isn't there?" I said. "I mean, there's an answer key in the back of my math book. Why isn't there an answer key for stuff we actually need to know?"

"That's a very good question. I suppose some would say the Bible is a sort of answer key."

"Oh," I said, trying not to sound disappointed. "Sure."

"I like to think of myself as a man of science, Miss Fisher, but I don't think it precludes me from believing there's something out there that we can't yet see or understand. Believing is one of man's basic needs. It's a form of hope. Even science requires hope. We don't get far in this life without it."

"Maybe it depends on what you believe in," I said.

He frowned a little. "And what do you believe in, Miss Fisher?"

"I'm not sure," I said and stood to go again. "The jury's still out."

He scratched his neck again, then loosened his tie. "Do you know about the canaries in the coal mines?" he said.

"Yeah, sure." My dad had told me about how after an explosion or fire, miners took those delicate birds down into the mines with them. Canaries are highly sensitive to toxic gases. If they showed any sign of distress, it was back up to the surface, pronto. "They use them to tell if there's gas."

"Correct. The interesting thing is, most people assume the

birds die from the gas. I suppose sometimes they do, that's true, but the miners don't want them to. The miners have those birds for years, you see. They're like pets. They love those canaries. I think that's why it works. They're both looking out for each other, you see—man and bird."

"I didn't know that," I said. My dad never told me that part of the story.

"Most people don't." Mr. Galpin yanked at his tie until it hung loosely around his neck, a ready noose.

I took my chance and moved to the door.

"You know, perhaps you should," Mr. Galpin said as I turned the doorknob.

"Sorry?"

He leaned back a little more in his chair and shut his eyes. "Participate in the dialogue, Miss Fisher. Perhaps you should."

I sat at the back of the auditorium that Thursday, wondering what the hell I was doing there. Most of the kids around me looked like they were thinking the same thing. Posters or not, Rona Blumberg had packed the place with the promise of extra credit to any of her students who participated. It said so on the flyers Missy had handed out. Students for Social Harmony Through Bribery.

Miss Blumberg was trying to get a brainstorm going. "Expand your minds," she told us, smiling under her blue beret. "The sky's the limit—within reason, of course. Our goal is to represent the full spectrum of voices. We don't want to make anyone feel uncomfortable. Every point of view is valid and valuable. There is no such thing as a bad idea in this room!"

"What about that beret?" someone cracked.

"If you're here, you keep it positive, okay? There's no extra credit for negativity."

A hand shot up near the front. "How about lip-syncing a folk song?"

"That's great. I love that. That's exactly what I'm talking about. What are you thinking—Bob Dylan? Joan Baez?"

Kids called out their favourite songs. Miss Blumberg nodded encouragingly while Missy wrote them down on a clipboard. I watched the side door, half expecting Carol to bust through it any minute, pocket Bible in hand, shouting scripture and calling everyone communists. This was exactly the kind of thing she loved to hate.

"We could do a skit," Joyce Peyton said.

"Okay," Miss Blumberg said. "I like that. That's good. A skit about what?"

"Freedom?"

"Okay . . . I think we're getting there . . ."

"Choices? The freedom to make your own choices and be yourself?"

"Choices. Yes, okay, choices. Good. That's the direction we want to go."

"What does that mean?" I said.

"What's that?" Miss Blumberg said, squinting to find the source of disruption.

"I was asking what that means—choices."

"Choices. Freedom. Free will. Can you hear me back there? Maybe you could move up a little closer. Don't be shy."

"What if you don't have a choice?" I said.

"We all have choices," Joyce said, turning around in her seat. When she saw me, her eyes narrowed. "This is America, in case you forgot."

"That's right," Miss Blumberg said. "That's why we're here. That's what we're talking about. Choices. Perspectives. Great. Okay, we've got a folk song, a skit—what else? Let's keep those creative juices flowing. I want to hear from everyone."

"What's so great about having choices?" I said. "Maybe you have a million choices, but that's just a million chances to make the wrong choice. One wrong choice can ruin every-thing. So you can choose to stay in your car or turn around and drive the other way, but either way, you could still get buried under all that dirt."

Everyone was looking at me. I had gone to school with these people my whole life and I still didn't recognize any of their faces.

Miss Blumberg squinted in my direction. "Who *is* that?"

"Pyro freak!" Joyce shouted as the auditorium door slammed behind me.

I had no idea where I was going. I thought about heading to the library to look up coal mining and see if what Mr. Galpin said was true, or maybe I'd bury myself under a set of encyclopedias and wait for the end of time. As I rounded the corner, there was Melanie, struggling with one of Missy's newly hung banners. It was still wet and stapled in a million places. There was paint all over her hands and clothes. I didn't know why she wanted it down, but I knew why I did. I walked over and grabbed a corner. The banner released and crumpled to the floor. We stood staring at it.

"Have you noticed how nobody around here ever says what they mean?" she said. "We're all hypocrites."

"Not all of us."

Melanie nodded. "Would you tell her I'm sorry? For last year? Freak or not, nobody deserves that."

"You could tell her yourself."

"But I won't," she said, wiping her hands on her sweatshirt, beautiful streaks of blue, red, and green. "See what I mean? Hypocrites."

I wrestled the paper noisily into a ball nearly as big as I was. Then Melanie went one way, and I went another, through a door that led, among other places, to the furnace room.

I walked to the gas station but it wasn't there anymore. It was just a hole in the ground where a gas station used to be.

Jamie's car was parked on the street. He was sitting behind the wheel, staring at the hole as if he'd lost his best friend down it. I dropped to my knees in front of the Pinto. "God damn you," I said, beating the ground. "God damn you all to hell."

Jamie laughed. I got up and walked over to him. I was covered in ash. My throat was dry with it.

"Aren't you working today?"

"I quit. Today was my last day."

"Me too," I said. "Can we drive somewhere? I don't care where."

He leaned across the passenger seat and pushed open the door. As I slid in, I saw the button I gave him stuck into the dash.

Ash had collected on the sides of the road like snowdrifts. We kept the windows rolled up to keep out what we could. Jamie turned the radio on, then off again. We cruised by the new golf course being built into the hills, and Jamie surprised me by knowing something about skid-steers and backhoes. We saw the gap left by the old bridge they'd finally blown up to make room for a new one. "That soil won't hold anything," he said. "They might as well backfill it and call it a day." We whipped past the stunted, shuddering palm trees out to the Joshua fields where the old-man branches shook their gnarled fists at the sky. When we reached the town limits, Jamie pulled onto the shoulder and parked between the two signs. One welcomed us to Golden. The other thanked us for visiting. As with most things, what you saw depended on which side you were already on.

There was nothing around but asphalt and road cut, that endless wall of red rock that ran alongside the highway where it sliced through the hills. Geologists drove up from the city sometimes to read its sacred layers. You'd see them standing by the side of the road in orange vests, gazing lovingly at their core samples. But that day it was just me and Jamie.

On the other side of the highway, Golden spread out like a monopoly board. It was about as good as views got in a town with a six-storey height restriction. We sat on the hood of the Pinto and pointed out things we recognized. You could almost make out our school and the hospital, but not individual houses, not anything you'd want to call home. In the distance, the wildfire smoke caught in the trees like hair on a brush. I felt bad knowing that somewhere out there was an old person with knots in her hair.

"The view's better when it's dark," Jamie said.

"It's nice now," I said, wondering who he brought there at night.

He took a joint out of his jacket and got it going. I stared at the glowing tip, a tiny wild fire.

"I want to try it," I said, taking the joint and holding it like a cigarette.

Jamie laughed. "Maybe don't inhale."

I inhaled anyway. It felt like somebody was scraping my throat with a melon baller. When I was done coughing, I took another drag. Maybe everything hurts the first time.

We passed the joint back and forth, not talking. Every couple of minutes a car drove by, coated with ash, windshield streaked with wiper fluid.

"My dad used to spray our whole house down with a garden hose," I said.

"I thought only crackpots did that."

"That's what my mom said. She'd say, 'How about if you just spray down your half?'" I started laughing, then I couldn't stop. I was laughing so hard my heart hurt.

"That's enough for you, Amelia Earhart. Maybe I should take you home."

When I shook my head, my brain sloshed around inside my skull. "Don't harsh my buzz," I said.

My fingertips were tingling. My ears were getting hot. I could see the scent of ash and motor oil and taste Jamie's apple shampoo. I could feel him start to smile at something. I could smell his smile. I could hear his dimple. That dimple was calling out to me. I'm not really a dimple, it said. I'm a button. I reached out and pressed it.

"Robin," he said. The dimple was gone. I had wrecked it. Jamie licked his fingers and put out the joint, tucked it into the pocket of his jean jacket. He pushed himself off the hood of the car.

I followed him across the highway to the road cut. When I stood beside him, he put his hands on the rock, read it with his palms. His fingernails were clean and trim. I wondered how he kept them like that, moving bricks around all day.

"These lines are made by the shifts in the earth," he said. "Cutting into this rock is like cutting into a person and seeing everything that's happened to them."

"Like the rings in the redwoods," I said.

"Yeah. Just like that."

My head was swimming. I put a hand on the rock to steady myself. A piece crumbled off in my hand. Everything was falling apart.

"We should go there," I said. "To the redwoods. I've never seen them. We should go there right now, before they're gone too."

Jamie shook his head. "It's too late."

"We can drive all night," I said. "We can take turns. I failed the test, but I know how."

He shook his head again. I leaned in and kissed him. His mouth was warm. I wanted to climb inside it and take a nap. I wanted to disappear inside that kiss. Jamie put his hands on my shoulders. I thought he was pulling me closer, but he was pushing me away.

"What the hell?" he said.

"Did I do it wrong?"

"Your timing sure is crap, you know that?" Jamie shoved his hands into his jean pockets. He didn't say anything for a long time. It was starting to freak me out.

"Why did you quit your job?" I said.

"I told you," he said. "I'm going to Vietnam."

"What?" I said. "What?"

"I couldn't stand waiting around doing nothing. Guys are dying over there, Robin. Kids my age."

"Some of us are dying right here too," I said.

Jamie shook his head. "I shouldn't have left you there that night. I should've broken the fucking door down."

I could hear my heart thumping inside my chest. It sounded like someone pounding on a door. Like footsteps on carpet, back and forth. Like a clock ticking. I put my hands over my ears, but it didn't help. Cars slowed as they passed us. Cars sped by. Time was spinning, rushing backwards, peeling away the layers of rock. I started crying. It was different from laughing. Crying hurt in a whole new way.

I ran into the road, flapping my arms at the cars. An old lady stopped and rolled down her window. "Are you okay? Did that boy do something?" I meant to shake my head, but I nodded instead. "It's not their fault," she said as I got in her car. "They're just made that way."

Jamie shouted my name as we drove away. Tears were Hope-sliding down my face. I covered my ears again and said the words in my head over and over so I'd know they were true. *He's going to Vietnam. He's going to Vietnam.*

He was the third boy I'd ever kissed.

The old lady drove with both feet. My whole life felt like that car ride. Stop, start, stop, start. She insisted on taking me all the way home. It was the Christian thing to do, she said. By the time we got to Carol's house, I wasn't high anymore, just nauseous.

Carol's little brother was in the front yard, pretending to water the flowerbed with a red jerry can. I sat on the grass and watched. I wanted to lie down and sleep, but I'd promised Mr. Galpin I'd look after his canary.

Carol's brother tugged on my sleeve. "Knock, knock," he said.

"Who's there?"

"Orange you glad," he said and fell on the ground, laughing. I leaned over and ruffled the little guy's hair. Having a brother wouldn't have been so bad, I thought.

The front door opened. Mrs. Closter was dusted with flour. There were marks on her forehead where she'd wiped at it, ghostly fingerprints on her dark green blouse. "Carol's not feeling well," she said.

"I have something to give her. For school."

Mrs. Closter studied me for a minute. I was covered in grass clippings and ash. I didn't even have my book bag. Then I remembered the flyer crumpled up in my back pocket. I held it out. Mrs. Closter read it and sighed. "All right, dear," she said. "Just, please, take off your shoes."

Carol was lying diagonally across her purple bedspread with her face mashed in Stuffed Jesus. She wasn't wearing a hat, and the lamp cast a small ring of light on her strawberry-blond curls. Otherwise, the room was dark. She lifted her head and sniffled. "What are you doing here?" Her eyes and nose were pink from crying, but the rest of her face was as pale and puffy as uncooked dough.

"I came to see if you were okay. You haven't been to school."

"I hate that place. I hate this whole stupid town. Nobody even cares whether I live or die."

"That's not true. I care."

"Why should you? I'm a big, stupid joke. Everyone laughs at me because I'm a joke. God's probably up there laughing too. Ha ha ha ha ha!"

"You're not a joke, Carol. Don't say that."

"I didn't save a single baby. Not even Melanie's. I can't do anything."

"My mom says the war will probably end for real soon," I said. "At least they'll stop killing babies in Vietnam."

"Who cares about gook babies?" she said.

"You don't mean that."

She took a tissue from the box on her nightstand and sat up to blow her nose. "I can't figure out what I'm supposed to do. I'm supposed to do something, but what is it?"

"You could do this," I said, holding out the rumpled flyer. If it would make Carol stop crying, I'd get up on that stage and recite a prayer myself.

Carol took the flyer, hugging Stuffed Jesus as she read. She studied me suspiciously. "You know, sometimes you're so stupid I want to scream."

"And sometimes you're so mean I want to punch you in the nose."

Her eyes widened. Her mouth made its little o. Then she laughed.

"You really are horrible sometimes," I said.

She stopped laughing and blew her nose again. "I know, I'm sorry. I don't know why I'm like that. You're the only person I can even stand to talk to." She grabbed my arm with both hands and tugged me down beside her on the bed. "Don't go yet, okay? You can hold Stuffed Jesus."

She moved over to make room for me. I wanted to go home, but more than that I wanted to sleep. I'd never felt so tired in my life. I had to sit down just to keep myself from falling. Stuffed Jesus was damp.

"Do you know why we moved here?" Carol said.

I shook my head. It was full of ash.

"I was called, Robin."

"Called," I repeated. I thought she meant on the telephone. I imagined Governor Reagan ringing her up, saying, "We need you in California, Carol. We've got a real situation down here." My body was so heavy, I sank into the mattress. I was practically on the floor.

"By God," she said. "I was called by God."

"Right," I said and closed my eyes. Just for a minute, then I'd go.

"Nothing's turning out the way it's supposed to," she said.

"It never does."

I heard the crinkle of paper being smoothed, a nose being blown. Then Carol snuggled up against me, small and warm. "You smell funny," she said as I floated away.

I dreamed of birds, hundreds of them, thousands, their wings tickling me everywhere, my arms, my face, the world a bright flurry of yellow. I reached up and tried to catch them. They stretched and darkened, whirring around me, thickening the air until the sun was gone and the sky was black with wings. I was buried under them, under the ground, inside the earth. I covered my face. My hands were wings.

A buzzer sounded. The birds scattered like buckshot. When I opened my eyes, Carol and I were coiled around each other, arms and legs entwined. Her hair was in my mouth, her thumb in hers.

Stuffed Jesus was on the floor. I lifted her arms off me and nestled him in beside her. Then I stood in the doorway for a minute and watched her sleep. She seemed so delicate lying there, like something you put on the top of a Christmas tree. It was hard to believe so much hurt and sadness could fit into such a little body. But bodies are good at keeping secrets, especially from themselves. I turned out the light and shut the door.

"Oh," Mrs. Closter said when she saw me. "You're still here."

"Carol fell asleep."

"Will you be joining us for dinner, dear?" It didn't sound

like an invitation. The oven timer was still ringing behind her. Mrs. Closter frowned, sniffing the air. "The biscuits!"

She leapt at the oven door and yanked out the tray. A dozen hockey pucks flew across the room. Mrs. Closter sunk to her knees on the linoleum and started to cry.

"You can scrape that black right off," I said. "My mom does it all the time."

Carol's little brother pulled on my sleeve. "I wish you were my sister. Carol's the meanest person in the whole entire world."

"Don't talk that way about your sister," Mrs. Closter said, sniffling into her apron.

"She's not my sister!" he yelled and stormed out of the room. "I'm a Martian! I'm from outer space!"

I remembered when Carol had told him that. He seemed happy about it now, anyway.

"Mrs. Closter? Why did you move to Golden?"

She glanced up through the smoke, head tilted in that June Cleaver way I loved, red eyes glistening. The timer was still ringing. "Mr. Closter was transferred, dear. Why do you ask?"

The Buick was in the driveway when I got home, but there was no Cardboard George on the lawn. Mom had conceded the territory, but not the principle. Now Cardboard George smiled at me from behind every window, where he would stay until

Election Day. "Your mother finally found the perfect man." Vera had told me. "He couldn't leave if he wanted to."

My plan to stay in bed forever was looking pretty good again. I definitely didn't want to be awake for any more of this day. When I reached my room, Mom was sitting on my bed with my shoebox in her lap.

"I'd like to talk to you about this calmly," she said. "Like adults." The line was thick between her eyes.

"You went through my stuff?"

"I bought you a dress for George's reception, and I wanted to make sure you had the right shoes." She spoke slowly, measuring her words. "I thought these might be pumps."

The dress was hanging on my closet door, a length of navy under a plastic sheath.

"I'm not going to the reception," I said.

"What do you mean you're not going? Of course you're going."

"They're not going to end the war, Mom. They're lying. Nixon's lying. McGovern's lying. You said it yourself—they're all a bunch of con men. Boys are dying and nobody's doing anything. Now we're supposed to ham it up for the cameras? You go right ahead. Be my guest. But I'm not going to be part of their circus act."

"You're sixteen. You don't know what you're talking about.

You don't know how the world works yet. I'm thirty-six and I barely know."

"That's obvious," I said.

Mom raised an eyebrow to let me know parental guilt wasn't going to save me this time. "You want to talk about lying, young lady? Tell me about this." She gestured with the shoebox, rattling the lighters. "I'm listening. I'm all ears. I'd really like to hear what you have to say."

"Why start now?"

She looked me over, stopping to frown at my feet. I'd forgotten my shoes at the Closters'.

"Where are your shoes?" she said. "Why are you always losing your shoes? What's going on here? Oh, God. Are you doing drugs? Robin, are you on the pot?"

I tried, unsuccessfully, not to laugh.

"You think this is funny? Because I don't think this is funny. First, I get a call from your vice-principal—"

"Mr. Galpin called? What did you say?"

I could feel the tears pressing at the backs of my eyes. That's why Mr. Galpin was so nice to me. Carol was just an excuse. I was the freak he was worried about. I took a deep breath and sat on my chair. My knees almost hit my chin. It was a child's chair and too small for me now, but at least I had one. Nobody had hauled it to the curb when I wasn't looking.

"I told him we had everything under control," Mom said. "But we don't, do we?"

I shook my head slowly. At least that was working again.

"I'm worried about you, honey. This isn't about the campaign or volunteering at the hospital. You don't want to do that? Fine. Maybe you're a Republican now. Terrific. School isn't your strong suit? That's okay. That's not the end of the world. What's not okay is you floating along, not caring about anything. If you don't decide for yourself what you want, other people will decide for you. Life will decide for you. I was like that when I was young, and I think that had a lot to do with how things turned out. If I'd cared about something—I mean, really cared—things might have been very different. Do you hear what I'm saying, Robin? You've got to decide for yourself who you want to be. You're not a child anymore."

I turned to the window, wondering when that had happened and why hadn't anyone told me.

"I'm sorry I ruined your life," I said.

"Isn't that supposed to be my line?"

I could feel the tears coming again. "I ruined everything."

"Oh," she said softly and reached out to touch my knee. She still wore her wedding ring. She didn't soak it in Alka-Seltzer every week like she used to, but the diamonds glittered all the same. "Is this about a boy?" she said. "Is that it? Is there a boy?"

"There's no boy," I said. "Why does it always have to be a boy?"

"Then what? Tell me."

I shook my head. Where would I start? Troy? The fire? She didn't even know who Carol was. I'd kept so many things hidden for so long, it was easier to leave them that way. If I were a canary, we'd be in real trouble.

"I'm just tired," I said. "I won't smoke anymore."

"All right, then."

We sat in silence. There was nothing else to do. The silence crystallized between us, solid as that diamond ring.

"I love you," she said.

"Okay," I said.

She patted my knee and stood up, taking my shoebox of lighters with her. I heard the front door open and watched through the window as she walked to the garbage can sitting empty at the curb. She stood there for a while, garbage can lid in one hand, shoebox in the other. Ash swirled around her as she tipped the box into the can. Did she see her own silver lighter among them? If so, she didn't let it show. The lighters rained down like cupcake sprinkles, pink, white, yellow, blue.

I told myself that this was it. The half-empty Bic in my pocket would be my last. There was nothing left to burn, anyway. I was actually feeling pretty good about it until I put my hand in my pocket and found nothing but lint. Mom tossed the empty box in the garbage can and put the lid back on. Cardboard George smiled at everyone, pleased, as always, with the way things were turning out.

18

We communicated through notes. *Please water the ferns. We're running low on milk. Have a nice day.* It wasn't that we were too angry to talk. We just weren't sure how to start.

Then Mom slid the newspaper across the table one morning. She stood at the kitchen window and lit a cigarette as I read. There was Governor Reagan on the front page, outfitted in state-of-the-art protective gear and surrounded by the brave men of the Golden Fire Department. Wildfires, it turned out, are a very good publicity op. Politicians were shaking hands with firemen all over the state that fall.

"McGovern isn't coming," Mom said. "There's no competing with a Republican in a fireman's hat."

"Sorry," I said.

"Well, anyway, you're off the hook. No more circus." She stared out at the driveway for a while, forgetting to smoke. Ash collected at the end of her cigarette, a long, grey finger pointing at the dirty dishes. "At least I kept the receipt for that dress."

When Vera Miller realized she wasn't going to meet the next president of the United States, she promptly abandoned McGovern's divorced women's club for an actual divorced women's club held twice a week in the basement of a woman named Trish. She'd been disappointed by enough Republican men. She didn't need to add a whole other political party to the list. But Mom wouldn't give up. She went door to door. She made her calls. She stuck George's smiling face in the Buick's back window and drove him around town.

A short typewritten letter came a week later from the real George McGovern. It thanked Mom for her contribution and asked her to keep up their important work. Citizens like her were the hope for America, he wrote. He couldn't do it without her. "It's a form letter," she said. "Everybody got one." And then, "Do you think the signature's real?"

She held the letter close to her face to scrutinize the handwriting, and in that moment I saw her at some future date, in bifocals with frizzy blue hair, clipping newspaper articles about pension reform and bursitis. I saw her all alone in this house, cats twining her slippered feet, the sole member of her own not-quite-divorced women's club.

"Give it here," I said. "I'll run it under the tap and see if it smudges."

"Don't you dare!" She lifted the letter high in the air, her face lit with laughter. The old woman vanished. That would never be her. Mom hated cats.

She stopped laughing. "There's something I've been meaning to tell you," she said.

"You have tuberculosis."

"What?"

"Wandering spleen?"

"You aren't supposed to read the files."

"They're everywhere. I glance."

"Mildred wants me to take on more responsibility, that's all." There would be a small modification to her title, she explained, and a modest raise.

"You mean a promotion?" I said.

"I suppose you could call it that."

"That's not as bad as tuberculosis."

Mom shook her head. "I haven't the foggiest idea why they'd want to promote me."

"Usually a promotion means you're good at something."

"Well, yes," she said. "I suppose it does."

Mom stuck the letter to the fridge with a magnet.

"The hope for America," I said.

There was a hint of line between her brows. A questioning grin twitched at the corners of her mouth. It was the same expression she had when she drove now, not happy or unhappy, simply astounded by the unexpected hairpin turns life could take. "Assistant manager, records and billing," she said and let the grin win.

The following weekend brought the final phase to the Great Fisher Purge. This time I helped. We gritted our teeth and said little as we toiled, felt the significance of our actions in our muscles and bones. A few hours later, the contents of the pool house squatted at the curb. From there, two men from the Salvation Army loaded everything into a big white van. They wore dark blue trousers and shirts. One had a cross tattooed on his forearm. Holy garbage men. When they were done, the one with the tattoo shook Mom's hand. "I'm sorry for your loss," he said. "Thank you," she said, trying not to smile. The merry widow. "Thank you very much."

As the white van pulled away, a blue truck arrived, two men in dirty T-shirts and jeans, tools slung on leather belts around their hips. They used sledgehammers to get it started. The rest they did with their yellow-gloved hands and steel-toed feet. They pushed and prodded. They jumped up and down. If they were little boys, they would have been having the time of their lives, but because this was their job they wore the grim faces of men who had seen too many things destroyed. The thin wood snapped and crunched under their boots. The sounds were sickening, like the shell of a beetle being crushed under your shoe. Slowly, slat by slat, it folded in on itself, the little house that Dad built reduced to firewood. They carted away everything except the hole in the ground.

Mom shook her head at the hole. "Happy now?" she said and went inside. Mrs. Houston started to say something to me from her side of the fence, but there was nothing to say. It wasn't a funeral, it just felt like one.

I went inside to get something to eat. I wasn't hungry, but there was something gnawing at me and I couldn't think what else to do with that. Mom was at the kitchen table, flipping through the college's spring catalogue that had come in the mail the week before. I'd thought she'd thrown it away. There was an unlit cigarette in her hand. Lately, she'd been forgetting to light them.

"We need to fill up that hole," I said.

"I'm working on it," she said and turned another page.

Growing up in a town that was in love with the appearance of progress, I'd seen more holes in the ground than anyone ever should. Lately, I'd started taking the long way home from school so I could pass by the hole where the gas station used to be. I wanted to tell Jamie that I'd made a royal mess of things, and if he would just not go to Vietnam maybe I could fix some of them. But he was never there. It was already November. The water planes were long gone and the birds had come back. Sparrows, thrushes, finches, towhees. There were dozens of them most days, hundreds sometimes, circling and swooping overhead, drawing their Spirographs all over the sky. I tried not to make too much out it. A kid at school with an older brother said that Jamie Finley was in basic training somewhere on the coast, but I liked to think that maybe he'd found a new construction site where they needed bricks moved around. I heard Missy Carter tell Miss Blumberg that they should invite him to the pageant. Maybe he could say a few inspirational words. I pictured him on the stage, wearing one of his dad's ties, a live version of the boys whose graduation photos would sit up there on easels come December. I stopped taking the long way home after that.

Carol still hadn't come back to school. I didn't see Melanie around much anymore either. Everybody I'd ever cared about was MIA. The only one I could count on was the person on the school roof. They were up there almost every day. I waved from Mrs. Maxwell's window once, but they didn't wave back. Whoever it was, I guess they had better things to look at up there.

Down below, Mr. Galpin and the janitor were peeling paper pumpkins and witches off the front doors. Behind me,

Moody was beating egg whites while Mrs. Maxwell explained to everyone else why it was important not to overwork the meringue. I couldn't bring myself to watch anymore. There was something sad about all the eggs we'd used in that room, all the breadcrumbs and flour, all the butter and lard. So much of it ended up in the trash. The whole place was starting to smell like garbage left in the sun, but I was the only one who seemed to notice. I thought maybe I was developing an allergy to home ec that had nothing to do with peanuts.

"See those lovely peaks?" Mrs. Maxwell said. "Very nice, Moody. Very nice."

My stomach didn't think it was very nice. As it twisted and flipped, I untied my apron, hung it on the hook near the door, and went in search of fresher air.

There was a Euclidean geometry to getting up to the roof, an intricate choreography of foot and hand placements to scale the wall of old pallets at the back of the school that served as makeshift stairs. Being neither dancer nor mathlete, I wasn't doing too well. My arms shook as the pallets groaned and creaked beneath me. Suddenly, a hand appeared before my grunting face, bitten pink polish on its fingertips. Melanie bent over the edge of the roof, her hair falling toward me like rain.

"You?" I said.

"Come on. I can't hang around here all day."

Her hand dangled, open and waiting. My own was white-knuckling a dirty length of pipe. I took hold of hers and let it pull me up.

I have read that the refurbished Reagan High has a green roof, replete with living walls, solar panels, and grey water collection for the sustainable herb garden managed by the Farm-to-Table Food Club. But back then it was, like all school roofs before it, a heat-absorbing tarpapered slab littered with wizened apple cores and tennis balls. Someone had rigged a canopy of golf umbrellas in the middle and laid two old gym mats underneath. Melanie settled on one of them, cross-legged, and picked up an old library copy of *Teen*.

"What are you doing up here?" I said.

"I wait for Moody," she said. "He brings me food."

"I thought Moody Miller was a loser."

"Who said that?"

"You did."

"Huh." Melanie adjusted one of the golf umbrellas so she was in the sun and lay back on the mat. The mound of her stomach pushed up between her sweatshirt and unbuttoned jeans.

"Melanie!"

"Oh yeah."

"But I thought . . ."

She shook her head. "I chickened out. I was in the paper

gown and everything. I guess I'm a good Catholic girl after all."

I wondered what Carol would think about Melanie's baby. Something told me it wouldn't make her happy. I also suspected that whatever made Carol unhappy didn't have anything to do with this.

I sat beside Melanie on the mat. "What do your parents think?"

"I thought I'd wait and tell them at Christmas, see how well the old Virgin Birth story works the second time around."

"If it was good enough for Mary," I said.

Melanie put her hand on her belly and tapped her fingers lightly like she was doing Morse code. Her boobs were huge now. I remembered how she used to sleep on her back because her sister told us that made them grow bigger.

"What about Troy?" I said.

"What about him?" She gave me a look and that was all we ever said about that. It was all we had to.

"Are you scared?" I said.

She shrugged. "Terrified. But what are you gonna do? If it wasn't for Moody, I'd probably jump off this roof right now. Don't laugh, but I think I might love him. I mean really *love* him. Isn't that funny? Me and Moody."

I pictured Moody in a grey jacket with one of those joke tuxedo T-shirts underneath and started laughing.

"It's not that funny," she said.

"I was actually thinking about Jamie Finley," I said, and laughed even harder. "He's going to Vietnam, you know."

"That's not funny either."

"I know it's not funny. It's the opposite of funny." But I was laughing so hard I could barely get the words out, so hard I could hardly breathe. Then I was crying, crying and not breathing.

"What's with you?" Melanie studied me, arms crossed tightly over her giant boobs. Her mouth fell open. "Oh," she said. "Oooooooh."

Her belly was as hard as a basketball when she hugged me. I hadn't been expecting that. More surprising was how tightly she squeezed, how she dug her fingers into my shoulders so fiercely it almost hurt. Something loosened inside me at the pressure and I finally let go, finishing what I'd started at the road cut, all those hurts and sorrys pouring out of me. Melanie held me even tighter.

"I hate this place," she said. "I really do. I hate this school, I hate this town, I hate everything. I wish someone would blow it all to kingdom come."

"Don't look at me," I said.

But she did. She pulled back just enough to look at me and smile.

———

The Monday before the 1972 presidential election, Mr. Jensen across the street lost his dog, a half-blind beagle that was always running away. "Here, Buddy!" he called. "Here, boy!" I heard him clapping and whistling as he walked down the street. It sounded like the world's saddest round of applause. I thought of the Pageant of Ideas! When Missy Carter handed out the final program the week before, Carol's name had been on it. *Carol Closter—A Dramatic Interpretation of the 23rd Psalm.* I wasn't surprised. If there was a way for Carol to humiliate herself, she'd take it. Not that I needed another reason to skip it, but I'd seen Carol humiliate herself enough already. "Here, Buddy!" Clap, clap, clap. I shut my window. Some people just didn't know when to quit.

It wasn't eight o'clock yet, but Mom was already up and dressed and burning a pot of coffee. She'd had her hair cut just above her shoulders. She'd told the hairdresser that she needed something sensible that she wouldn't have to fuss over, but I thought the way it bounced and swished when she moved was glamorous. She'd even bought a new suit. Her blouse had a small ink stain on it, but she said it was fine, she'd keep her jacket on. It was her first day as Golden General's assistant manager, records and billing.

"What do you think?" Mom said. "Too much?"

"You look beautiful," I said, because she did.

She smiled softly. "So do you," she said. I glanced down to make sure I hadn't accidentally put on a dress. Ripped jeans, faded rainbow T-shirt. When I looked up again, Mom was ruining her mascara. Her words were choked. "You're just growing up so fast."

"I was going to say the same thing about you."

She laughed and swiped under her eyes. Instead of her wedding ring, a pale strip of skin circled her finger. I didn't know when she'd taken it off, but I'd have bet good money it was sitting in a thrift store display case somewhere next to the gold-plated tie clips and cultured pearls.

I stood on the front step to wave Mom off. As she backed the Buick out of the driveway, Mr. Jensen whistled and clapped across the street. I joined in now. A standing ovation, long overdue.

Mrs. Houston came outside to see what the commotion was, and I told her about the missing dog. She said the Fosters down the block were missing a cat. I scanned our street. There were no animals anywhere, no tabbies climbing fences, no birds in the sky, only a low November sun and the cozy scent of burning leaves. Mrs. Houston pulled the two halves of her cardigan together. "Do you think it's an earthquake?"

My dad always said pets could predict an earthquake about as well as they could pick winning lottery numbers. I wasn't so sure. If canaries could detect poisonous gas, why couldn't a beagle sense an earthquake? But I was trying to be more optimistic about things.

"That's just an old wives' tale," I said.

"Well, I'm an old wife," Mrs. Houston said and went inside to wrap up her crystal.

When I got to school, I went straight up to the roof. Everyone would be getting ready for the Pageant of Ideas! Moody was on spotlight duty again, but Melanie and I were going to stay on the roof all day and do nothing. We called it our Pageant of Idle! She was already up there with Moody, the two of them lying side by side on the gym mats, feeding each other the cookies he'd made the day before. "They're like little drops of heaven," Mrs. Maxwell had called them. Melanie said she and Moody were going to open a bakery in the city some day. She talked about it the way she used to talk about her dream wedding. She never talked about the baby, I noticed, but I liked to imagine Melanie Junior snuggled in a basket under the cash register, happy and fat from all that heavenly food.

After Moody left for the auditorium, Melanie and I made up a game involving a tennis racquet and a deflated soccer ball. It was easy to play. No matter what you did, you got a point. I wondered why there weren't more games like this. Winning wasn't any less fun for me because Melanie was winning too. We were both all-state champions and feeling really good about our achievements until we sent the soccer ball over the edge of the roof, across the parking lot, and under a yellow Pinto. The driver's door opened and someone in a soldier costume got out. I shut my eyes, took a breath, and opened them again. It didn't work. He was still there, standing in his dress uniform. Jamie Finley, a week too late for Halloween.

He reached under the car for the ball. As he scanned the parking lot for its owner, something caught his eye. We followed his gaze to the football field. Someone was crossing the end zone, carrying a red suitcase. When he couldn't see them anymore, Jamie looked up at the roof. I ducked behind the little wall that kept juvenile delinquents like us from tumbling over the edge. I'd been searching for him for weeks. There were things I needed to tell him. Only now I realized that telling him these things would mean actually having to talk to him.

Melanie followed my lead, crouching beside me with her feet wide apart to accommodate her stomach. She wouldn't be able to hide it much longer. In a few weeks, she wouldn't even be able to climb up to the roof.

"Why don't you just talk to him," Melanie said.

I shook my head. I could feel the flush on my cheeks. I'd been so stupid for so long, I didn't know how to stop.

Melanie straightened up and sat on the wall. "Hey, Thinly! Robin says you look really sexy in that uniform." She laughed, pleased with herself. Being pregnant hadn't made her any more mature. Under that belly, she was still just a sixteen-year-old girl.

"What's he doing?" I said.

"He's checking his watch . . . Now he's going inside the school." She frowned and went back to her gym mat, broke a little drop of heaven in half and pushed it into her mouth. "Sorry. I should probably just stay out of your love life, huh?"

"You and me both."

While Melanie finished the cookies, I considered what to do. The longer I stayed crouched there, the more stupid I felt. When I couldn't take it anymore, I climbed down from the roof. He already had his dress uniform. Ready or not, I knew that time was running out.

I took the shortcut between the portables. Mr. Galpin was standing in the narrow dirt passage, leaning against the aluminum siding, a small bottle pressed to his lips. When he saw me, he slipped it inside his blazer.

"You caught me," he said. "I'm playing hooky today too."

"I was just going to the auditorium," I said. I could smell the booze from where I was standing, sharp from the bottle and tangy from his pores.

"I'm afraid you've missed most of it. Though I wouldn't say you missed much. What those kids don't know about life could fill an auditorium." He laughed like he was choking on something, then shook his head. "I'm sorry. I didn't mean that. Or maybe I did. I'm sorry either way."

"Carol signed up for it," I said, hoping to cheer him up. "I guess she's feeling better now."

Mr. Galpin nodded. "I'm sorry, Miss Fisher."

"What for?"

"We should practise what we preach, but it's not always easy. I'm no good at this anymore."

"You're a great vice-principal," I said.

"Just a lousy human being. I've got a hole inside me, you see. A great big hole where a person used to be. People said it would close up in time, but it doesn't. That hole only gets bigger. Eventually it gets so big that everything falls into it. One day you wake up and there's no light at all. There's nothing but blackness. There's only that hole."

I wanted to say something that would make him feel better, but I was on unfamiliar ground. Teachers were supposed to give kids pep talks, not the other way around. I said the first thing I could think of, the thing I needed to tell Jamie. It would have to do for Mr. Galpin too.

"Do you ever think about time machines?" I said.

"Time machines?" Mr. Galpin leaned back against the wall and closed his eyes. He looked like someone who hadn't slept in years. "No. No, I can't say I do."

"I've been thinking about them a lot lately. I was thinking about how if you went back in time and changed something—a mistake you made or something—then when you came back to the present, things might be better."

"I believe that's one idea, yes."

"But then I thought how that one change would change everything else, right? So everything would be different, not just the thing you want to be different."

Mr. Galpin turned his head. "It's called the butterfly effect," he said, interested now, seeing the potential for a lesson. "It's actually an explanation of how a weather system, even something as significant as a hurricane, can be affected by the slightest change, such as a butterfly's flight."

"Right, okay, so let's say that even though you made that one mistake, you did some other things that turned out all right. If you went back in time, you might end up changing the good stuff along with the bad. See what I mean?"

"I do."

"So maybe you wouldn't want to change anything at all. Not even the bad stuff."

"I suppose that's right," Mr. Galpin said. "You'd have to leave it. You'd have to let it be."

I glanced over his shoulder, thinking of Jamie. "That's what I was thinking too."

"Go on," Mr. Galpin said. "Tell Miss Closter to break a leg."

At the end of the portables, I looked back, hoping he'd be gone. But Mr. Galpin was there still, leaning against the wall, bottle hovering near his lips. "I would, though," he said to nobody. "I'd go back and change everything."

The distant bleat of the school band greeted me as I pulled open the side door—that and the scent of cleaning fluid and gasoline. There was always graffiti to deal with, I thought as I pulled the neck of my T-shirt up to cover my nose. I wasn't special that way.

The Thanksgiving decorations had been hung in the halls, pilgrim hats and turkeys, chains of green and orange paper. The plastic tree would go up in a few weeks. I wanted to look forward to the holidays, to imagine a bright, shiny new year along with everyone else. But I would have to think about all that later. Right then I had to find Jamie. I didn't want any more holes in my life where people used to be.

I was so focused on my task that I almost didn't see her. She stood at the foot of the auditorium stairs, hugging a small red suitcase in front of her. When I said her name, she turned slowly. The suitcase was too heavy for her, and she listed to one side like a sinking ship.

"I knew you'd come," she said. "I knew you wouldn't miss it."

"Of course not," I said. The clock over the office door told me it was almost three. The pageant would be ending soon. I pointed to the red suitcase. "What's that?"

"Guess," she said.

When she put the suitcase down, it made a hollow metal sound. Something splashed onto the floor. The smell of gas was so sharp it made my eyes water. I noticed the puddles on the linoleum all around her, the toes of her Hush Puppies stained black with it. It took a few more seconds for my heart to catch up with my head. The red suitcase wasn't a suitcase at all.

"Carol, what are you doing?"

"Don't act like you don't know."

"What? What don't I know?"

She scratched her head through her yellow hat, then took it off and scratched some more. She'd shorn her strawberry curls to a couple inches all over. Lopsided bangs sprung away from her forehead. "You don't like it," she said.

"No. It's nice."

"I look like her, don't you think?"

"Mia Farrow?"

She rolled her eyes. "I'm Joan of Arc," she said and put her hat back on. Then she dipped a hand into the right front pocket of her cords and held out her fist. When she opened it, my red lighter lay flat in the middle of her palm.

"That's mine," I said, stepping closer to take it. Carol closed her fingers again and tucked her hand behind her back. "You gave it to me," she said.

"I lost it."

She shook her head. "Why are you being like this?"

The music in the auditorium stopped, followed by applause. Someone spoke too closely into a microphone. Carol opened her hand again. We stared at my lighter. "I wasn't really given up for adoption," she said. "They found me at a gas station. She'd left me in the trash."

"I didn't know that."

"You didn't want to know. Nobody wants to know anything. Everyone sticks their heads up their you-know-whats and pretends the world is just peachy-keen."

"I don't want to pretend."

"Don't you?" she said. "That day in the showers, they held me down. Do you want to know about that, Robin? Because you never asked. Not once. They held me down and made him touch me while they laughed. They *should* laugh at me. I'm garbage." Carol tried to laugh but it came out like a cough. "Every time I think, He'll take me now, I've suffered enough. But He never does, Robin. Why doesn't He take me? Why isn't it ever enough?"

"We'll fix it, Carol. We'll tell someone."

"You never told."

I didn't say anything. There were no words to fix this. The clock over the office door spun toward three. Beside it, the dead soldiers smiled at us blandly from their class photos. They'd seen worse.

"They'll be here soon," Carol said, watching the auditorium door. "I've changed my mind. I don't think you should see this after all."

"See what, Carol?"

"Thank you for coming, Robin. I really appreciate your friendship. But I think you should go now."

"Let's both go," I said. "Let's leave right now and never come back."

Carol looked at me hard for a minute. "Where?"

"Wherever you want. We'll go anywhere you want in the whole world. There's a really ugly Pinto in the parking lot with our name on it."

"I get car sick," she said.

"You can drive."

She smiled a little, so I took a step toward her. I held out my hand, begging it not to shake. She reached out her empty hand, then reconsidered and lifted the one that held the lighter.

"No, Robin," she said. "This is where I'm supposed to be. Don't you see? This is where it started and this is where it will end. I'm not a joke. They'll see that now. They won't laugh at me anymore."

"Nobody's laughing. I'm not laughing."

"I baptize you with water for repentance," she said. "He will baptize you with the Holy Spirit and fire."

"What does that mean, Carol? I don't know what that means."

The bell screamed. Three o'clock. A thousand feet thundered against hardwood, louder, louder as they moved toward the door.

Carol lifted the lighter higher in the air, knuckles white, thumb ready. When the door banged open, the Bic stabbed the air between us and she flicked the wheel.

I thought her hand was trembling, but it was me. My whole body shook. The wall of lockers behind her swayed like hula dancers. The fluorescents rocked side to side. Everything whirled around us, all the signs I had missed, all the words left unsaid. Only Carol was still and focused, as steady as that little blue flame. As she brought it toward herself, I saw how everything had led to this moment, how everything led to everything back to the beginning of time. Dreaming of time machines is about as useful as watching a rerun and hoping for a different ending. Our choices are carved in flesh and rock.

"The Lord is my shepherd," she began. "I shall not want."

"Please, Carol," I begged. If I'd known it would be the last thing I'd ever say to her, I would've tried to think of something more profound.

"You should probably close your eyes now. You don't want to see this."

I shook my head. She was right, I didn't want to, but I owed it to her. This time I would not look away.

Carol smiled strangely, wholly, full of rapture I'd think later, finally understanding what beatific meant.

"Don't cry, Robin," she said. "I am God's special lamb."

As far as last words go, they were pretty damned good.

19

In November 1972, at a high school in a quiet, affluent Californian suburb, a sixteen-year-old girl set herself on fire. Damage to the building was serious but not catastrophic. Five hundred people ran to safety. Many recalled a loud boom and a flash of white light. The girl suffered third-degree burns over half her body. Two other students were injured trying to help. All three survived. A miracle some called it, including one girl who shared her near-death experience on a local talk show. "I see them everywhere now," a teary Joyce Peyton told the studio audience. "Our whole lives are miracles. This television program is a miracle."

The details of this particular miracle were cobbled together over the next few months from eyewitness statements, private correspondence, church confessionals, and wishful thinking. A photographer from the local paper got a heart-rending shot of what was left of the melted jerry can silhouetted against a scorched hallway. Papers around the country ran it on their front pages, below the election results, but few reporters managed to get beyond the who, what, where. There were several theories. The melodrama of the teenaged mind. Unrequited young love. Drugs were implicated, of course, then quickly abandoned as a possible cause once people got a look at the alleged pothead in the paper. They ran Carol's junior yearbook photo, taken that September just before she'd stopped coming to school. A cherubic face framed by a cloud of curls. For once, she hadn't worn her hat. When the anti-abortionists got wind of our afternoons in Dr. Winkelmann's parking lot, they put a stop to the conjecture and claimed Carol for their own. They called her a martyr for the cause. They declared her a saint. Carol neither confirmed nor denied their claims, but I'm sure she objected to them. Beatification is serious business, as she always said, and there are proper channels and procedures one simply doesn't skirt.

My part of the story, I kept to myself. My black box, a therapist would later call it, a fitting phrase as the memories often hammered me with violent flashes of light and sound not, I imagine, unlike a plane crash. There is a lot I've forgotten, but I can still feel my hair blowing back with that tremendous exhalation of heat just before the school seemed to fly at me. I slammed against a bank of lockers, metal twang ringing in my ears. Under that was screaming, mine, hers, other people's. Carol had disappeared inside the flames. I froze. Just like that night, I froze and watched her burn. It was my dad's voice booming in my head that yanked me back into that hallway. *Stop, drop, and roll! For Christ's sake, kiddo, stop, drop, and roll!* I threw myself at her and we crashed to the floor.

I beat her clothes with my hands. I wrapped her in my arms and squeezed her to my chest. The smell was horrible, but I wouldn't let her go. Then someone was running toward us, shouting my name, one of the dead soldiers come to life. He pulled me to my feet, then scooped up Carol and carried her to his car. We were whizzing through red lights when I remembered poor Mr. Galpin. Who would watch out for him now?

At the hospital, angels in green scrubs and shapeless white shoes swirled around us, barking at each other in a secret language. Carol looked so helpless on that giant gurney, so tiny and broken and wrong. What was it? "Her hat," I yelled out as they wheeled her away. "We forgot her hat." My hands were raw and shaking. They were somebody else's hands. They sat me down and gave me a shot of something. The hours after were like watching an episode of *M.A.S.H.* underwater. When I surfaced again, Mom was beside me in her black slacks, crying against a woman who reminded me of my dad's old secretary. The nurse showed her where to hug me so it wouldn't hurt and then Mom really blubbered. Katy May mascara ran down her face, but her hair still looked nice.

The Finley boy was fine, the nurses assured me. He'd been treated for smoke inhalation and released. Me, I would need to stay put a while longer. The other girl was in the ICU. That was all they said about Carol, and I was too scared to ask for more.

"Could've been a lot worse," the police officer said. He was wearing his sunglasses inside. While he spoke, I studied the girl in the mirrored lenses. Her red skin was as shiny as a poison apple, her eyebrows all but gone. The officer's own thick unibrow bounced up and down behind his glasses as he spoke. Or maybe it was a moustache. I was body-surfing another shot of morphine. Everything around me was doing the hokey-pokey. Everything except my mom, who sat rigid in a hospital chair while he took my statement. She refused the nurse's Valium, drank gallons of cafeteria coffee instead.

"I don't understand why this happened," she said. "Who is Carol Closter? Why would she do this? Why would anyone do this?"

The officer saved me from having to answer. "You wouldn't believe some of the things I've seen kids do, though I'll say this one is a real wacko. She used one of those plastic lighters you get at gas stations, if you can believe it." He took off his sunglasses and rubbed the bridge of his nose. "Damned thing had a sticker on it."

I can't say what Mom believed at that moment, but she didn't ask any more questions after that. The only questions I heard were from the nurses. Did I need more juice? A second pillow? Another one of those little pills? I was so brave, they told me, so lucky. I was a brave and lucky girl. My hospital room overflowed with balloons and stuffed animals, good wishes from strangers who agreed with the nurses. The pain arrived between doses, after cleanings and dressings, and in the seconds before I opened my eyes. I listened closely to what it had to say. *Remember*, it told me. *Never again*, I answered. I wasn't sure about the brave part, but I sure as hell believed the lucky.

After a week, I was allowed visitors. To my surprise, they came regularly and in droves. The Sisters brought carob bars and a portable turntable. They sat on my bed and played folk music guaranteed to heal my soul. Mildred Howard and the women from Mom's office joked with the nurses and kept me well stocked in Rice Krispies squares. Vera Miller brought Moody's Monopoly board and an old photo of herself in roller skates. My grandparents flew in from Canada, drank tiny bottles of airplane liquor, and stuffed homemade beef jerky under my mattress where the nurses wouldn't find it. My grandfather didn't talk much, but my grandmother had a lot to say about religion, California, and the general mess of things on our side of the border. She told Mom that the bags under her eyes were bigger than the ones they'd brought with them. "So you're staying for a while, then?" Mom said, rubbing the line between her brows.

When Jamie Finley came, he brought flowers and two cans of pop from the vending machine. I made him wait in the hall while Mom drew on eyebrows for me with her Katy May eyeliner. By all rights it was our first date.

We couldn't go for a drive, but there were stairs and a roof. We sat with our legs over the edge and willed the sun to go down. Jamie put his coat around me, then his arm. We didn't talk much. The things I'd needed to say before didn't matter anymore and what mattered now was too hard to hear. So Jamie didn't tell me he'd be gone before Christmas, or that I was the first girl he ever loved. I didn't tell him I had wanted it to be him all along, or that he was my first everything. Instead, we sat shivering and holding hands, and let ourselves believe we were lucky just a little while more.

The day before Thanksgiving, they said I could go home. "Don't worry," Mom told me. "Your grandmother will cook." She left the room to fill out the paperwork while I dozed off the last of the morphine drip. When I opened my eyes, one more visitor stood at the foot of my bed in a rumpled sports coat.

I thought how disappointed Mom would be that she'd missed him. George McGovern at long last.

"You came," I said.

"Hi there, kiddo."

My eyes filled. I couldn't breathe right. Something fluttered inside my chest, a bird caught in a house. I had done that. I had closed her in that small empty room and locked the door. All this time she had been waiting for someone to set her free.

"Daddy?" she said.

He buried his face in his hands and sobbed like a baby. It wasn't a bad start.

Dad and I would be okay. We would begin awkwardly, stumbling and stuttering over old hurts. There was no other way to do it. Once or twice a month, he would drive up from the city where he lived now. He would let me pick the movie, take us for fish and chips, buy me things I didn't need. It would take time, but eventually we would fill up the chasm with these handfuls of sand.

Years later I would visit him on my way home from college for the holidays. He had a one-bedroom condo near the beach, a lady friend named Bev. He still sold insurance, but he'd finally given up golf. He'd started a small potted garden on his balcony with great success, squat flowering succulents, towering agave, and Mexican feather grass. I brought him a piece of Jasper for it from my graduate dig. It reminded me of those old road cuts on the edge of Golden. Maybe Dad saw what I did in that red rock, or maybe he just saw the stuff his life was built on. Either way, he turned it over in his hands and told me one last story.

They'd met at a party off-campus. She was on a cultural exchange semester from Alberta, playing volleyball and studying American drinking habits a thousand miles away from her parents. He had his first business card in his pocket and a flask of bourbon in his blazer. She was the only girl at the party who he didn't have to stoop down to talk to. They dated for a few weeks. He made her grilled cheese sandwiches. She made him laugh. Then she'd gotten knocked up and he panicked, asked her if it was his, drank himself into a stupor. She fled home before he knew what time it was. When he sobered up he bought a ticket to Red Deer, wherever the hell that was. They were married two days later in in her parents' backyard. He'd borrowed my grandfather's suit. "We were just dumb kids," Dad said, "but we meant well." Which I think sums up most people's failures and victories well enough.

I got in my car to go home. As I started the engine, Dad leaned down to ruffle my hair. "I wanted you, kiddo. It just took me a while to know it, that's all. So don't you ever question that."

"I won't," I said. It was a promise I've kept for the most part. I could spend my life digging around for people to blame. I'd find plenty of fool's gold that way, if I wanted to. I prefer my Jasper rocks.

With Mom it was harder. When I finally confessed to the fire—my fire—nobody wanted to hear it. The Place had been demolished long ago, along with any evidence. Both the police and the developers preferred to let it be. Digging up the past would only complicate the present. They were right. Once it all came out—The Place, Troy, Dr. Winkelmann's—Mom would devote whole days to staring out the kitchen window again. This time I guessed she was looking for the daughter she thought I'd been.

Then one Friday afternoon, she turned around and said, "Let's drive somewhere." We didn't talk about it, we just threw a bag of clothes in the car and drove. We took back roads and scenic routes, kept going until it got dark. We found motels with swimming pools and diners with jukeboxes, ate too much, and went to sleep with wet hair. Then we woke up and got in the car and did it all again. Nothing was going to stop us from seeing those trees.

On the way home, we passed the road cut. Gazing out over a sleepy Golden, thousands of houses stretching to the hills, I thought about all the families they contained. Some were happy. Some weren't. Some had lost a parent or a child. Some

368

didn't know all that they'd lost. But everyone was still going. Little bursts of lamp and TV light told me so. I said a prayer, the only way I knew how. I found a star in the sky and made a wish. A week later, Jamie Finley left for Vietnam. As Carol liked to say, "God hears all prayers. He just doesn't always answer them."

Melanie came to see me before she was sent away. There was an aunt in New Jersey willing to take her in and help with the arrangements. After that was anyone's guess. Plans were being made without her. She still didn't talk about the baby. She said she would come see me when it was over, but she never came back to Golden. Moody left town shortly after she did. Vera doesn't know where he went, but I like to think there is a bakery somewhere out east where you can buy little drops of heaven anytime you want.

Carol was sent to a hospital in Buenos Aires run by nuns who agreed to care for her for the rest of her life. The State of California was more than happy to let her go. She was God's problem now. She never spoke or wrote another word. Her fingers were too badly burned to save. She can talk, but refuses to. I've been told she communicates by pointing to words in her Bible with a pencil in her mouth. For everything else, she has her nuns.

The rest of us were scattered like refugees across the Golden school system. I gave up home ec, to the relief of Mrs. Maxwells everywhere, and took up choir. I couldn't carry a tune but at least no one got hurt. I buckled down, sights set on colleges in towns where it rained once in a while. I started swimming again, did lazy laps with Mom in the evenings sometimes. By then my skin had calmed to cotton-candy pink. Baby skin, Mom called it. I slathered on the sunscreen. There was a store-bought sheen to me that I was eager to protect.

As the months passed, the nightmares came less and less frequently, though they were just as potent when they did. I dreamed I was being burned at the stake. I was shredded to pieces by rusty kitchen knives. I was held underwater by a thousand hands. I screamed sometimes, Mom told me. I'd wake up with a damp cloth on my forehead, her voice soothing in my ear. My doctor said the anxiety was normal, that the mind was slower to heal than the flesh. My body had rushed ahead of my brain again. He'd seen something similar in soldiers coming back from Vietnam. Try to relax, he told me. Settle into your old routine. I told him about the lighters. "You might want to find some new hobbies," he agreed.

Nixon beat McGovern. Roe beat Wade. The war ended. Some things stayed the same and some things got better, not by giant leaps, but by small human steps.

For a long time, people called the house at all hours. Reporters, lunatics, well-wishers. Mom finally had the number changed. The flood of mail was redirected to a PO box. She collected it every Friday and helped me decide what to keep and what to toss. People sent tear-stained letters about things they'd done and regretted or not done and regretted more. They asked for my advice, my forgiveness, a blessing from the girl who'd saved a living saint. I replied to as many as I could. They thought I was a hero, though it seems to me that heroes are the ones who need our prayers.

What surprised me were the items they sent. The photos of loved ones who'd died, the locks of hair, the baby teeth. I kept them in a shoebox under my bed. Mom said they were morbid, but I couldn't bring myself to throw these strange gifts away. When I was little and Dad talked about the aftermath of a disaster, it made me think of the remainder left over from my long division exercises. Later, I thought how funny that was, how childishly I'd seen the world. But I'd been right all along. The aftermath is what remains.

Like Mr. Galpin, widow, misplaced father, vice-principal. When he came to see me in the hospital, he told me about the night his wife and daughter died. I've never repeated that story to anyone and I never plan to. Knowing something like that is like being given a glass egg. You don't pass it around. You wrap it in tissue and put it in a box and set it on the shelf of your teenaged heart.

Or Jamie Finley, the first boy I ever loved, who went to Vietnam and never came back, a hero too many times for one young life. He wrote me seven letters before his helicopter went down in the Andaman Sea. I have them still.

Carol, that tiny girl who contained so much anger and sadness. Carol Cloister. Jesus Freak. Patron saint of teenaged arsonists. One Saturday, sifting through the envelopes and tiny boxes, I found a postcard with an illustration of Saint Lucy, who was stabbed to death because she could not be burned. It bore a stamp from Argentina, my name written in purple ink by an immaculate hand. Was it an apology? A thank-you? Whatever it was, it was her story, not mine. I didn't want to be a martyr and I was certainly no saint. I preferred the Sisters' story of the phoenix, a mythical bird that sets herself on fire every thousand years so a new phoenix can be reborn from the ashes. Still, I put the postcard in the shoebox with other people's baby teeth. My ninth grade chemistry teacher told us that you measure the strength of covalent bonds by how much heat you need to break them. But, of course, heat bonds things too.

And what about Elaine Johnson Fisher? Swan diver, college dropout, diehard Democrat, doting grandmother, abysmal cook. I keep her ashes in that old enamel box on my bookshelf, surrounded by her wild women, and a photo of us on the windowsill above my kitchen sink. It's from our day among the redwoods, taken for a dollar by an industrious hippie with a Polaroid camera and no shoes. In it, Mom and I stand together in front of a great tree. The sunlight is yellow on its bark, the forest around us glows like fire. I am holding her hand. I smile widely, but my chin is tucked. I am still learning that we all have scars. If you search that photo for mine, you won't be disappointed. Don't search. See instead our sunlit faces. See how brave and lucky we are. We are all just dumb kids—me, her, him, everyone. But we are phoenixes too. We flap our wings and caw at the stars. Some days we even remember that we can fly.

Look at us. Look at us.

ACKNOWLEDGEMENTS

First thanks must go to my readers, whose praise for a very early draft gave me the courage to plod on. Thanks to my sister, Danielle Rockel, who wouldn't let me stop plodding when I wanted to, and to my parents, Elizabeth Rains and Al Hyland, who gave me a room with a view where there was little to do but plod. Thanks also to my fellow chickens at the Castro Writers' Coop and to my personal cheerleaders, Christie Rae and Masa Takei. You know the importance of friendship and bubbly, and supply both in a bottomless cup. And to the outstanding team at McClelland & Stewart, who mid-wifed this manuscript into print with speed and grace—tribute must be paid. A debt of gratitude is owed to my agent, Carolyn Forde, for seeing what I did in this story, and to my wise and tireless editor, Anita Chong, for helping me see so much more. Finally, eternally, thanks and love to my husband, Hugo Eccles, for inspiring me, and doing the laundry, and helping me see more in everything.